Lucy Banks is the author of the *Dr Ribero's Agency of the Supernatural* series, and has won or been short-listed for several literary awards and competitions. Originally from Hertfordshire, she now lives in Devon, with her husband, two children, and extremely boisterous cat.

Also by Lucy Banks

Caged Little Birds

Lucy Banks

SANDSTONEPRESS

First published in Great Britain in 2022 by
Sandstone Press Ltd
Willow House
Stoneyfield Business Park
Inverness
IV2 7PA
Scotland

www.sandstonepress.com

Sandstone Press is committed to a sustainable future.
This book is made from Forest Stewardship Council ® certified paper.

ISBN: 978-1-913207-93-9
ISBNe: 978-1-913207-94-6

Cover design by Stephen Mulcahey
Typeset by DataWorks, India, www.dataworks.co.in
Printed in the UK by CPI Group (UK) Ltd, Croydon CR0 4YY

ACKNOWLEDGEMENTS

Thank you to my husband Al, who always gently nudges me onwards. His knowledge of birds has been incredibly helpful, and if my questions about the migratory habits of skuas in the Scottish Isles drove him mad, he was kind enough never to show it. Thank you also to my boys. They're both incredible cheerleaders, and I'm so blessed to have them in my life. I'd like to thank the cat, but to be honest, there's always an element of risk when he's around: that he'll step on the keyboard and add letters or delete entire sections. Thanks to the rest of my family; their support is always appreciated. I'd like to say a big thanks to my friends too – especially those who read the book and who took the time to give constructive feedback. A special shout-out to Lou; her positivity meant an enormous amount!

My agent, Greg Messina, deserves a special mention – for making the dream happen, and for his unshakeable confidence in this book. Thanks also go to the wonderful team at Sandstone Press, who have been incredible to work with. Moira did a phenomenal job of editing the book.

Special remembrance goes to a friend of my husband's, who highlighted how the prison system (and society) can sometimes fail those who are in need of support. While criminal acts must be acknowledged and dealt with, sometimes the answer isn't as simple as locking the door and throwing away the key.

CHAPTER 1

The gulls are screaming. High, repeating notes. Low croaking beneath; the seabird colony at its most swollen. My head is stuffed with the sound, to the point of combustion.

Watch the sea, Daddy orders. *Eyes outwards, not at me.*

But he points to the sky, high above our heads.

I follow the line of his finger and see the bird, wings spread, trowel-feet dangling towards the ground. It's a bigger bird, darker than the rest of them. A skua, searching for eggs to steal, or a chick to tear into.

It's wrong. I say nothing; Daddy's scorn would be the answer to my stupidity. This is nature, after all. This is our purpose here, to observe without judgement. He's teaching me his ways, and it's important that I listen, learn, absorb it entirely.

(This is a dream. I know it, even as it's going on. Isn't that always the way?)

There's elegance in the skua's bullet-bluntness, in those slippery-smooth feathers. But her beak is cruel. It gapes open, like the mouth of a panting dog.

I look to the cliffside and see you. Not as you looked on that last day, but as you were before. Healthy, awkward in your own teenage body, holding out your hands to me. But you can't be here, because this is another time and place, far from where we met. You don't exist any more.

(It's a dream. Wake up, Ava, wake up.)

There's something cupped in your hands. Something round and grey, soft at the edges. A chick. You're holding a chick. Of course you are.

The skua circles closer and the chick cranes upwards. *Eyes outward*, Daddy says, from somewhere far away. *Eyes outward, not at me. Never lose your focus, girl.*

I scream. The chick screams. The colony of gulls scream with us and there is no room for anything else; no sight, no touch, no smell. All is noise.

The skua dives downwards and I close my eyes. When I finally dare open them again, you are gone. Everything is gone: the colony, my father, the rabble and the noise. Nothing remains except the chick's bones, cleaned to parchment-white, lying on the ground at my feet.

The alarm squawks its note, again, again, again. My head's in a puddle of menopausal sweat. Sometimes I feel like a husk, a hollow vessel of what I once was. I wonder what I'll be left with, in the end.

The sleeping pills have glued my eyes half-closed. I took too many as usual, though fortunately I've still got plenty left; more than I should have, in fact. I slap at the clock and the noise stops, thank goodness.

I know I shouldn't complain. I'm waking up in my own house; my private space to do as I like. There are no prison guards here, bellowing down the corridor. No metal doors clanging, no shouting inmates. Only this cosy bedroom with a little bathroom down the hallway, just for me. No queuing for showers. No scrabbling for soap or squabbling over bottles of shampoo. The list of little luxuries seems almost endless.

I can make myself breakfast – whatever food I choose, at whatever time. Porridge today, I think, as I used to have it as a child back on the islands, with a tablespoon of honey drizzled in the centre. It's a shame I can't stare out to calm, endless sea, as I did back then. The vista of my little courtyard garden will have to do instead.

Why do I always dream of you? I wonder, as I climb out of bed. Why do I always see your lanky young body, the earnest frown on your face? But I already know the answer to that; it's because you're still *there*, knotted tight in my memories. You continue to haunt me, even though I hoped to leave all thoughts of you in my old prison cell and to emerge into the world as a woman reborn.

I'm still determined to make this happen. It doesn't do to dwell on what happened; I would much rather push you from my mind until you finally disappear altogether. There's no benefit to letting you clog up my every waking hour, not after all this time.

This is freedom at last, and that's all that matters.

I spend the morning reading *Nature's Home*. The article on ringing plovers takes me back to my childhood, to days spent slipping through tufts of sea-grass, grasping puffins and clipping plastic around their legs. I struggled with the task, when we first moved to the islands. My fingers bled with the constant nips of angry beaks. Yet after a while, it became the easiest of manoeuvres. The quick grab. The pinning down of the rustling wings. The deft ringing before release. Daddy never used to praise me, but then, he never really noticed any of my achievements, such that they were. However, I like to imagine he must have felt a certain level of approval towards me, on occasion.

Sipping at my tea, I marvel at the delicacy of its taste. Earl Grey, after so many years of prison-issue builder's tea. Fresh milk, instead of UHT. Even a sprinkle of sugar, to provide depth and sweetness. It's almost too much.

This will all take getting used to but I suppose, in time, it will feel as commonplace as ringing those birds. The house is run-down and dreary, but it's mine for now, until the council decree otherwise.

I've only dared to go outside a couple of times so far, to grab some essentials from the corner shop. Everything has changed out there; even the shops are alien now. The shelves are cleaner.

Food packaging is shinier than I remember it, and everything comes in far larger sizes. Even paying is a mystery: the till beeping rather than ringing.

Baby steps, that's what's required. No panicking. No ruffled feathers. It will all work out fine, as long as I maintain my focus.

The doorbell rings just after I finish washing up my lunch plate. It's my probation officer, Margot, right on time. Solid-boned Margot, chest an uninterrupted cliff-ledge above a wide, no-nonsense waist. She settles onto one of my kitchen stools like a walrus alighting on a rock, then places her phone on the table. I've yet to get used to these devices; miniature televisions they seem to me, somehow dangerous in their diminutive proportions. Margot is the brusque sort and ignores my furtive glances. She accepts a biscuit, but declines a drink.

We discuss the house, then Universal Credit, which I confirm I'm now receiving. She asks if I've met the new neighbour, who has been busy moving his belongings into the property next door. I laugh when she suggests I get a pet for company. It wouldn't do to have another living creature share the space, but I don't tell her that. Alone is best for me.

She calls me *Robin*, and I wish I'd chosen a different alias. At the time, I liked the bird connotations, but a robin is too domestic; too small and rounded. *Robin Smith*. However, it's a forgettable name for an unmemorable person, and that's what I need to be, in this new existence. *Ava Webber* must be stored safely away. I understand why, but I still wear my real name inside me, like a blanket around my heart. It won't ever slip away, not completely.

It's nearly time for the visit to end. Margot recommends that I look for some voluntary work, to ease me back into the habit. Something to get me out of the house. A position in a local charity shop, perhaps. This is, of course, an impossibility. I live in terror that someone will recognise me, because if that happens, they will relocate me. I'll have to start all over again, and transform into yet another new person.

4

'Give something back,' she tells me, nudging her glasses up her nose. 'It'll be good practice for when you enter the world of employment again, and it's nice to make a positive difference.'

I think of all the things I've done in the past. The truth is, I've probably made enough of a difference as it is. No further input is required, in my opinion.

It is so easy to rest out here, in the quiet of the garden. I love sliding into stillness and ignoring the thoughts that churn around in my head. It is a privilege, and I should feel grateful.

A noise breaks the silence, though it's not the sound that makes me jump. Rather it's the sheer force of movement on my left, not to mention the swearing that follows. The clematis on the fence is shuddering; someone on the other side is wrenching it free.

I sit up, squinting in the sunlight. Half a head peers over from the garden next door: a bald scalp shining in the light, and a pair of crinkling eyes. My new neighbour, I presume.

'Sorry about that, I was giving the garden a bit of a tidy-up.' The eyes wrinkle further. Perhaps he's grinning; it's difficult to tell without seeing his mouth.

'It was mostly dead anyway,' I reply, noting the deep lines etched on his forehead. An older person then, like me. That's a relief. Younger people are often more inquisitive and I can't tolerate questions.

'I've just moved in,' he says.

'I know.'

Another tug and the clematis is free. The fence is naked without it, its parched panels exposed to the air.

'I'm Bill.'

So you are, I think, then realise he's waiting for a response. I was never good at social niceties, and twenty-five years in prison has only made my ineptitude worse. Taking a breath, I stand up, move closer, and extend my hand.

'Robin,' I say, stumbling over the soft centre of the name, the alien roll of the *R* at the start. 'Robin Smith.'

My hand is taken, albeit awkwardly, and we shake. The fence is higher than I'd realised, and Bill is by no means a tall man.

'So,' he says, releasing me. 'Is this a good neighbourhood?'

'I've not been here long myself. It seems decent, though, for a run-down part of town.'

'Ha, indeed. Are you originally from around here?'

I immediately remember islands, endless islands. Then my little prison cell, with its tiny window. Space, so much space, then hardly any space at all. 'No, I'm from all over,' I reply.

'Me too.' His eyes crease again. 'Well, I suppose I'd better get back to my unpacking. All my rubbish won't sort itself out, will it?'

'Probably not.'

'Nice to meet you, Robin.' He touches his forehead. 'Great name, by the way. I love garden birds.'

I smile, in spite of myself. 'Really? I've always favoured larger varieties myself.'

'What, like birds of prey?'

I nod, but he's taken a step back. Conversation over. That must be my cue to do the same. I need to familiarise myself with social signals all over again.

'Enjoy your new home,' I call out lamely, as the top of his head retreats towards the house.

He says something in response, but I miss it. His throaty chuckle cheers me. I realise that I haven't made anyone laugh in a long time.

Later that evening, I make myself some pasta. The saucepan still feels odd in my fingers, too heavy and substantial. It reminds me of the comics I read as a child, of men being walloped about the head by fuming wives. A weapon like this would easily take a grown man down, providing it connected with the right part of the skull.

I wonder what Bill is doing, on the other side of the wall. Perhaps he's cooking his dinner too, though probably most people would consider it too early to eat. Pouring himself a glass of wine, maybe. No, he looks more the type to drink beer, a manly, no-frills drink. Maybe there's a wife there too, or friends who have come over to see the new place. Or perhaps he's sobbing because he's lonely. People do feel that way, sometimes. Personally, I'm used to being on my own. After Mother died, *alone* was the standard way of things. One learns to cope with isolation, especially when there's no other option.

There was Henry, of course, once I'd reached adulthood. But it wouldn't do to think about Henry, not here, in this house. Not while I am attempting to carve out this new life, this *Robin* existence. Henry belongs in the past, and so do you. You with your skinny jeans and clumsy posture, and that baby chick in your hands. So different to the other teenage boys, so much more interested in the world around you. I'm sure that, if you were still here today, you wouldn't have stared constantly at screens, as young people seem to do now.

You. The only child I've ever enjoyed spending time with. I miss your face sometimes, though I see it often enough when I'm sleeping. But I must stop my mind from racing through these old tales of you, and of Henry. Of being in Bristol, too, and of when everything went so wrong. There is no point thinking about it. As Daddy always said, we should look forwards to the future, not backwards into the senseless, meaningless past.

I spoon the pasta into the bowl. It's lifeless and limp; I must have boiled it for too long. The tomato sauce spatters it with a sheen, but doesn't disguise its unappealing nature. Still, it's sustenance. Survival. And that's what my psychologist said, back in the prison. The focus will be on surviving, to begin with. Then, I'll be able to start living again.

I lie in bed, and think in the darkness. It's the time when my thoughts are most clear, when they dance and tilt like leaves in a storm. I've always been like this. Sleep is often elusive, and so I use this time to remember, or else fight against remembering.

Before I was sent to prison, I had a vague notion of what it might be like. Cold brick walls. Bars across the windows. Meals served in steel trays. Threats of violence reflected in every stare. There are elements of truth in this perception, but it doesn't capture the reality of the place. For instance, others would struggle to imagine the ceaseless stink of too many people trapped in an airless building, or the pressure of that much oestrogen, like volatile gas in a canister. There's also the slick of grime coating every surface. In a prison, negativity swiftly spreads. It's there in every brick and tile, and it's dangerously infectious.

The hardest thing was the desolation of waking up in the same cell, each and every day. Of forgetting what day of the week it was, or what month. What year, even. It was the pain of having the mind tethered to a single location, which was far worse than the presence of bars and bricks. Waiting out every hour in a state of tedium. Breathing in, then out, then in again. Wondering what was the point of it all. But Dr Holland would insist that these are unproductive thoughts, so they must be stifled.

I think about Ditz instead. Ah, Ditz. The other spectre that persists in plaguing me. I suppose it isn't surprising, given my thoughts just now. She was an integral part of my life there, if only for a short while.

She arrived only a few months before my release. New inmates, whenever they came in, were usually fragile, wide-eyed and frightened by the new environment. Some of the other women enjoyed tormenting them, shouting a few expletives, rattling at the doors to make them jump. It was cat-and-mouse play, and gave them something to brighten up their otherwise grey and repetitive days. I confess it used to amuse me, to see that unfettered cruelty. People are nastier than they realise, and prison simply pulls all the poison to the surface.

Ditz, or Ditsfield, was even more timid and terrified than most new inmates. She was childlike in stature. Elf-hair, squashed close to her head like a skullcap. Big blue eyes, containing too much watery grey to be attractive. Her skin was bad, especially around her mouth, probably because of the drugs. It was usually related to drugs in one way or another – not that I ever touched any while I was in there.

8

They put Ditz in the cell next to mine. I pressed my ear to the wall and listened to her crying. It sounded like a chick, a high-pitched *hyuk-hyuk*, rhythmic and slow. She used to call out the name *Babs* a lot. I later found out that was her sister. *Babs*. What a name.

She needed someone to hold her up, otherwise she'd have slipped, fallen and disintegrated. It'd happened before in prison; I witnessed it several times over the years.

She became a project, I suppose. Something to take my mind off things, to stop me thinking about the past. And she reminded me of you. Hollow-chested as a teenage boy, crop-haired and spotty, and so cowed by the world around her. It angered me at times, as though she'd deliberately chosen to take on the form of you, merely to drag me back to that time, again and again.

But you were so long ago. A footnote in a few dusty books and some archived newspaper articles, buried in ancient websites. Ditz is in the past too now, blown away with the dust of passing time. It frustrates me that it still rages so brightly in my head, the memories sharp as needles.

They called me *Butcher Bird*, after she died.

Butcher bird. The colloquial name for a shrike, due to its habit of impaling its prey on thorns. How clever the inmates thought they were to name me that, because of my background. All it did was show how little they knew me. I am nothing like that at all, and I refuse to accept blame for Ditz. We are our own people, after all. Some people are strong, others weak; that's the way of the world.

I shouldn't dwell on this. My sleeping pills will help. I need some rest, and this is the only respite I know. I used to call them *my little friends*. That's inappropriate, I know, especially given what happened. There's nothing friendly about them, as I'm sure my doctor would go to great pains to remind me. Still, I can't help but be comforted by the sight of all those bottles and boxes stacked in the bathroom cabinet, both prescription and over-the-counter. It's surprisingly easy to hoard medicine these days.

Sleep. It will come soon. Then another day of freedom, or nothingness. I'm not sure how it will be yet.

Sometimes, the pills send me into a pit of unconsciousness. I like it when this happens. The emptiness is a blessed break from thinking, and is worth its weight in gold. But last night, this absence of thought was denied me.

Instead, I dreamt of my cell. In reality, it was roughly the size of my old bedroom back in Bristol, in the flat I had before I was sent down. In the fog of the dream, the cell was even smaller, the walls pressing against my shoulders, the floor and ceiling so close, my chin and knees were forced to meet. I'd been compressed, diminished. Unable to stretch and be free. The pictures on the wall were the same ones I had during my time there. Bird images torn from magazines, because they reminded me of more peaceful times. A sea eagle, talons outstretched to seize a fish from the loch. A gannet plummeting into the water. Clusters of terns lining the cliffsides.

In that muddled mess of a dream, you were there too, somewhere. Although I couldn't see you, I was aware of your presence, hidden under the bed, hugging yourself for comfort, begging me not to do it. Ditz was there as well, sobbing from some unseen corner. Crying for Babs, for the holy saviour sister to help her. Asking me to *stop saying that, stop it please.*

I might be free from that cell, but the dreams are reluctant to leave me be.

Still, it's morning now. I must get up and get moving, regardless of how hard it is. I intend to sort out the spare room today, to clear it of the piled-up junk and create a reading nook, or else a place to sit and watch the birds in the garden below.

I have a job, of sorts. A purpose. The thought fills me with mild pleasure: a childlike anticipation of productivity. This is how life should be; this is how other people do it. I'm becoming like them, I can feel it. More *normal.* More palatable to others. At times like these, I almost believe that I could fit in.

For the first few hours, I am lost to it. My elbows are deep in cardboard boxes, fishing out long-forgotten books that have been in storage for as long as I was incarcerated. I find a few notepads, with figures about bird counts in various locations. Other more random items. A pair of oven gloves soft with mould. A sleeping bag, for camping trips that were never taken. Most of it is unsalvageable, grimy garbage that's fit only for landfill.

There are other things too, buried in those boxes. I find a pack of playing cards. The sight of the white and red box jolts me back to you. Your trusting gaze, as you watched me deal them out. That laugh of excitement as you won another round. The cosy fun of it, and how confiding you were with me, when I asked you questions about your life, your family. Your father. I taught you Gin Rummy, then Old Maid and a few others that I forget now. You were a quick learner, smart, without a hint of arrogance. A perfect child, in many ways. Then I offered you some food, and that's when it all went wrong.

No, I mustn't think of that now. I hadn't intended to keep these cards: they need to go to the tip, like everything else. They shouldn't be in the house.

A shrill buzz startles me. The cards drop and scatter on the carpet like red and white feathers. My fingers tingle with the sudden emptiness. It's the doorbell, I realise. Just someone at the door, nothing else. But it can't be Margot, I won't see her until next week. It isn't the postman either; my weekly delivery of *Nature's Home* was two days ago. I don't know who it could be. I haven't got a clue what to do in these situations. My skirt is dusty, and my forehead damp with sweat.

Answer it, Margot would tell me. This is all part of the experience, the process of survival. Take each moment as it comes. Deal with every situation in turn. I can do this. I can answer a door, for goodness' sake; it shouldn't be hard. But what if it's someone who knows who I am, what if they've come to shout abuse at me, what if there's an angry mob out there, ready to throttle me, what if the whole street knows what happened in the past and now they want to – no, stop, don't think of that.

My feet march down the stairs, though my mind protests. I won't be afraid. I can't be. That's what Dr Holland keeps repeating to me. A life lived in fear is no life at all.

The silhouette at the door is bulky around the shoulders. A man then, not a woman. Somehow that's better. Women are more unpredictable. I unlock the door and inch it open, noticing the bald head first, then the crinkly eyes. A roll-neck sweater, despite the warmth of the day, and a bottle of something in his hands.

'Hello,' the man says uncertainly. 'I hope I'm not disturbing you.'

'No, no,' I reply, losing track of my thoughts. 'I'm not disturbed.'

He laughs. 'It's Bill, from next door. I just wanted to pop round to introduce myself properly. Talking over the fence isn't the best way to chat, is it?'

He holds out the bottle. *Pinot Grigio.* I'm no wine expert, but it doesn't seem expensive.

Henry always liked Merlot. My cheeks redden at the thought.

'Would you like to come in?' I blurt.

'What, for a cuppa?'

'Yes, I can put the kettle on. We can have tea.'

Bill grins. He has a pleasant smile, crooked at one side, with a broken tooth. 'That'd be lovely.'

The hallway seems to shrink around us as we walk through it. I sense his gaze travelling from wall to wall, taking in the pictures, the crassly patterned carpet, the dated woodchip on the ceiling. It's impossible to tell whether he approves, or is shocked by the spartan nature of it all. If he's taken aback, he's too polite to show it.

'You really do like birds, don't you?' he says, as I pull out a kitchen stool for him to sit on. It's yet another item that's cheap and nasty; the furniture grant didn't stretch very far.

'Are you referring to my pictures?'

'Yes. Lots of seabirds, I notice.'

'I grew up by the sea,' I say, then wonder if I've said too much. No, that statement is safe: there's nothing to be deduced from revealing I was raised near the coast.

'That must have been nice,' he says, shifting on his seat. 'I've always been a city man, myself.'

'Which city?'

'London. Cardiff. Bristol. A few of them.'

Bristol. I freeze, kettle in hand, wanting to ask when, wanting to know if it was back then. If there's any chance that he'd remember me. He can't. He mustn't. I'd have to move again if he did: that's the whole point of me having this false identity.

'Where in Bristol?' I ask cautiously.

He pauses. 'I'll be honest, it was mostly in hostels, or on friends' sofas. Failing that, it was the streets for me.'

'You were homeless?'

'I was. For a long time.'

This news is a relief. If he was homeless, he wouldn't have followed the news, surely. He would have had bigger problems to focus on, so he would never have read about me. Besides, his manner is guileless, friendly even. If he knew about what happened, his expression would have betrayed something.

'Living on the streets must have been very hard,' I say, fishing the teabags out of the cupboard.

He shrugs. 'I brought it on myself. I'm lucky that my daughter still wants to see me. She'd have every right to tell me where to stick it. Bless her, she's a good woman. Not without her own challenges in life, you understand, but her heart is in the right place. You know what I mean.'

No, I don't know. I fail to understand normal family relationships. My father never showed the slightest bit of interest in me other than as an apprentice to assist him on the islands, and until I reached my early twenties, I presumed that was how it was for everybody.

I hand him a mug. 'What about your wife?'

'Dead wife, now. And she was an ex-wife before that. I never blamed her for leaving me.' He chuckles, and again the sound warms me. 'But listen to me, babbling on about my past, and we hardly know each other. What about you, Robin?'

There's that name again. The little innocent bird. It surprises me every time I hear it, though I know I must get used to it quickly, or risk giving myself away. I rearrange my expression into something more neutral. 'I'm not very interesting,' I say, sitting on the other stool. 'So there's not much to tell.'

'The ones who say they're not interesting are always the most interesting of all.'

'Not in my case. I'm genuinely dull.'

'What about the birds, then? Are you an environmentalist?'

'I just like birds,' I say quietly. I used to work for the Society for Bird Preservation, many years ago, but I can't tell him that. Again, too much information.

He senses my discomfort, and wisely moves on. 'Well, your house is cosier than mine, I must say.'

'Really? Don't you find it a bit basic?'

'Not at all. It's got a homely feel. Clean, too.'

I smile. 'I'm not clean. I was clearing out my spare room before you came over. That's why my clothes are so dirty.'

'That's not dirt, that's a sign of hard work.' He grins again, and I realise who he reminds me of. The actor Clint Eastwood, back when he starred in those old cowboy films. Henry made me watch one once, told me it was a masterpiece of its time. Bill has the same narrow, alert eyes, and a similar expanse of smile. He's handsome I suppose, in a lean, weathered way.

The thought panics me. I shouldn't be finding anyone hand-some, not any more. The thought alone is ludicrous, especially at my age. 'I should get back to my decluttering soon,' I say, drinking my tea quickly, even though it scalds my tongue.

He nods. 'I can't stay for long either. I'm still unpacking, and my daughter is coming over later, to help. She split up from her boyfriend recently, and I think she likes the company.'

I smile, though I don't want to hear about his daughter. Offspring make me nervous; they often complicate things. But these thoughts I keep to myself. Positivity, that's the word they kept repeating before I left prison: stay positive and avoid confrontation at all costs. Remain invisible, and make no trouble.

After he leaves, I return to the spare room. The isolation is welcome after so much chatter. I'm unused to small talk, especially when the attention is partially focused on myself. Where there were once scattered boxes, there are now piles. A pile of things to keep, not so large. Another to discard, which is overflowing. It will all go in the bin, and that will be the end of it. I am good at taking decisive action.

There isn't much more to go through now. As I loot onwards, I find a box, hidden inside a pillowcase. It feels as smooth as I remember. How paranoid I must have been, to think that anyone would have cared about it. They'd already condemned me by that point, and the contents of this box wouldn't have offered anything further to their investigations.

Its surface is blistered, more than it was before, I'm sure. The mother-of-pearl inlay is missing in several places. It was my mother's, one of the few items of hers I was allowed to keep.

The hinges squeak as I lift the lid. Only a few things rest inside, nestled in the worn velvet corners. A necklace, with a gull in flight as a pendant. It seems such a cheap, nasty thing now, and feels sticky under my fingers. There's also a pair of tickets for the theatre: Ibsen's *A Doll's House*. An old cork from a wine bottle. Red, not white, evident from the staining. Why I saved these things, I don't know. I wanted to forget all about Henry, but I clung to these knick-knacks. Perhaps to prove that I was capable of love, regardless of what people said.

I sit back against the wall and close my eyes. It's painful to remember him, even though I know it shouldn't be.

Sometimes, Henry's face is a blur, a shapeless mass of pink skin and beard, a vague impression of eye sockets, cheekbones, laughter lines. At other times, it comes to me with piercing clarity. I remember how he seemed to me the first time I met him. Not just the warmth of the eyes and the open smile, but the swagger of him. The confidence. The way he held my gaze for a fraction too long.

It started as a single request, shouted from one landing of a staircase to another. His voice echoed up the stairwell, asking me to help him to carry some files. I was so young, back then. So stupid. Fresh from my father's funeral, back on the mainland and still struggling to adjust. His request for assistance took me by surprise. I scurried down the steps towards him, eager to please, hobbling in my calf-length skirt, and he handed me the top few files, grappling with the rest while I stared at him. We talked while we climbed the stairs together. Idle chatter about his department, the boredom of the job. Probably some other nonsense too; I can't recollect the details. I told him I worked in outreach, and I remember how he chuckled, a deep, throaty sound from the back of his throat. Going into schools and working with kiddies, then, he said, and I winced. Even then, I was never one for mingling with young people.

He introduced himself twice: first by his desk, then later, as I turned to leave. That was significant, I think. A sign that he wanted to be known, even at that first meeting, that he wanted me to absorb him, to store the memory of his face away for the future. At the time, it seemed so completely, entirely harmless. Nothing in the exchange to indicate anything more than mutual, casual interest.

But it didn't remain that way. Even a small pebble can change the course of an entire river, and that's how it was for me. The mess of everything after was a direct result of that meeting, and I'd give anything to go back and do it differently. Ignore his call, rather than answer. Refuse to help carry his ridiculous files. Shove him down that stairwell if necessary, and watch as he tumbled backwards and cracked his skull on the floor. Anything would have been better than what followed.

I squeeze the gull pendant in my palm. It leaves red marks, which then fade. If only Henry would fade as quickly. But he'll never leave me be. He'll always be at the edges of my memory, ready to move to centre stage.

I hate thinking of these things. I hate him.

And I hate you too, sometimes. Even though you were just a child, barely a teenager when it happened, and none of this was your fault.

CHAPTER 2

Going outside shouldn't be so hard. I used to do it all the time. But it's difficult to recall how easily I used to slip out of the front door, joining the throng of people for the morning bus, squeezed alongside suited men, women with pushchairs. How did I manage it back then, to be so fearless around others?

I yearn for empty space, that's the problem. I need vast swathes of fields and rough cliffs to stop the rest of the world from blundering in. This city is smaller than Bristol, but there are still too many people out there for comfort. However, I'm not permitted to go somewhere more natural. My parole conditions tether me here.

I'm procrastinating, putting off the inevitable. I know it, even as I water my kitchen herbs for a second time, and rip off another sheet of kitchen towel to blow my nose. These psychologist's visits aren't optional; they're part of my post-prison requirements. It *has* to be now. I pull open the front door and step outside. It isn't so bad, now it's done. The sky is an inviting shade of blue, the street is quiet. Mercifully, it's still early, so there's no one else around. This is fine. I can do this.

The walk into town is pleasant enough. In fact, I almost forget myself for a while. My steps are quietly confident, my eyes fixed ahead. I pat at my hair. It feels so different to how it did before I was locked up. Back then, I had silk-soft curls. Now it's brittle as a scouring pad, not that it matters much. Who'd look on me with desire now? Certainly not Henry, if he saw me. He'd probably delight in my diminished state, tell me it was nothing less than I deserved. Actually, I'm deluding myself; he'd prefer to see me dead. Nothing but annihilation would quench his desire for revenge, I'd imagine.

Dr Holland's office is suburban, a semi-detached property with only a small brass sign to mark it as a business. It takes me by surprise, each time I come here: there's nothing professional about it. I ring the bell and wait.

He appears swiftly, as he always does. There's a smear of yellow on his shirt. Perhaps egg yolk from his breakfast, or a tiny splash of orange juice. Either way, it doesn't reflect well on him.

'Ah, Robin.' He steps aside. 'Do come in.'

I follow him to his room. One chair for me, the cheap polycotton semi-reclining sort, facing away from the window. An executive leather chair for him, by the desk. It's an effective way to establish hierarchy through the medium of furniture, I'll give him that.

I settle, then watch him do the same. The room smells over-poweringly of vanilla. Probably he was told on his psycho-therapy training that it calms the nerves, or some such nonsense. Personally, I find it cloying and artificial. In short, the perfect accompanying scent to these meetings, which are inevitably pointless.

'How have you been this last week?' he asks, skim-reading his notes.

'Good, thank you.'

'That's excellent news.' He meets my eye, then looks away. 'And how are you adjusting to civilian life? Last week, you said you had some struggles with visiting your corner shop.'

'It's better. I walked here this morning, and it was pleasant.'

'Wonderful, wonderful. Exeter's a nice place to live in. Cosy, yet bustling. Have you been into the city centre yet?'

'No, I haven't.'

'Maybe that could be part of our action plan, give you some-thing to aim for. What we don't want is for you to feel nervous about going outside. It's better to beat those fears before they take root.'

'Perhaps.'

He waits, then nods. 'How have you been sleeping?'

'Fine,' I lie.

'You've been finding it easy to go to sleep?'

'Absolutely.'

'No bad dreams? Your notes from Dr Resner mentioned that you suffered from nightmares in prison.'

'That's just being in prison, isn't it? It's a nightmarish place.'

'Not like it is in some countries, believe me,' he replies, lips twitching. 'So, you're sleeping well, not having bad dreams, and you're getting out of the house. This is a good start. Remember, Robin, if you're having issues, we can look into medication. There are options available.'

'Can you call me Ava? At least in here?'

'No, that wouldn't be wise. As part of your protection, you were given a new name, so we must keep using it. Anonymity orders are rare, not to mention expensive; no one wants to go through the hassle of getting you another.'

'Robin is such a small name.'

He laughs. 'It's two letters longer than Ava.'

'It's restraining.'

'Let's talk about that, then. How does it restrain you?'

I feel myself slumping inwardly. These conversations are tiresome. There's nothing I want to communicate to him, and I can tell he has little genuine interest in me. It's yet another hoop to jump through, that's all.

'I don't feel like me,' I say.

'Okay. So, what would you prefer to feel like?'

'Like myself again. I'd prefer not to live here.'

'Really? Where would you choose to go?'

Somewhere remote. Somewhere where there are no other people. Where I can live as myself and not be frightened of others. I don't say any of this, of course. Instead, I give a non-committal shrug.

20

Dr Holland doesn't care anyway; as long as he receives his payment for this half-hour session, he'd be happy to talk about anything.

'I'd like to be free to go where I want to,' I say carefully.

He leans forward. 'But you understand why you can't, yes?'

'I understand why the law says criminals can't.'

'That's not quite the same thing. Do you regard yourself as a criminal, Robin?'

Ava. Damn that false name, even the mere sound of it is irritating. 'I've served my time,' I remind him.

'That's true. But your answer is interesting. We've discussed culpability before; in our last session, in fact. It's so important to accept when we've done something wrong, and to own our actions. It's actually an empowering thing. Do you accept that you did something criminal?'

'I was in prison, wasn't I?'

'Yes, but that's not quite the same thing. Do you accept your crime?'

My crime. Always it leads back to this. It happened over twenty years ago, and still they won't leave it alone.

'I said I did, during my release hearing.'

He studies me hard. I feel like an insect under a microscope.

'Do you often think about what happened?' he asks.

'You mean before prison?'

'I mean the incident that put you in prison, Robin.'

Stop calling me that! Anger rises, thick and sudden. I could pick that paperweight off his desk, smash it into his rigid, smiling teeth. Break each one into shards, and make him look like the shark he is. At least then he'd have something authentic about him, something genuine.

'You're talking about the murder,' I say, without looking at him.

'It's good that you can now call it that. That's progress.'

'It's what everyone else calls it.'

'Words have power, don't they? Sometimes it's hard to use a particular word, because it's so laden with meaning, and because it makes us feel a certain way.'

21

I shut off. This session is more excruciating than the last. Instead, I focus on the paintings behind his head. A whitewashed cottage sitting in a rolling meadow. Waves lapping at a cove. They could be shots from my childhood, laid open for me to slip back into.

It would be so much easier to be there again, and not here.

As I walk back, my mind turns to prison again. How strange it is these days, to wear a skirt, rather than regulation trousers. To take a breath and for it to be full of fresh oxygen. To pace on pavement rather than pocked grey linoleum. It should feel better than it does. Instead, it makes me think of the women I left behind. None of them were my friends. Most of them were positively vile, in fact. But don't humans deserve a better life than that? Probably not, in the eyes of everyone else. It's easier to lock a problem away than it is to try to resolve it.

I close my eyes and imagine Ditz walking behind me, shoes squealing against the floor. She was so mouselike. So high-pitched and weak in every move she made. I noticed that even on her first day, when she entered the recreation area, how her eyes flitted from wall to wall in a state of panic. To be fair, it wasn't the most welcoming of places: a vast, echoing space, with clinical plastic chairs and cheap tables scattered around the floor. And of course, there was the endless hum of women, muttering, grumbling, occasionally laughing out loud.

She interpreted it as a hostile environment, a place to fear, and she was right to do so. The whole prison was a cage, after all. A big, dangerous cage where hiding wasn't an option, and where there were plenty of untamed creatures, all lethal and waiting to pounce. She didn't have a clue. I talked to her for the first time in the yard, as we stared through the fence at the road in the distance. Asked her what her name was, even though I knew it already. Wondered, for a moment, if she'd simply vanish when I spoke, if she was you, come to haunt me in a different form.

I was frightened of her, just briefly. How prescient, given how badly things turned out. How the inmates hounded me after she died, how those calls of *Butcher Bird* echoed down the prison corridor after the lights went out. I would have left Ditz well alone, had I known what would happen. Instead, I moved closer, told her we were cell-neighbours. She blinked those bovine eyes of hers, then gave me a smile of relief. The wall inside her crumbled with no further resistance, tumbled by her desire to have someone to protect her. That was all she ever wanted, I think. To be sheltered from the painful storm of living.

That trusting, blinkered hope reminded me so much of you. You believed I was a friend, that you could talk to me about how your mother ignored you, how your father was too busy with work. You were right to trust me, despite how it ended. I liked you, and that's the truth.

I won't think of you now, though. I will turn my thoughts back to Ditz instead; the memory of her is somewhat less painful. It was only a few months ago. Strange, it seems like far longer. It was a different existence back then, and I showed Ditz who was in charge, just as Daddy would have wanted me to. Her precious sister Babs was no longer around to look after her, so it had to be me instead, and she needed to be taught the ways of the world. *You're the one in the driving seat*, Daddy would have said. *Their survival depends on you. Remember that, and stop being sentimental.*

I believe he was talking about birds at the time, but the same equally applies to humans.

Love is a strange concept. No human seems immune to it, even though it makes little rational sense.

Henry loved me once, I think. No, that's the wrong word. It's too ardent, too clean. He desired me, wanted to take possession of me. I was a thing to be enjoyed, for a time.

He used to make excuses to pop down to our office. To linger by my desk, look over my shoulder and read my notes. It wasn't long before his hand grazed my neck, those dry, roughened fingertips stroking my skin. Outwardly, it was a show of comradery; a small squeeze to demonstrate support or commiseration. But I'm sure he knew exactly what he was really doing. When Henry first asked me if I was free after work, I genuinely believed it was for a friendly chat, nothing more. How naïve I was. What the people said about me afterwards, and the newspapers – they were all wrong. I was the victim, not him.

I agreed to Henry's suggestion to meet. But my response wasn't a come-on, absolutely not. I suppose I may have found it flattering. After all, Daddy had scarcely taken the time to say more than ten words to me each day, when I was a child. And here was this man, broad-shouldered, narrow-waisted, handsome and charismatic, listening to what I had to say, rather than glazing over.

I was easy pickings.

In prison, the doctor said that I should glean some positives from the past. As such, I take this from my experiences with Henry. His seduction technique proved useful in the long run. His devoted attention, the way he made me feel worthwhile; all of that I replicated with Ditz, many years later. My relationship with her was purely platonic of course, but nonetheless I had the necessary tools to bring her to me. It felt good, after so many years of being alone.

She saw me as a replacement for her sister, the infamous Babs, she of the ridiculous name. Short for babble, probably, if she was anything like Ditz. Foolish, empty babble. It's a kindness when a mother tells her child the truth about the world. That's all I ever imparted to Ditz. Less babble, more plain, honest talking. I fail to see how that's a crime.

This computer is both a marvel and a menace. Margot recommended that I invest in a second-hand one, a laptop, which sat on my kitchen table for a week before I summoned up the courage to use it. Computers were around before I was incarcerated, and they were in the prison itself, but none like this. This modern contraption is something quite different.

The internet is a limitless world of knowledge. It staggers me that I can type in any word and instantly have endless reams of websites at my fingertips, waiting to be read. I search for images of Lundy, Rum, Sark, all the islands I lived on before. None of them has changed. My chest aches for them, so much that I can't stop myself from touching the screen, reaching towards those tumbling cliffs and navy-blue waves.

I find a photo of a huddle of Manx shearwaters, nestled into the loose soil by the edge of a cliff. Their black eyes, so watchful and unreadable, pull me in. I remember the feel of their wings in my hands, the fragility of their necks beneath the feathers. The flap of webbed foot against my palm as I attached the rings to their legs.

We ring them to understand them, Daddy said. *Then we know when they come back.*

But what if they don't come back?

Then they have abandoned us. Either that, or they are dead.

Like Mother?

No. Not like that at all. Some creatures matter. Others don't.

I wondered which mattered more. Mother or the birds.

We never stayed in one place for very long, as ours was a nomadic existence. Daddy's career demanded it. He was the larger planet, tugging me, his little moon, behind him. The few people we encountered, his work colleagues, fellow ornithologists, all treated him with the respect he commanded. Me, they hardly ever gave a fleeting glance to. Those birding types were all very single-minded.

There were advantages to being ignored. I was free to roam as I wanted, to explore without question or interruption. My knees were mud-crusted from slithering through bog-water and crawling in caves. My fingernails were usually black-rimmed and cracked. I was an animal, enveloped and encircled by the wild, permitted to roam. Daddy's only request was that I wash myself occasionally, especially when he was entertaining an eminent scientist at one of our rented cottages. Like her, of course. The notable researcher and later much more, Professor Jean Marshall. It was the opinions of others that he was concerned with most. As such, appearances had to be maintained when it mattered.

It's getting dark outside now. Beyond my kitchen window, the garden is a wash of grey, bleached of colour. So small and insipid, compared to what I knew before.

As a young girl, I wandered on those cliffs alone, groping at the ground, peering in tiny burrows for nesting birds. I can almost hear Daddy, shouting to me from somewhere in the dark. The thwack of a hand around my ear if I was making too much noise.

It was a strange way to grow up, I suppose.

I didn't kill him. Daddy, I mean. After everything that happened, people threw all sorts of accusations at me. Elaborate theories abounded about how many other deaths there might have been in my past. Murder, made to look like an accident. Of course, they found no evidence, those spiteful accusers. I had nothing to do with his passing. That is the truth. Of all the people in the world, he was the one that I never could have hurt, regardless of how much I might have wanted to. Ultimately, life and death are all about who matters more, but no one else has ever seemed to understand that, aside from him.

You, I could never have willingly hurt, either. I had such fondness for your honest, upturned face, the awkwardness of your near-teenage limbs. Only I did hurt you, somehow. Things went badly wrong, but it was Henry's fault.

Nobody believed me. As Daddy said, some people matter more, others less. It was perfectly clear which category they wanted to put me in.

CHAPTER 3

It's another glorious day, unseasonably so for this time of year. I take my book outside and settle onto the lounger seat. It was left behind by the previous tenant, and though the fabric is grimy, it holds my weight just fine. My backside eases into it like cake mix into a tin. It is a pleasure, it really is.

Time passes. I yawn. Perhaps it's the indolent thrum of the bees, pressing themselves against the lavender next to me, or the low drone of a passing aeroplane, high above. The sun glows red in my private world as I close my eyes and, for a moment, I think I know peace.

A crash yanks me back into reality and my book tumbles to the ground. I look around, blinking stupidly, and see that the garden is suddenly the wrong shape. An unfamiliar lawn is now visible through a gap and two faces are peering in at me, both with mouths in perfect circles of horror. Bill, plus a female, perhaps in her late thirties. Girlfriend? Unlikely, too young. Her hair is pure white, her chin sharp and somehow defiant.

It's the fence. I see it now. One of the panels has fallen, landing barely inches from my lounger. Luckily, I hadn't moved it closer to give myself some shade, otherwise I'd be nursing a sore head right now.

'I'm so sorry!' Bill says, stepping forward, then deciding against it. 'I don't know what happened; one moment I was hanging a flowerpot on it, and the next, it—'

27

I wave his comment away and quickly smooth myself down. 'It was an accident. It just made me jump, that's all.'

'I'll get it fixed.'

'Honestly, it's no problem.'

Bill sighs, then points to the woman standing beside him. 'This is my daughter, Amber. Amber, this is Robin, my new neighbour.'

Amber smiles tightly. 'Sorry to drop in on you like this.'

I laugh, perhaps too forcefully. The truth is, I feel invaded, a besieged castle surrounded on all sides. It's as much as I can do to stop my hands from curling into fists.

'It's one way to say hello, I suppose,' I say.

'I might be able to get it back up,' Bill says, reaching forward and grabbing the fence panel. 'It's in good enough shape. It's possible it only needs some new brackets.' He smiles. 'Glad to see you're making the most of this lovely weather.'

His daughter eyes me, starting with my slippers and ending at my face. I detect a steeliness, a tension in the jaw, a hint of cold surveillance in those pupils. I should know, I've seen it often enough in prison. I can't read what she's thinking, though, and that worries me. Her hostility is a folded map; there's no interpreting her.

'We should leave,' she says, turning back to the house. 'Dad, maybe you can prop the fence back up for now and give this lady some peace.'

He gives me an apologetic smile.

As if I'd ever really know peace, I think, watching him as he crudely seals the gap, until only the top half of his head is visible. His daughter is the possessive sort, I suspect. So many offspring are. They believe they own their parents, simply because they gave them life. As far as I'm concerned, they're the ones who should be paying the debt, not the mother or father.

I pick up my book and head inside. The garden feels different now, less secure. I'd rather get back into the safety of the house.

I can't stop brooding on Bill's daughter. Women are peculiar creatures. Being locked up with so many of them only cemented that fact for me. They're beings in endless motion, emotions jostling for space in the chasm of their minds, thoughts all piled up on one another like rubble. They're tricky to read, with a tendency to overshare trivial opinions. Contradictory, intense, but often empty. Empty. Funny, that's the word Daddy used to use to describe Mother, back in the day. I must have inherited my views from him.

My spare room still looks like a tip. Books are scattered haphazardly over the carpet, mildewed clothes spew over the sides of the boxes like innards on display, and the pile of things to discard seems too enormous for any bin to contain. It reminds me of the storage facility Daddy used just after Mother died. It possesses that same sense of overwhelming tension, as though the stacks of useless items might detonate at any moment.

I remember seeing her armchair in that storage unit, sitting in the corner with my toys piled beside it. It still had the faint indentation of her on the cushion, a shadow of absence, of someone who'd perhaps never really been there in the first place. You won't need those toys where we're going, Daddy told me, as we walked back to the car. It was true, I never missed them, not one bit, and we never returned for any of our belongings. So much of it is meaningless junk, once you get down to it.

I don't remember much about the boat journey to the first island, only the spray of salt water on my face as I stood on the deck, and how bracing it was. But I do recollect that first house by the cliffside. Stone-built, with only four rooms inside. A walled garden in the front, one parched picnic bench in the middle of the scrubby lawn. But most importantly, the vast expanse of sea, right in front of us. The kittiwakes woke me each morning. They reminded me of the school I'd left behind; the same excited lilt of their chatter, the rabble of their squawking. I was hundreds of miles from the children I'd known, and I didn't mind one bit. They'd never meant anything to me anyway.

That first island was where Daddy introduced me to Jean Marshall. Professor Jean, he said reverently, as if her title was an award to be displayed. They'd worked on projects together in the past. She reminded me of a horse, with thrusting front teeth and a lengthy nose. Plaid shirts in every colour, khaki wellingtons, sensible jeans on most days. She visited our cottage too often, made herself comfortable in our lives, and this was evident in all the little things. Mud from her boots scattered over our doormat. The ghost of her lip-salve on our coffee mugs. The essence of her had seeped through the place like gas, quiet but unmistakable.

Looking back, it was obvious they'd been intimate for a long time. Years, perhaps. Had Mother known? There was no way of saying for sure. But one thing was certain. I'd thought that it would be Daddy and me, a lonely pair, starting a new life together. Instead, we'd become three again. Worse, they were a duo, and I the spare, singular one, whether I liked it or not.

Home schooling, which Daddy had promised, turned out to be assisting with his research, or else reading a few tattered books he'd collected for me. He didn't enforce any of it. I don't believe he had any interest in my development whatsoever. But I loved the birds as he did, so it didn't matter. The island was small and I spent my days traipsing over every part of it. I knew with loving intimacy each overhang of precarious cliff, every grassy, sloping hillside. I peered over rocks to see nesting seabirds and found eggs secreted in sandy holes. Aside from the occasional visiting enthusiast, striding past me with rucksack and binoculars, there was never anyone else. I was silently, blissfully alone.

This is why I struggle with company now. It has nothing to do with perceived psychopathic tendencies or anything else the lawyer levelled at me in court. Just a lack of practice around others, which is why Henry found it so easy to take advantage.

Yes, that was how it was. When I think about it like this, it is so obvious. I believe I'd make a much better psychologist than most. I certainly do a far better job of analysing myself than they ever could.

I venture to the corner shop again. There are people around, which isn't surprising, given that it's now mid-morning. A young woman meanders along the street, grasping her toddler's arm

30

while staring at her phone. An elderly man, leaning on a crutch, aggressively avoids my gaze; a younger fellow, with a mass of dreadlocks bundled under a cap, wears earphones blocking him from the world. It seems so much easier to isolate oneself from the rest of society now. Acceptable, even.

I pick up a chocolate bar. They've definitely got bigger over the years; some of them look positively indecent. The woman behind the till scarcely raises her eyes.

'Eighty-five pence.'

It's a shocking price. Everything shocks me now. I remember them costing a quarter of that, back in the day. It's a marvel how anyone affords anything. I hand over a pound coin, another thing that has changed. Everything is an adjustment.

Small steps, I tell myself. Soon, this will feel normal.

Outside, a child hurtles towards me on a scooter. The father frowns and says nothing. I fight to contain my disgust. People have no manners these days and no sense of decency. But maybe it was always that way. Perhaps I've glorified politeness, imagined it to be more prevalent than it was, as a contrast to the foul behaviour of the inmates I was surrounded by for so many years.

I wait, motionless, as the child skids the scooter around in one deft flick, then hurtles in the other direction. It's the only thing to do, otherwise I risk being mowed down. You were the only child I ever liked. Even the few children I knew growing up were never friends. In my opinion, most youngsters are untamed savages, greedy, grasping and unpredictable. Parents seem unable to shape them into functioning adults, which explains why our species is ultimately doomed.

What a world we live in, I think, as I stride back home.

Margot is late, which is unusual. She seems out of breath when she arrives, though her car is parked directly outside.

'Would you like a cup of tea?' I ask.

She bustles past me, all business already. 'Not for me. I'm in a rush.'

'Busy day?'

She laughs, eyes narrowing. 'Every day is a busy day. They work us hard you know, and it's only getting worse.'

Niceties over, she takes a seat, then pulls out a form from her satchel. 'I need to complete a report on your adjustment, Robin, so I'm going to ask a few questions. Let's see, how long have you been out now?'

I place a plate of biscuits in front of her. 'Twenty-three days.'

'Very precise, that's excellent. How would you say you've found it? A difficult process? Fairly easy?'

'Fairly easy.' I know she doesn't really care how I respond, so I'll aim to make it as hassle-free as possible for her.

'That's wonderful.' She ticks a box. 'How have you found the support that you've been offered?'

'You mean *you*?'

'And your psychologist.'

'Yes, all good, thank you.'

She scribbles for a minute or two, then munches on a biscuit. 'There's a government push on better after-prison support, so we need to make sure you're not feeling depressed or anything. We have to make sure the media doesn't keep painting us as the villains.'

'No, I think I'm doing well.'

She nods, satisfied. 'I haven't had a chance to read Dr Holland's latest notes yet, I've been rushed off my feet. How are his sessions going? Are you finding them useful?'

It's hard to keep a straight face. 'He's been helpful,' I tell her. 'You know, with providing tips for how to cope in the future.'

She raps her pen on the paper. 'That's good to hear. It helps that the victims aren't making life difficult for you. Sometimes that can cause real complications.'

'Victims?'

'You know. Henry and Miranda Hulham.'

I stiffen at the names. Victims? I don't deny that they lost something, but I lost twenty-five years of my life.

'How would they make life difficult?' I ask slowly.

'Protesting your re-entry into society, getting in touch with the media. That sort of thing. It does happen, on occasion. I know you had that run-in with Miranda in prison, too.'

'That was a long time ago.'

She gives me a strange look. 'Well, it's good that everything is going smoothly.'

'Where are they living now? Surely they can't still be in Bristol, can they?'

'You know I can't give you that information, Robin. That's strictly confidential.'

'And they can't find out where I live?'

'No.' She makes another note on her paper, covering her pen with her other hand, so I can't see what she's written. 'I'm sure that if they were going to attack you in any way, they would have done so by now. They probably just want to move on with their lives.'

Henry always liked to sweep things under the carpet, I think, remembering his all-too-easy laugh, the way he rolled through existence like a boulder down a hill, oblivious to those he squashed beneath him. As for Miranda? That poisonous creature would like nothing more than to make me suffer.

'Are they still married?' I ask.

'Henry and Miranda?' She picks up the paper and stuffs it back in her bag. 'I can't tell you that either, and you really shouldn't ask.'

I bet they are, I think. I bet they still pretend they're the perfect couple, while he has affairs with any woman that he can get his hands on. I was nothing special to him. Nothing at all.

Margot's hand hovers over the plate of biscuits, as if debating the decision, then is withdrawn. 'You're not thinking of trying to get in touch with them, are you?' she asks, keeping her voice light. I hear the threat beneath it.

'Of course not.'

'That's good. We fought hard to get you a new identity, Robin. If you were to do anything like that, it would jeopardise everything.'

'This new identity won't stop other people from recognising me, will it?'

She frowns. 'I'm sure that won't happen. It's been twenty-five years; you look very different. Now, I need to be confident that you won't try to contact Henry or Miranda Hulham, or their daughter. Can you assure me of that?'

I nod, like a good little girl. The truth is, I have no desire to see any of them again. Though if they were to come near me, if they did try to hurt me in some way, I'd give them cause to think twice about it. I remember what Daddy once said to do. Watch the seabirds. They have beaks. Beating wings. But they only use them to defend, never to attack.

Apart from a few, I thought at the time, watching the arctic skua circling overhead, searching for a chick, or else a puffin to drown at sea, in exchange for a morsel of fish. The skua has no issue with taking other creatures down. It's a survivor.

'Robin?' Margot says, eyes narrowing.

Skua, I think, then laugh.

She sighs. 'Just stick to the rules of your parole, okay? That's all that matters.'

'Of course.'

She smiles, believing she can see inside me. She thinks she knows my thoughts, all because she's studied a few books, attended a few lectures. It would be endearing, if it wasn't so deeply offensive. She doesn't speak my language, and she certainly can't read me.

You silly woman, I think, while smiling back at her sweetly.

CHAPTER 4

My mind is uneasy today. I'm sleeping even worse than usual, though it's a comfort I've barely made a dent in the sleeping pills in the bathroom, or my supplies in the bedside drawer. Still, I feel I should get more, to be on the safe side. That means another trip outside, this time into the city itself. I shouldn't have taken so many last night, but the need was urgent. I kept hearing Ditz, crying out in the darkness, and even saw her watery eyes, shining somewhere in the corner of the bedroom. Moving, shifting around me, hanging from the ceiling light, she was everywhere, her head at the wrong angle, feet dangling to the floor.

Sometimes I feel I must be going mad.

I need to think of something positive. I turn my mind to the small pleasures in life, which isn't so hard. There's sitting in the lounge with my book. Watching television programmes that I enjoy, rather than ones that have been deemed suitable for me to view. Having a bath, even though the grouting around the edge is rather mouldy.

But none of it seems to be doing the trick. I think back to how I used to cope as a child. I used to simply walk from whatever cottage we were staying in at the time, and stride through the fields and woods. I did that a lot, especially when Professor Jean Marshall was around. God, I hated that woman. I shouldn't think of her, I really shouldn't. But sometimes it's difficult to switch the memories off.

Daddy was never demonstrative towards Mother. Even when she was at her sickest, he always kept his distance, with no sign of charity or care. Jean seemed to bring out another side to his character. He chose to touch her often. Fingers at her elbow, or else lingering on her waist. Across her cheek, and over her lips, especially as the months progressed. I loathed her flushing, simpering face, and the snicker of a giggle she had, like a mule whinnying. Not that she smiled much at me. Whenever I entered the room, a wary, guarded look would close her face down in a heartbeat. Even though it was my home, she always made me feel like the stranger. I understand, now, that children are frustrating. But I was there first, not her. Territory is the most important thing of all, and she'd invaded mine.

After we moved on to the next island, I imagined we'd never see her again. How pleasant it was to think that she'd remain back on those cold beaches, washed up like dirty flotsam on the tide. But there she was on Lundy, and again on St Helens. It transpired she was working on the same project as Daddy. It was all rather too convenient.

I am brooding. I must stop; it's not necessary any more. I did enough of that in prison. Instead, I pull my coat out from the understairs cupboard, cursing its lack of hood. Rain is on the way, and I've no way of protecting myself. An umbrella, even a lightweight anorak with a hood: these are things I'll need to buy for the future. But that means another journey into the outside world, which I'm reluctant to put myself through.

The clouds roll uneasily above as I close the door behind me. Another front door echoes my own, close by. *Bill*, I think, looking next door, but it's a woman. His daughter Amber. I can tell by the brittle posture and the striking white hair. She sees me and her gaze flits away almost immediately, a sure sign that she wishes she'd left the house a few minutes earlier, or else later. Anything to avoid conversation, which I completely agree with, naturally.

'Good morning,' she says curtly, eyes still fixed elsewhere. Her hair is wispy, I notice; almost transparent in its whiteness.

Angel hair, my mother might have called it. There's nothing angelic about this woman though. She's flint, through and through.

'Are you staying with your father?' I blurt.

I can tell that she longs to tell me it's none of my business. Instead, she nods.

'Dad likes company from time to time,' she says. 'I take it he told you about his past.'

'Yes. It must have been hard.'

'You have no idea.'

And neither do you, I retort silently. I've seen her type before, back in prison. They present themselves as street-smart and tough, merely because they've encountered turbulence in the past. Admittedly, an absent father must have been hard, but still. She had a mother, a house to grow up in, which is more than Bill had benefited from.

'Is he around?' I ask, peering over her shoulder, half-expecting him to emerge from the doorway at the sound of our voices.

'No, he's catching up on his sleep. He doesn't sleep well.'

'I know that feeling.'

Again, that look. She's sizing me up, viewing me as competition. Silly little creature. Then her eyes narrow. 'Have we met before?'

Her question takes the breath from my body. A hundred frantic whispers travel through me: she knows, she knows. She can't know. It's impossible. It's possible. I've been discovered.

'What do you mean?' I ask, keeping my tone light.

'I'm not sure. You look familiar.'

'I probably look like a thousand other women.'

She doesn't reply, only nods. 'I'm off into town,' she says, pointing vaguely behind her. 'Hopefully Dad will get the fence fixed soon, then you won't have him peering into your garden.'

'I honestly don't mind,' I say, but it's too late, she's already walking away. I watch her swaying back as she paces along the pavement. It's not just her words that are unsettling, it's everything that's unsaid, hidden behind her impassive expression. She's a closed book, even more so than other women I've met. There's something off

37

about her, but I can't quite put my finger on it. She has the ability to be vicious, I'm sure. I know the type when I see them.

I've lost my appetite for going to the shops now. The pills will have to wait; I'd rather try it again another day. In answer to my thoughts, the first fat drop of rain falls from the sky, catching me directly on the nose.

It's better to be inside, for now.

The rain hasn't stopped all morning.

It reminds me of when Henry and I spent our first night together. It was the same drizzle then as it is now. I was worried that my hair would be ruined; it was always prone to frizzing. He pulled his jacket over my head as we ran to the bus stop, but the lightweight cotton did nothing to stop the damp seeping through.

I'll come back with you, he told me, boarding the bus. It's not safe to travel alone, not at this time of night.

I should have known what his motives were. It seems so ignorant now. The hand around my shoulders should have been another clue. But I was young, and probably far more innocent than other women. I don't recall liking it. I'm sure I can't have liked it. After all, he was taking liberties, making a move, despite the fact that he'd spent a long time in the bar beforehand telling me about his two children, about his wife, Miranda. He'd sold himself as a family man, then casually slipped through my front door like smoke through an air vent.

That was my introduction to physical intimacy. Fingers, tugging my blouse from my skirt as soon as I closed the front door. Hot mouth, tracing moisture down my neck. Hands, hands everywhere, cupping my buttocks, forcing my head back, running along my sides. I felt like a fish in the arms of an octopus. So many limbs, wrestling to subdue me.

He didn't even bother to take me to the bedroom. Instead, he pressed me to the floor, just by the welcome mat. My shoulder blades chafed against the carpet. Isn't it odd, the things that stay with you, after so many years? The experience reminded me of swans mating. The male bird holds the female down, often below the waterline. He cares little for the fact that she is submerged, suffering presumably, while he has his wicked way.

I chuckle at this bitter thought. I'm echoing so many other prison women, hardened against men, keen to dismiss them as the more brutal, less human gender. Of course, it doesn't help that they make it so easy for us to hate them sometimes.

I believe in being useful. Regardless of one's situation in life, one should always contribute. Since coming out of prison, I've felt distinctly ineffectual, and this needs to be addressed, in order to re-enter society successfully. Baking is the answer, I decide. I used to enjoy making cakes and pies; I taught myself as a child, on those dark evenings when it was apparent that no one else was going to do the cooking.

My first attempt at a sponge cake is disappointing. To be fair, it's been a while since I last tried. The bottom is a touch soggy, the edges have stuck fast to my tins, and the overall taste is slightly bitter. I shall have to practise; making cakes is a good skill to have. We all need some sweetness from time to time.

The doorbell rings once, then again. I almost drop the cake in my surprise. It's an unwelcome intrusion. I'm not in the mood for *thinking* this evening, much less talking. But the sight of a balding head, glistening in the evening sunlight through the frosted glass, is enough to change my mind. It's Bill, holding another bottle of wine. He smiles, then performs a sheepish half-bow as I pull the door ajar.

'Would it be intrusive of me to invite myself in for a drink?' he asks.

Normally I'd refuse. But his smile is gentle – womanish, even. I notice a scar, curving around his neck, just below his ear. A sign of violence on the streets, perhaps. This makes him safer. He knows the impact of suffering, the damage that unkindness can do.

'Of course,' I say, stepping aside. 'I've been trying to bake, but you're welcome to come in.'

'Anything tasty?'

'A cake, but it didn't turn out too well. The next one will be better. I'll make sure to give you a slice.'

'You're a friendly sort.' He follows me through to the living room, then settles into my old sofa, as though already well acquainted with it. 'I'm glad we're neighbours.'

I hold up a finger, stemming his flow of conversation, then quickly run to the kitchen and grab two glasses. I only possess two, so it's fortunate they're both clean.

He unscrews the cap, then quickly pours, passing me the first glass. A gentleman, I note approvingly. Not that Henry wouldn't have done the same, but he would have done it with a leer, a suggestive glance to indicate that he'd be expecting something in return. Bill seems more innocent. His eyes are round, peaceful as an infant's. I sense no risk from him.

'Thanks for being so happy to share a drink with me,' he says, leaning closer. 'Not everyone would be.'

'What do you mean?'

'Because I was homeless. I had a drug problem. I'm not exactly the sort that people want in their houses. And I'm on benefits. Everyone out there would call me a scrounger.'

'I'm on benefits too,' I blurt, then redden.

'Are you? Disability?'

I nod, then quickly drink.

He's too polite to ask, which is a blessing. Instead, he gestures to the room. 'You keep this place very clean. You haven't been here long, have you?'

'Not very,' I agree. 'But what about you? Where were you before?'

'Ah, not so fast. I want to find out more about you, Robin. Seeing as we're friends now.' He chuckles, then clinks his glass against mine. 'What were you doing before you moved here?'

'I lived in Herefordshire,' I say. My throat feels dry, despite the wine. I'm telling the truth: that's where the prison was.

'Was it nice?'

'It was hellish,' I answer honestly.

'I suppose if you grew up by the seaside, anywhere seems like a poor second-best, eh?'

'That's right.'

The flow of words ceases, and I feel his gaze on my cheek. My skin tingles in response. 'It was a horrible day today, wasn't it?' I say, to break the silence. 'You wouldn't guess it was still summer.'

'It forced me to stay inside and get some jobs done, so I can't complain.'

'It must have been awful on the streets when it rained.'

He narrows his eyes. 'It was. But I don't think about it much now. I focus on the future instead.'

'That's what my—' I start, then falter. I can't mention that Dr Holland regularly says that exact same thing. Bill mustn't know about any of that. He wouldn't understand; no one would.

'I sense that you don't like to talk about yourself much,' he says, filling the gap in the conversation. 'I won't pry, don't worry. I'm too much of a gasbag, I talk about myself all the time. Amber says she wishes I'd give it a rest sometimes.'

'She seems nice,' I lie.

'She's a good lass. She mentioned she'd seen you earlier. It's funny, she's convinced she knows you from somewhere.'

My breath catches in my throat. She's old enough to remember what happened, just about. But I've changed, I'm virtually unrecognisable. I've got a new name, I'm a different person, and surely that's enough. Perhaps it isn't. I know that all it takes is a single rumour for people to start digging for dirt. That can't happen. I'm finished if it does.

'Are you all right?' Bill asks, breaking the silence.

I bring myself back to the present, force a smile. 'Yes. Of course. I don't know your daughter, so she must be getting me confused with someone else. Could you tell her that?'

'I'll be sure to pass the message on. So, do you live by yourself, Robin?'

'I do, yes.'

This isn't a good idea. I can't navigate conversations like this, it's too hard to come up with lies and keep track of what I've said. Every word that drops from my lips is a breadcrumb, leading to the truth. It's dangerous.

'No kids?'

I think of you. How can I not? You were like a son to me, albeit for too short a time. I shake my head quickly. I can't start dwelling on you now, not here. It'll show on my expression, and Bill will notice.

He nods sympathetically. 'Sorry, that was a nosy question. I'm just struggling to make you out. You've got no personal photographs in here either, so I can't do any guesswork from that.'

'Apart from the birds,' I say, pointing to the images of the fulmars on the mantlepiece.

'I figured out you were very fond of birds.' He smiles. 'But no man, or woman, can live off birds alone.'

'I think birds are a lot more sensible than most people I've met.'

'Where does the love of birds come from, then?'

'My father,' I say, then quickly lie, 'and my mother.'

'Did they work with birds, or something like that?'

Too close to the truth. I quickly shake my head. 'No, they just liked watching the ones in the garden.'

'And that led you to have a career in all things avian?'

'What makes you think that?'

He gives me a strange look. 'You told me, the other day. Didn't you?'

'Yes, that's right.' My face feels hot. I can't remember what I said or didn't say before. This is the problem with being around Bill; he's too affable, too easy-going. It's worryingly simple to drop my guard.

He laughs, then holds up his hands. 'I can see there's no cracking you, Ms Robin. You're a woman who likes to keep things private. That's fair enough – I'll stop asking questions. Now, would you like a top-up?'

I accept the wine with a smile, but my stomach knots. This is meant to be normal, a casual meeting with a new acquaintance. Social interaction. But this will *never* feel normal, I can tell.

I'm not even sure I know what normal is.

Ditz loved me, I'm certain. I *know* it to be true, as I lie here in the bath, in the cooling water, letting the moist bubbles tickle my limbs. I remember how she used to look at me, that dopey haze of adulation, the relief that someone would take care of her while she was in prison and make everything all right. She was right to think that. I kept her safe, steered her away from the malign influences of the other inmates. I took her under my wing as tenderly as a hen with her chick, and showed her how to survive in there. How not to let the cramped, dingy cells break her. How to maintain a face of stone and hide her fear. I cared for her as a parent would. In those moments, I knew I would have made a wonderful mother. I would have, definitely. That's not to say I ever wanted it.

Then she started to take advantage. It's always the way with people: you give a little, and they push for more, then more again. Perhaps I was a little cruel in the things I said, but it was all true. She was never going to amount to anything in life, regardless of whether she got a job after prison, or got married. Some people matter, others don't. It's one of life's brutal, simple truths.

Butcher Bird, I think, then shudder involuntarily. I hated that name.

The tap is dripping. Only every so often, a sombre *plip* against my foot. If I listen carefully, I can hear the bubbles popping softly, as they slowly fold in on themselves. This is another luxury I struggle to adjust to. Showers in the prison were timed: three minutes of sputtering water, in which both hands had to be constantly active, rubbing off soap before the whistle blew for the next person in the queue. Now, I have all this time. Endless hours to sink into the heat, and to wallow.

I run my fingers over my breast, then towards my stomach. My body isn't bad for a woman of my age. I've seen many that are worse. Admittedly, my tummy is no longer flat and taut. Now my belly button is lost in a sagging cushion. But my breasts are firm enough, and bigger than they once were. People imagine that prison makes you thinner. Actually, the lack of activity ensures that the hips spread rapidly and the skin becomes pasty and loose.

I am under no illusion that Henry would find me desirable now; nor would I want him to. I never really did. Each time we met, he took me roughly and against my will. I'll maintain that until the day I die, despite what everyone else thinks. The court called it an affair. They used that word repeatedly, savouring the elongated f, stretching it to vulgar proportions. I'd argue that it was abuse. A continued, protracted abuse of a young woman who knew no better. After all, what is abuse, but the assault of someone against their true will? No one was prepared to see it from a vulnerable female's perspective, which was the standard way of things back then, I suppose. I'm not convinced that things are any better now, beneath the facade of equality.

I vividly remember Miranda in court. She sat a few rows behind me. The whole time, I felt her eyes at my back. *In* my back, rather, peeling the skin, unpicking ribs, scratching at my organs and muscles, over and over. All that silent accusation, and why? It wasn't as though I was the one to do anything wrong – or at least, not in the way she thought.

Henry once teasingly told me that I had none of his wife's natural poise. But I never regarded Miranda's composure as *poise*. More like a serpent, waiting to strike. After all, she wasn't so composed when she screamed in my face, in the prison visitors' room.

I never warmed to her. She was poison, through and through. And for the record, I believe she was a terrible wife, and a bad mother too.

Especially a bad mother. You told me that. Or implied it, at least.

CHAPTER 5

'Sometimes it's useful to delve into the past,' Dr Holland tells me.

He's moved all the furniture around since I was last here, though goodness knows why. Now, his desk is by the window, his head framed by the landscape outside. Dull clouds loom over the opposite rooftops, pushed along by a strong wind. It takes me a while to unglue my eyes from the sight of it, and look back at his face.

'I understand that,' I say.

'I'm glad to hear it. As part of our sessions, I'd like you to have the chance to explore your history. We often pick up negative learned behaviours as we travel through life, but they can be unlearned, if you understand the root triggers.'

It sounds like well-worn psychobabble to me, but I nod nonetheless. It's not as though this process is new to me; the prison doctor was exactly the same. They look entirely different, but it's there in their expression – the same impassive yet watchful gaze, minus any real emotional interest. It must take a certain breed of person to enter this sort of career.

He leans back, stretching his legs across the rug. 'Let's go back to your childhood. Obviously, you had an unorthodox lifestyle while growing up.'

'I liked it, though.'

'That may well be the case. But how did you feel after your mother died and you moved to the islands?'

I consider it. In all honesty, I don't remember feeling much. I'm not sure I was even completely aware of what was going on. 'I felt fine,' I reply. 'I liked living out there, on our own.'

'How did the absence of a mother affect you?'

My instinct again is to answer as Daddy would have wanted me to, to say that she slipped from my life as carelessly as a discarded ribbon. She wasn't that much of a presence even when she was alive. She took up minimal space, shrinking into corners, living silently and in a state of continual avoidance. Daddy used to mock her passivity and shout at her for holding him back. He made sure I saw it, too, and that I was in agreement with him at all times. He could be like that: authoritarian, unyielding. That's how he got where he did, I suppose.

But I know this isn't what Dr Holland wants to hear. It's important to supply him with the correct answers, the ones that prove I have natural, normal emotions.

'I missed her,' I say. 'I cried a lot, afterwards.'

He accepts this with a nod. 'What about your relationship with your father?'

'He taught me all he knew about birds, which was useful.'

'What about emotionally? Do you feel he was emotionally present in your life?'

I want to laugh. My father's face comes to mind: earnest, eyebrows compressed in a frown of concentration. I don't think *present* would be the right word at all.

'He cared for me,' I say, struggling to maintain a veneer of conviction.

'How do you feel about him now, looking back on it all?'

'I feel fine. I don't regret a single day that I spent on the islands. Not ever.'

'Do you feel the isolation affected you?'

My irritation is rising. I must fight to conceal it, and to remind myself that there are consequences to my outbursts. 'Not negatively,' I say slowly. 'I liked being alone. I always have, even before my mother died. I'm a solitary person.'

'Yet you entered into a relationship with Henry Hulham?'

'A person can enjoy solitude and still be with other people.'

He draws his legs under the chair. 'What did you feel that Henry Hulham offered you?'

'I thought this was a conversation about my childhood.'

'I said your history, Robin. That encompasses all the experiences that have led you to this point. But we can focus on your childhood, if you feel more comfortable doing so.'

I nod.

'Was it always just you and your father?' He examines his notes. 'Did your father ever meet anyone else after your mother died?'

I think of Jean Marshall. Of her grating laugh and long, hard face. How she invaded our quiet existence and tried to take my place. Swiftly, I shake my head. 'No,' I say emphatically. 'There never was anyone else.'

I tell this lie with a clear conscience. She wasn't important anyway, and no one knew she was ever with us. They always worked hard to keep their relationship private, to maintain the illusion of professionalism, which certainly worked out advantageously in the end. I attempt to keep a clear head, not to dwell on this line of thought, then miss Dr Holland's next question, a fact which I'm sure he'll draw unfavourable conclusions from.

'Are you all right, Robin?' he asks. 'I feel that I've lost your attention.'

I give him my brightest smile. 'I just spotted a bird outside the window. A great tit, on your tree. I'm back with you now.'

His eyes crinkle in quiet surveillance. It's an uncomfortable notion, being scrutinised from the inside out. But I can rest easy. He thinks he knows me, that he's got it all figured out. But really he's only seeing the tip of what lies above the surface. The rest is hidden, and it will always stay that way.

I think of Henry as I walk back home. How can I not? Dr Holland's rummaging around in my past leaves me open and exposed, and the memories come slipping out, regardless of whether I want them to or not. The relationship only lasted a couple of months, three at most. There weren't that many dates, only a few meet-ups in seedy bars, a safe distance from his home. The cinema, a couple of times. Once, a trip to the theatre, when he spent the evening looking around, checking the crowd for people he knew. Then afterwards it was always back to my apartment. It had to be mine, of course, there was nowhere else we could go. Each of those occasions was worse than the previous time. A mad, savage groping in the dark, which seldom made it to the bedroom. Looking back on it now, I think he wanted to keep it animal and emotionless. It was always on his terms, never mine.

I remember seeing him with her, for the first time. Miranda, his long-necked wife. She reminded me of a cello: smooth, made up of polished lines and a big, teardrop bottom. They were in the museum with their children, peering into cabinets, pressing their fingers against the glass. I said hello and, for a moment, Henry looked haunted. But he kept his composure, maintaining eye contact with the wall, rather than with me. Miranda was civil enough, I suppose, though I read the hostility, veiled behind her distantly polite demeanour. His daughter wasn't interested, skipping off to some other part of the room after a few seconds. But Henry's son remained with us, gawkish and narrow for his years, light shining off his glasses. I recall noticing the hint of wispy hair on his upper lip. A boy, just on the cusp of puberty. He was the only one polite enough to say goodbye to me afterwards.

I mustn't think of that. I can't bear it. He mustn't enter my thoughts. You, I mean. You.

Instead, I force myself into the present and study my feet, pounding beneath me. Then the puddles gathered in the uneven paving slabs. The swoosh of cars passing in the road. Anything to stop myself thinking. Sometimes, I believe that even physical pain would be better than this. I *hate* Dr Holland, and I realise this with sudden, vicious clarity. These sessions, they're not helpful; they're designed to trip me up and make me feel less certain of myself. Perhaps the prison service is trying to trick me into revealing new information.

I know all the things they suspect me of. The more I ponder it, the more it feels true. I should know better than to trust people.

Bill comes to mind, unbidden. That head, so unashamedly smooth and hairless, like one of the bubbles in my bath. The crooked, smiling teeth. The thought of him makes the resentment subside, just a little. I believe he's a nice man, someone who's lived through much, just like me. Maybe I can make an exception. Perhaps I can even put my trust in him.

You'll look after me, Ditz whispers.

(I know this is a dream. Don't look at her. Don't—)

I look. I always do.

She seems the same at first glance, but her tongue protrudes, bloated with blood. Her eyes are larger than they ever could have been in life, bulging orbs that stare and stare. I am trapped. There is no door in this cell, only grey walls, grey floor, grey ceiling. It's all closing in on me, dragging me closer to her.

Help me, she begs. *I want my sister.*

Her feet jerk and dangle and all the while I wonder why she didn't want me. Then I remember what I said, and how she cried afterwards.

You are there too, though I can't see your face. I know where you are, lying beneath the sheet on the bed. I can see your narrow shape, the jut of your nose, the awkward lumps of your knuckles and knees. The tiny bones of a chick rest at your feet. Always, it's the chick. I can't ever get away from it. I can't scream. I have no throat, no mouth, no body. I'm here but not.

Why won't you both leave me alone?

Why won't you—

I sit up. Sweating again, shivering in the dark. The duvet cover is glued to my legs and it's cold, so cold in here that if I was more fanciful I'd believe that you and Ditz have followed me out of the dream, that you're here, still staring, still dead, still blaming me.

I won't turn on the lamp. I refuse to. I'm not a child, I don't need reassurance that the dream isn't real. But still, I struggle to calm the pounding of my heart. There are shapes in the black; I sense them shifting backwards. As long as they leave me, that's the main thing, because I can't bear their presence for much longer.

In the morning, I know I will feel silly about this, but that knowledge doesn't help me now. I need to calm myself quickly, for the sake of my health. Women of my age are at an elevated risk of cardiac arrest and I don't want to die like this, another sad statistic, a lonely corpse on a bed. And of course, you might find me after death. Ditz and you. You might be waiting patiently, ready to— Such thoughts are not helpful; it's time to focus on something else instead. Going to the bathroom: yes, that makes sense. It's an excuse to switch on a light. I'll fetch my sleeping pills; just a couple more. It doesn't matter if I don't wake up until midday – I'm not expecting any visitors.

Dr Holland told me I should only take the pills when absolutely necessary, because of the associations as much as anything else. He doesn't understand how it is; no one does. Without them, there *is* no rest. There's no break from it all.

I have to take them, despite what they remind me of.

It's close to one in the afternoon when I eventually wake up. Even I am shocked by the lateness of the day; usually I never lie in past twelve. My head aches, so perhaps I took three pills instead of two.

I make myself an omelette and burn the underside to blackness. The pulled curtains reveal rain, the plants in my garden shaking like frightened things in the wind. I'm out of teabags and orange juice, but I have no desire to venture to the shop, not today. I feel raw, naked somehow, and I don't wish to be seen.

Sometimes I loathe this existence, and the unfairness of it all. It's painfully easy to see how things could have been, if I'd have been more fortunate, or other people less cruel to me. If I'd found a man who loved me, rather than one who took advantage. If my womb had borne a child. If I'd secured a great career and become a respected professional, like Daddy. There's a myriad of possible paths that should have been open to me, but the gates were always closed when I reached them. Sometimes, cleverness and attractiveness aren't enough. You have to have luck on your side too. Without luck, life is like this. It's worse than prison in some ways. The bars are still there, they just can't be seen any more. I'm a caged creature nonetheless, and my wings have been firmly clipped.

Clipping. I haven't thought about that for a while. Father always said it was unethical, that birds weren't made to be restricted in such a way. He had to do it just once, to an injured short-eared owl that we found in a disused barn, squalling and screeching, hopping in circles. It refused to accept its damaged status, something that impressed me at the time.

Jean Marshall wrapped the towel around it, then turned her back so I wouldn't see, although it was only the primary feathers they snipped, not flesh or bone. But Daddy wanted me to watch, and pointed out the blood feathers, explained how vital it was not to cut through them. The owl would bleed to death otherwise. I studied the veins in Jean's neck, and wondered if they were like blood feathers too, apt to flow if severed. They protruded from her skin as though conscious of my attention. She released the owl onto the kitchen table when it was done, then rubbed at her neck with her hand. At the time, I imagined that the slice of my gaze had made an impact. Of course, I know now that was childish fantasy.

It was around that time that she started mentioning boarding schools. Jean was clever in her approach, I have to hand it to her. It was insidious, veiled beneath a veneer of false concern, beginning with *how lonely little Ava must be*, then growing to *how unhealthy it is for a girl to be on her own so much. Think of the disadvantage*, she said, *if she doesn't get a good education*. Not that Daddy was worried about that. He always maintained real life was the great educator, not the four walls of a classroom. I thought I was safe, that her wheedling on this matter was futile. But I was wrong. Jean was far more cunning than I realised.

The owl nipped me that day, sharply on my forefinger as I reached to its head to settle it. The blood dropped to the table, and the owl's foot trampled it to a messy swirl. I should have taken it as a sign. Never offer yourself willingly to a dangerous animal, and *never* trust in anything or anyone.

CHAPTER 6

The day is miserable, so I sit, stagnant, in the living room. I watch a few television programmes but skip the news, as I never was one for watching the world's tragedies play out on the screen. I eat some digestive biscuits, then drift off for half an hour or so as the mantelpiece clock ticks with solemn insistence.

The doorbell rings. I startle. The leftover biscuits tumble to the carpet.

Bill? It's nearly five, perhaps he's come over with another bottle of wine. Excitement and panic flush through me in equal measures. I'm not presentable. My hair is no doubt stuck to my head and my eyes feel gritty and swollen.

I peer around the doorframe to the end of the hallway. The figure behind the frosted glass is not a man. It's shorter, with white hair. Now they're pressing their nose to the door, I can see their flesh in sharp relief. Peering into my house like an impudent child – who would do such a thing unless they know who I am, unless they're here to hunt me down and—

I force myself to take a breath. The figure looks familiar, and then I realise. It's Amber, Bill's daughter. I sense that she knows I'm here, watching her from my hiding place. Suddenly, the ridiculousness of the situation hits me. I smooth my jumper and walk firmly to the door. She eyes me frankly through the glass, and I don't like the suggestion of disapproval behind her gaze.

'We need access to your garden tomorrow,' she says, without preamble, when I open the door.

The statement sends me momentarily off-kilter. 'Why?'

'The broken fence. Dad says it needs a fresh pole in the cement, otherwise a new one won't hold. So he's got a man coming over to do it. They'll need to dig up the ground, then carry the fence through. Dad's kitchen has a breakfast bar built in the middle and there's not enough room, so they want to come via your house because you don't—'

'Couldn't Bill have told me?'

Her forehead wrinkles. 'He can't come out at the moment. Post-traumatic stress. Sometimes it does that to him. Don't worry, it's not personal.'

I bristle at the tone of her voice. 'I didn't take it as such.'

'Can we, then?'

'Can you what?'

'Have access to your garden?'

'Yes. No.' I feel my cheeks starting to heat. 'Hang on, when are you talking about?'

She squints at me. 'Tomorrow. Morning sometime.' A pause. 'What's your name again?'

The hallway seems narrower, suddenly. The walls tighten inwards. It reminds me of last night's dream. 'Robin,' I reply, too quickly.

'Your face is so familiar. I wondered if you were a teacher in my old school. You have that look about you.'

'What look?'

'You know. *That* look.' She waits a beat, then laughs with no real humour. 'You look like you've worked with kids in the past.'

Again, the certainty floods me that she knows. My fingers curl in on themselves, tense to fists. If she does, she could ruin everything. She could tell people, she would tell Bill, he'd be repelled. They'd spread the news and I'd be torn apart by everyone.

Just shut her up, a quiet voice inside me orders. Silence her.

No, no, that's foolish, overdramatic talk. She doesn't know. She wouldn't be talking to me about fences if she did. I'm reading far too much into it, and I've allowed paranoia to get the better of me. The prison doctor talked to me about that; the advice was sound and I must follow it. People aren't out to get me, they really aren't.

'No kids,' I whisper, then say more loudly, 'I've never worked with them.'

She shrugs. 'Fair enough. So, tomorrow around ten, is that okay?'

I nod, unable to think of a response.

She nods too. 'Good night,' she says curtly. The relief at seeing her leave is almost intoxicating. She's a spiteful thing, an over-privileged creature concealed beneath an attractive face. I can't stop myself from wishing her ill, from hoping that a car will plough into her, or a tree topple down upon her. Anything to finish her off.

These are bad thoughts. I must remember that they're not appropriate, even if they're trapped in the silence of my own head. Her death would make Bill unhappy, for starters. That would be a shame. Dr Holland would say I need to recognise that, and to understand that every action has a consequence. But aren't some actions worth it? Don't the positives outweigh the negatives?

I've always been utilitarian in my beliefs. Moral codes were merely falsehoods perpetrated by the church, or that's what Daddy always said. Put in place to control the uneducated masses, and entirely meaningless in reality.

In short, they weren't for people like us.

True to Amber's word, the doorbell rings at ten the following day. I am better prepared this time: hair brushed properly, the shape-less jumper replaced by a shirt and cardigan.

Bill smiles apologetically as I wave him and his workman through. He looks older, somehow; perhaps due to a bad night's sleep. If that's the case, he has my sympathy.

'Sorry about this,' he says, as they follow me through the house, towards the back door. 'I hope it's not too much of a bother.'

'Goodness me, no,' I reply, in as bright a voice as possible. 'I'd much prefer the fence to be mended. Can I make either of you a cup of tea?'

The workman shakes his head, then heads out into the garden. Bill gives me a thumbs-up and a ready grin. Already, he looks younger. I like to imagine it's the effect I have on him. I hand him his mug and the leftover biscuits from yesterday.

'This is just what I need,' he says, exhaling in appreciation. 'Something to perk me up.'

'What's the matter?' I ask, gesturing for him to sit at the table.

He eases himself onto the chair. 'The usual. I suffer from depression occasionally. It doesn't help when I get flashbacks from the streets. I was beaten up, you see. It left a few scars – physical and mental.'

'That's terrible.'

'It was. It's a dog-eat-dog world when you're homeless.'

'I can imagine.' I can, only too well. In prison, it was exactly the same. A fight for survival, each and every day. Not that he needs to know that, of course. The last thing I want him to know is how I suffered when I was in there.

He sips at his tea, a strangely dainty manoeuvre that's at odds with his weathered skin and large hands. 'I thought one of them would kill me,' he says, conversationally. 'A drunk fellow; he had a knife with him. Got me good and proper, right in the ribs.'

I glance instinctively to his side. 'But you survived.'

'Luckily, one of those street angels found me. You know, those people who volunteer to talk to the homeless? They called for an ambulance. The wound still gives me grief though, and it was close to a decade ago.'

'Thank goodness for the kindness of strangers.'

'Too true. I don't understand the mentality of it, do you?'

I pause, mug close to lips. 'What do you mean?'

'Of wanting to kill someone. Some people just aren't right in the head, are they?'

I say nothing, not because I don't want to, but because at that moment I'm physically unable. I feel laid bare, carved open for him to see. I must keep my expression neutral.

'Are you okay?' he says quietly. 'Have I upset you? I'm ever so—'

'No, not at all.' My response is more abrupt than I intended. 'I have a bit of a headache, that's all. The pills I took have made me a little bit woozy.'

He reaches over and touches my hand, just for a second or two. 'I know what that's like. We can just sit here quietly, if you like. Until we've finished our tea.'

I smile. He understands. Of course he does; his good nature is etched in every crevice of his face. He cares about others. He doesn't see them as commodities, to be used and discarded at a whim. He understands *me*, perhaps. I am sure of this, even though he has a wolfish grin at times, and his gaze lingers a little longer than is appropriate.

He is a hundred times the man that Henry was. No, a thousand. Not that it's hard to be a better man than *him*.

For Henry, affection was always displayed via physical items. A cupcake, purchased from the canteen and left on my desk. A cheap bracelet with a few gaudy charms. He liked to showcase his generosity, and I believed it to be a vital part of him, like a limb or an organ. Then I realised how easily those things could be taken away. How swiftly he could pull the storefront down, hide those trinkets of his caring, and leave me on my own again.

He'd probably be delighted to know that I'm alone now. That even though I'm out of prison, I'm still isolated from everyone else. He never understood that it's in my nature to be solitary. Like the hunting bird, I am more than capable of surviving without others. If he thinks this existence bothers me, then he never really knew me at all.

He admitted as much, the day he told me it was over. The comment came with a pile of other platitudes. It wasn't me, it was him. He couldn't commit, it would devastate his family. It had been fun while it had lasted, but hey, these things were never meant to last forever. I reminded him that albatrosses mate for life. His lip twitched, then he said neither of us was an albatross, and this was the real world. Then he picked up his work jacket from the armchair and departed in a hurry. He left me alone in the semi-darkness, blouse still unbuttoned to my waist. He'd made sure that he got his final session of passion before leaving, because that's the sort of person he was. A selfish taker, through and through.

I remember crying, but not much. Henry was a cruel, vile man, and not worth shedding tears over. I wept at the indignity, though, at the humiliation. How I'd succumbed, over and over, to his will, and was left with nothing of any value in return. I hadn't even got pregnant; not that I wanted to. Women are perfectly capable of enjoying happiness without children, and I'd have loathed carrying his offspring for nine months. But still. It was strange, how life worked out.

Ditz and I spoke about it once or twice, during those cold mornings out in the prison yard. Babies. How thankful she was not to be pregnant, after her next-door neighbour raped her when she stayed at his house one night as a teenager. How relentless motherhood must be. We had a kinship then; a moment of shared femaleness, which no man could intrude upon. During those times, I think I considered her almost a friend.

I told her it was better to be alone, that I should know. But she never believed me, not really.

It is a good day, I have decided. Bright and cold, sharp as crystal. Unseasonably cold for early autumn, some might say, but for me, this is welcome. It takes me back to those brisk sea-breezes on Jura or Sark, with their wild winds and the tang of ice carried from the distant Arctic.

I have my shopping list. It's longer than I'd like, but I've been lazy of late, and I've allowed my outstanding requirements to pile up. There are teabags, milk, digestives, and some lemon slices as a treat. They'll have to be shop-bought; I've lost enthusiasm for home baking after my last failure. Perhaps I'll summon up the courage to call on Bill later, and see if he would like to share them with me. Wine: two bottles this time, as the habit of drinking is wonderfully easy to slide back into.

I feel almost happy today. Fresher, somehow, as though that old life is slowly sloughing from me, revealing a shining new version of myself. I have my shopping bags ready and my purse is in my handbag. Life is good.

At the shop, the young man holds the door open for me and smiles as I thank him. This is a larger store than the one near my house, with aisle after aisle of frozen food cabinets, shelves, racks of fruit and vegetables. I navigate slowly, taking my time with my selections. There is so much nowadays that wasn't available before my time in prison. The range of nuts, for example: pistachios, cashews, macadamias. Before, only peanuts would have been on offer. Stacks of olives in different flavours, of different sizes. Bread that I haven't even heard of. Sourdough remains a mystery; I shall have to sample it. In the spirit of positivity, I place a loaf in my basket.

It is a simple pleasure. Perhaps things will be all right after all. As Dr Holland told me, it's the small steps each day that make the difference. I pay with my card, then place my shopping in my bags, leave the shop and step into the sunshine. It's all so wonderfully easy.

It's the screech of brakes that I'm aware of first, followed by the scream. Movement, a car too close, too quickly, then a woman's voice screaming a name. *Jordan* or *Jayden*. A child streaks in front of me, a blur of dark hair and oversized anorak. Instinctively, I reach out, seize an arm and pull the child backwards. The car, the windscreen, is overwhelmingly close. The old man at the wheel looks too large to be real, with sunlight glinting off his glasses. The child wails and I gasp. The car stops, an inch from my leg. Somehow, I've managed to keep hold of my shopping.

Nothing is broken, nothing is broken, I tell myself, looking from my knees to my bags. A hand reaches in front of me and grasps the child. I hear muffled sentences, sobbing, then someone is saying *thank you*. Someone else says *you saved her life*.

It's a girl, then. I finally look at the creature, now enveloped in what must be her mother's arms. She has an upturned snout of a nose and scrunched-up eyes, and there's something red and sticky smeared around her mouth.

'You saved my baby's life,' the mother says. She is thin, her collarbones jutting like two knives. 'Jordan just ran, I don't know why she did it.' Without pausing for breath, she turns on the driver and bellows a torrent of abuse at him. The old man is shaking, trying to get out of the car without losing his balance.

'Are you all right?' another woman asks me. 'Your reflexes are amazing – the way you just swooped in there.'

'I've never seen anything like that,' a man adds.

I nod without looking at any of them. I feel as though I'm submerged in water; I suppose I've gone into a state of shock, as it all happened so fast. Another person, a young man this time, points his phone in my direction. Something flashes, making me blink. He nods, puts it back in his pocket, then leaves.

'I'd better be going,' I mutter. There's a crowd growing around me, and the attention is unsettling. Besides, I didn't do much, only grab the child as it ran by. I'd scarcely known what I was doing.

'I'm so grateful to you,' the mother says. 'I don't know what I would have done if you hadn't—'

'Honestly, it was really nothing.' I start to walk away.

I hear muttering as I go. Awed comments. On the one hand, there's something about their admiration that heats me inside. I haven't had praise in a very long time. But their gaze is making me nervous. I'm supposed to be invisible. This goes against every-thing that I've trained myself to be: unremarkable, colourless and uninteresting. This isn't what *Robin* is meant to be.

Someone calls after me, but I ignore them and quicken my step. It's best that they forget me straight away. The last thing I need is for anyone to take a particular interest in my face, even if it has changed a lot since that time. I need to go home. I must get there, and fast. The joy I felt earlier seems ludicrous now; a childish fantasy that I should never have indulged in. The truth is, I am never safe, not while I'm out here. And I'd be a fool to risk what I've already achieved.

CHAPTER 7

The next day I remain in bed until the sun is high in the sky. The snugness of the duvet is too much to resist; the feel of being enveloped in something secure and soft. Then, just before eleven, the doorbell rings. It makes me jump. I am still shaken by my experience in town yesterday, and every unexpected noise convinces me that someone has come to hunt me down.

Then I remember, and swear under my breath. Margot. It's her weekly visit and I haven't even got dressed yet. She'll not only think I'm a slattern, but she'll make other, more worrying judgements: that I can't cope, that I should never have been released into the world again. I can't have that; I fought too hard for my freedom, with all those useless psychotherapy sessions, and all those false smiles and nods.

The doorbell trills again, just as I tug out a sweater from the wardrobe. Margot's urgency is unmistakable; she's a busy woman and hates being made to wait. Plus of course, my presence is a legal requirement. At this stage, I must be here every time she calls. In future, I will be expected to visit her office instead.

I pull on some trousers and nearly trip over in the process. Then I trot downstairs as fast as possible and open the door. I hope I look presentable, though my hair must be sticking up at all angles.

She frowns at the sight of me, then raps her wristwatch. 'Did I wake you up?' she asks, entering without being asked.

I wince. 'I was awake. Reading in bed, actually.'

'All right for some.'

'I'm so sorry, I'd forgotten you were—'

'It doesn't matter.' She marches through to the kitchen and, with a sigh, takes a seat at the table. 'I've got no time for tea today, I'm already behind with my calls.'

I sit beside her. This is the normal routine of our meetings, but I feel woefully unprepared for the onslaught of her brusque, no-nonsense presence. I'd much rather be back in bed, letting the remnants of the sleeping pill carry me gently to semi-oblivion.

'What's on the agenda today?' I say, sensing her anxiety.

'Glad you asked. We need to discuss getting you a job.'

'Who'd want to employ me?'

She snorts. 'It's always an obstacle with ex-offenders. That's why the rate of reoffending is so high: none of them can get work, so they return to a life of crime.'

'I'm not going to offend again.'

'I'm glad to hear it.' She rifles through her bag and pulls out some papers. 'I want you to read these. They're about searching for jobs, filling out applications. That sort of thing.'

'I'm not ready to return to work.'

'In order to start receiving your full benefits, you'll need to show that you're actively seeking employment.'

I examine my fingernails. It's easier than meeting her eye at this moment.

'Robin,' she says eventually, in a voice that sounds more like a warning than a call for attention. 'I understand that it's a nerve-wracking prospect, but the idea is to get you to feel like a normal member of society again.'

'But I'm not, am I?'

'Normal?'

'A normal member of society. I never will be.'

She places the papers beside me. 'Just read them. Then I can get the necessary boxes ticked.'

I glance down. They look like typical government documents, with the same navy blue, no-quibble fonts. In fairness, I've always appreciated their lack of frills. At least they tell it like it is, which is more than I can say for Margot herself at times. She means well, but has a tendency to drift off on a tangent.

'I'll look at them later,' I tell her.

'Good.' She forces a smile. 'Who knows, you might find the perfect job in a shop in town. I could see you working in a shop.'

I stifle a sarcastic response. If she can see me working in a shop, then she knows me far less well than I'd imagined, which already wasn't very well at all.

Bill's outside, painting the fence. I can see the shine of his head just above it, bobbing from side to side, plus the occasional tip of a brush, as it rises to the top. It's comforting to know he's there. I may even go out and talk to him later – perhaps even invite him over for a drink.

I've started to think of him as a friend. It feels strange, to like a person in this way. Ditz was a friend to begin with, I suppose, before the relationship turned sour. The sheer weight of her dependency was like a stone-filled sack around my shoulders. I said as much to the wardens, even asked for her to be moved towards the end, as she exhausted me so. Not that they paid any attention. They never listened to what I had to say.

I wonder if it would be possible to be friends with someone like Bill. I'm not even sure what the protocol is for developing a friendship. If it requires me to divulge information about my past, then that's not an option. I must remain Robin, not Ava, regardless of how much I would like him to know my real name. I don't want him to know that I was in prison. Images will come to his mind of unwashed women in shapeless clothes, trapped in cells. Mouthy, unpleasant females with tattoos and violent minds. I know he's lived on the streets and that he's probably encountered those sorts of women before. But I don't want him to think that I'm one of them. I want him to know I'm better than that.

Above all else, he mustn't know what they accused me of. He must never know about you, and what happened that day. If he found out, he'd start prying. He'd read old newspaper articles and look things up on his computer. He'd access all those lies that the journalists spun, and swallow them all, because *everyone* did. And last of all, he'd hate me. My lawyer, a worn, grey man supplied by the state, let slip to me, just before the trial, that he'd received death threats. Not just aimed at me, but him too, for taking my case on. A few were posted through his workplace letterbox. One went to his home, threatening his children, of all things. Those judging people, so keen to point the finger.

I don't want to discover that Bill is like that too. It would break my heart. However, that doesn't mean we can't have some sort of relationship. We could talk about the present, about our gardens, our houses, and how we're finding it, settling into our new lives. We could even watch a film together sometime, perhaps. I wonder if he likes the old classics, as I do? I should ask him; it'll be another thing we can chat about.

I needn't have worried about going outside to talk to Bill. He disappears from his garden halfway through the afternoon, then half an hour later there's a knock at the door. I can already tell it's him, just by the jaunty rhythm of his fist. He's wearing a checked shirt, unbuttoned at the neck, sleeves rolled up to the elbows. A box of chocolates is tucked under his arm. His face lights up in a ready smile and I feel my own mirroring his instinctively.

'Are those for me?' I ask, letting him in.

'Both of us,' he says with a laugh, wiping his feet carefully on the doormat. 'My sister sent them in the post. She likes to send me care packages from time to time, to make sure I'm not wasting away.'

'That's sweet of her.'

'Sweeter than I deserve. I wondered what you were doing today, and if you fancied a stroll? It'd be nice to make the most of the sun, while it's still here.'

I consider it. In truth, I'm still nervy about going outside, but I know I have to face my fears, as Dr Holland says. I can't stay indoors all day – I'd starve to death, plus I need to pick up my next prescription. I can't have my stock of *little friends* running low.

'Okay,' I say slowly. 'Just a short walk, though. My legs aren't what they used to be.'

He grins. 'Mine neither. Isn't it depressing, getting old?' He leaves the chocolates on the stairs, then gestures outside. 'Shall we?'

'What, now?'

'Yeah, why not? Then we can come back and have a natter.'

A hidden part of me warms slightly at the idea. *A natter.* It sounds so free, so easy. Something that people do when they have friends. A cosy image comes to mind of us sitting on the sofa together, laughing at a joke, him patting my shoulder, touching my hair with his fingers, maybe— No. Not that. What a silly idea. I feel my cheeks redden at the thought, and I quickly retreat to find a jacket. It's warm, but I often feel the cold regardless. Plus, I feel a sudden need to barricade myself, to feel safe.

He waits patiently until I've readied myself, totem-like by the door. The lines on his face almost appear to be carved in place, like etchings in a woodblock. Stoic. Timeless.

'Shall we?' I say, jiggling my house key.

'After you, ma'am,' he replies with a wink.

The day is hotter than I'd realised, the last of the summer fighting for supremacy over the coming autumn. The air is still, too, quiet apart from the lilting notes of a blackbird somewhere close by. A few gulls wheel above and I feel like a child again, just for a moment.

'You're lost in thought,' he says, as I lock the door behind us.

'Am I?'

'Yes, you often are. You're a curious one and no mistake. It's almost like you're concealing something from the world.'

I stiffen involuntarily. 'I'm not.'

He follows me down the path and onto the pavement. 'I wonder if you used to be a Hollywood starlet, then you decided to lead an anonymous life in the UK. Amber says you look familiar, so I reckon we've discovered your secret.'

No, no, no. This conversation is wrong already. My stomach is clenching with every word, and I wish I could run back inside. Living a normal existence is impossible, despite what Margot and the others tell me.

'Have I found you out, Robin?' His voice is uncomfortably loud in the quiet of the afternoon.

'I couldn't act to save my life,' I tell him. It's not strictly true: every day in prison was a performance of sorts, fuelled by a drive to survive. Life itself is a performance, in fact.

'Maybe a singer, then? Or an eminent scientist? Amber was curious—'

'Amber's a curious girl, isn't she?'

He scratches his chin. 'What do you mean?'

Take a deep breath, I tell myself. I sense a brittleness, in unconscious response to my own defensiveness. He's just being friendly. Amber is nosy and irritating, but she isn't out to get me. I need to keep all of this in mind.

'I mean curiouser and curiouser, like Alice,' I say, forcing lightness into my voice. 'She seems like a nice girl.' I keep the smile in place.

'She is. She's going to stay with me for a bit, actually. Help me paint the lounge and kitchen. She's just gone through a messy break-up, so she could probably do with the support. She finds it hard to be with people, sometimes.'

If he expects me to soften at the news, he's badly mistaken. Still, I know I need to display the correct response. I try to look as though I give a damn.

'That's sad for her,' I say. 'Was he abusive?'

He gives me a look. 'Nothing like that. She just struggles with relationships, and I wasn't exactly a great role model in terms of what a partner should be.'

'You couldn't help it,' I tell him. I reach for his arm, feeling suddenly bolder, surer of myself.

He looks at my hand, and smiles. 'Are you sure you weren't a Hollywood starlet, Robin? You've got a touch of that glamour about you.'

Glamour. An ironic choice of word, given that its original meaning was to enchant someone. To place them under a spell. Is that what I'm trying to do? Entrance him, make him mine? Perhaps I am, in spite of everything. He stirs something within me that I thought was long dead and buried.

'I don't think anyone would pay to watch me in a movie,' I tell him.

'Oh, I think you're wrong. You've got a classic beauty. Poised. Elegant.'

'You're being far too generous. I'm a middle-aged woman, nothing special.'

'I disagree. Anyway, beauty doesn't have an age.'

Now I really am blushing. This feels dangerous, but also exciting, uplifting. I feel air-filled, light, as though I could rise upwards without impediment. It's only harmless flirting, but it suffuses me with emotions I haven't felt in a long time.

Haven't *ever* felt. What Henry made me feel was very different.

'You're an old charmer,' I say.

He gives me a knowing look. 'Does that mean you think I'm charming, eh?'

'Perhaps,' I say quietly. 'Just a little.'

Overhead, a gull shrieks. Bill reaches for my hand, tucks it through his arm, then smiles. His body is warm against my palm. 'That'll do for now,' he replies, with a look I can't decipher.

I feel like a young person again. It's terrifying and exhilarating, in equal measures.

Later, when I climb into bed, I notice the emptiness of it. The stretch of double mattress, the sea of cotton sheet covering it. All of it just for me and no one else. When I first moved in, it thrilled me, all that space. Now it seems somehow vacant. I feel shrunken by comparison.

I imagine Bill lying in it, duvet pulled down to his stomach. He'd have some muscle definition, I believe; he has that wiry look, though there is a hint of paunch. I wonder if his chest is hairy, whether dark hairs clamber past his nipples towards his neck, or whether he's pale and pocked as a plucked chicken. My mind moves to other areas of his body. Parts I haven't given a thought to for many years. I feel silly, both for my prudishness and my wanton thoughts. I'm in my late fifties. My body has become a thing of function, not beauty. *But he called you beautiful earlier*, I remind myself.

It would be so easy, at this moment, to reach downwards. To touch myself and think of him, of him touching me, kissing my neck, sliding against my body. But I know how absurd I'd appear. I'd see images in my head, even as I was doing it, I'm sure. My father's sneer, his disgust at my lack of control. Henry's look of pity at what I've become: a sad, middle-aged creature desperate for contact. I ease between the sheets and tuck the duvet around my chin. Wrapped up tightly as a mummy, ready for burial. A sexless, dead thing, after all.

You come for me again, somewhere in the black of the night. It doesn't surprise me, even as I'm dreaming. I know that I can't ever have happiness, that somewhere along the line, life decided that I should stay miserable forever, as penance for my sins. My sins. What about your father's sins? How does Henry fit into all of this? I think I scream these words at you, through the muddled fug of the dream, but you don't answer. Perhaps you don't even hear me. Your eyes are closed. You won't wake up. You're on the carpet, just as you were then, and you won't open your eyes, even though I'm shaking you hard. I feel bones break under my fingers. No, that's not right: they crumble, rather. Ease into dust, along with the rest of you. And I shout *I'm sorry*, because I am, I really am. Why won't you believe me?

Ditz is here too, dangling limply from the ceiling. Her feet are suspended near my face. But she's laughing, pointing at me because she knows that I can't bear this much longer. Her face shifts; she's a million women, woven into one. The prison bitches, hatchet-hard and scarred. My mother, weak-chinned, looking away at some distant horizon that doesn't feature a soul but her. Jean Marshall, smug and horse-faced as she was in life. Miranda, long neck stretched to breaking point. All of them, all of them laughing and laughing and laughing—

(Wake up, you have to wake up.)

You won't wake up. Nor will the others. I don't want to, either. I want to. I need to.

My eyes open. I'm in my bedroom, after all. There are no hanging feet. No pubescent boys, too still and too sad to bear looking at. It's just me, alone in this big, cold bed.

It's been a while since I've seen you dead in my dreams. I'm normally spared that particular horror. But then, I was happy during the day, with Bill. Perhaps this is life's way of creating balance, of reminding me that I have no right to be content. I remember thinking that, at some point in my sleep. I lost that privilege a long, long time ago.

I look at my bedside clock. It's only just past two in the morning. There are endless dark hours until I can legitimately get out of this bed, and I can't take any more pills – it would send me over the edge. A muffled creak breaks the silence, followed by a low cough. For a moment, I think it must be you, that you've slipped out of my subconscious and into reality. Then I realise it's Bill, just about audible through the wall. His bedroom must be directly next to mine, as is so often the way with terraced houses. He is there. That offers some level of safety, perhaps.

I switch on the lamp, then pick up my book. A tale of a lone wanderer, exploring the Outer Hebrides. An old one, slightly mildewed with the passing of time; one I'd liked as a younger woman, now liberated from my meagre storage boxes. It provides an escape, in a way. And it's all I've got at the moment.

The doorbell rings again bright and early the following morning. It's getting to be something of a habit, having visitors. I can already see Bill's grin through the frosted glass of the door, and he's waving something around. A piece of paper, perhaps.

I smooth down my hair and wish I had time to apply some salve to my dry lips. I only hope I don't look as tired as I feel, and that Bill isn't immediately repelled by my appearance. I pull the door open, then recoil as he pushes a newspaper towards me.

'You're famous,' he says, stepping inside. 'Look!'

'I most certainly am not,' I snap, without meaning to. His presence overwhelms me, in the narrow confines of my hallway. I feel small, trapped as a tethered falcon.

He jabs at the paper. I peer closer, then gasp.

It's me. The photo is of me. A little blurry, perhaps, and my hand is raised partially over my face, perhaps to protect myself. But it's unmistakably my face that I'm staring at, my eyes that are glaring back at me.

'It's not what you think,' I blurt, stepping back. 'I don't know what it says, but—'

'It says you saved the little girl's life, Robin. That's amazing!'

I take a deep breath. His words jangle at a thread, somewhere in my memory. A little girl's life. Saving someone. People talking around me. The car, screaming to a halt. *Jordan.* The mother thanked me. There was a flash, someone held their phone up at me; that must have been where they got the photo.

'It wasn't anything much,' I say, weakened by the surge of relief that races through me. 'I just reached out instinctively to grab her.'

'It says here that the girl would have been hit by the car, if it wasn't for you.'

'No. She would have been fine.'

He raises an eyebrow. 'You really don't like attention, do you? If this was me, I'd be singing it from the rooftops.' He points at the newspaper again. 'Says here that you're an *anonymous hero.* Look at that. Hero!'

'I'm no hero,' I tell him. I don't want to look at it – it bothers me more than I can say to see my face spread out over the paper – but something compels me to read it anyway. I need to know what's

71

been said, and if there's any risk to me. It's certainly not good to have the image in print: it might trigger memories for people, then lead them to start nosing into my life.

The article is mercifully short. Thankfully the editor buried it on page twelve, along with a tale of a small fire on the other side of town and a story about an adopted dog. Random words jump out before my eyes. *Kind woman. Lifesaver. Humble. Walked away without sharing her name.* I'm horrified at the exposure, but there's something warming about it, I must admit. The people *liked* me. They appreciated what I did. Prior to this, the only appreciation I ever received was from small chicks, when I fed them crumbs in their scraggy nests. By contrast, humans have always taken me for granted.

'I doubt anyone will read it,' I say, handing it back to him. 'It's a bit of a non-story, really.'

'I don't think it is.' He takes the paper and folds it under his armpit. 'You're a more remarkable person than I thought, Robin Smith.'

Remarkable. That's something I've never been called before. I can't stop the smile from blossoming on my lips.

'Thank you,' I mutter, then look away. The sudden burst of emotion is almost too much for me.

He places a hand on my shoulder, waiting patiently until I lift my chin and let my gaze comfortably lock with his. 'You are most welcome,' he says. 'And may I be so bold as to take you out sometime, to celebrate your kindness? A proper evening out, I mean, not just popping over for a cuppa.'

'Do you mean a date?'

'I mean exactly that. A meal, perhaps.'

'Can either of us afford it?'

He chuckles. 'My benefits might just stretch to a special occasion. What do you think?'

I swallow. Not just the moisture that's gathered at my throat, but my fears, my defences, my self-doubt. I stuff them deep within me, because I want to live again. I want to be the person I was all those years ago. I don't want to be burdened with sadness and fear any longer.

'How about tomorrow night?' I suggest.

'Sounds like a plan. I'll come over at six; we can walk into town together.'

We can walk together. Remarkable. It's all quite remarkable. All I can do is grin like a lunatic while he retreats down the path, waving merrily as he goes.

CHAPTER 8

'So, how do you feel about going on a date?' Dr Holland asks, leaning forward, resting his hands upon his knees. He clearly relishes the change in topic. I don't blame him – talking about things that happened years ago can be dreary work at times.

I shrug. 'I feel good about it, I suppose.'

'It's certainly a step forward, I'd say. However, have you considered how you'll share your past with him?'

'What do you mean?'

'In terms of what information you'll share with him, if the relationship becomes more serious. It's a difficult conversation to have.'

I feel my jaw tense involuntarily. 'That's rather getting ahead of ourselves. This is just the first date, after all.'

'But you suggested earlier that you'd already become fond of him.'

'He's my neighbour. He's a nice person.'

'Indeed. How do you feel he'll react, when he gets to know you better? That might be something you want to explore here, in a safe place.'

'I don't think we need to worry about that yet,' I tell him. The truth is, I don't *want* to think about that. It's unnecessary. In my head, Bill and I could move away, travel to one of the Scottish isles, somewhere remote. We'd be on our own, just the two of us, and it wouldn't matter if I was Robin or Ava. He'd never need to know about the mistakes that were made in the past.

Dr Holland eyes me shrewdly. 'This is part of a wider issue. Part of this process involves acknowledging what happened. We've spoken about that many times. If you become close to this man, he has a right to know the details, don't you think?'

A right. He talks about rights – the man who, by virtue of his gender, skin colour and social situation, has had everything handed to him on a plate. What is a right, anyway? Did I have a right to not be treated as I was, by Henry? Or the right to not waste my life in prison?

He frowns at the sight of me. 'Did what I've just said upset you, Robin?'

My name is Ava. I will always be Ava. I force a smile. 'No, I'm just processing the information,' I say, glib as a schoolgirl. 'I'm sure you're right. You normally are.'

'That's kind of you to say. Remember, true healing lies in being honest with yourself. And with others.'

'Of course,' I say, while wondering how seldom people have ever been truly honest with me.

I cannot decide what to wear tonight. My crimson skirt seems too suggestive, and the corduroy slacks ride too high on my waist, giving me a matronly look. I bought a plaid blouse when I was released, but still can't wear it. It's far too similar to the clothes Jean Marshall used to wear. A pair of black trousers and top, perhaps. Something neutral. A backdrop for that silver necklace I kept in storage all those years, one of the few things of my mother's that I was allowed to keep. Black is a slimming colour, too; that's something women always say.

Staring in the mirror, I see a hint of my mother staring back at me. My face is fuller, but there's a concealed terror in my gaze that reminds me of her. What if I embarrass myself tonight, or say the wrong thing? What if he somehow guesses I was in prison? Maybe I've developed some rough manners without even realising it. An uncouth way of using my fork, or dabbing my mouth with my fingers, that marks me as an ex-criminal.

I can't think these thoughts. They will erode me, and I've come too far to let that happen. I've proved my resilience in the past, and I shall do it again. That's my nature, after all. That's how Daddy taught me to be.

I wonder if I felt like this before meeting Henry outside work for the first time. Suspenseful. Excited. Panicked. It's so long ago, I can't remember. Only the amber lights of the bar and the moisture running down my wine glass. The scent of cigarettes, the low clamour of others around us. Little details rather than the big picture, which is probably for the best.

Henry's face flashes through my mind – another time, another terrible, upsetting time. Furious, lips pressed tight, fingers clenched around the edge of his front door. *What are you doing here?* he hissed. I heard voices from somewhere within his house. The daughter, asking where her ballerina Barbie was. Miranda's brusque response, muffled through several walls. I don't remember what I replied. Something accusing, I'm sure. He told me to go, as Miranda's head appeared from a doorway down the hall, frowning, tense, suspicious. *What's going on?* she asked; not a question, but an accusation aimed at me. *Henry?*

I wanted to deliver hell to his doorstep, to make him see that he couldn't just pick people up only to dump them a few months later. It wasn't fair; it was morally offensive, low human behaviour. Daddy would have said that a man deserved to be gutted and plucked for such a thing, I'm sure. *Or would he?* I think of Jean Marshall, her flashing smile. The way he curled his arms around her waist once, when she was washing up.

No. Daddy and Henry were not the same. Henry and *Jean*, now that was another matter. Parasites, draining others dry. They were two of a kind.

God, I wanted to kill Henry for what he'd done. I'll never share this with Dr Holland or anyone else, but I often lay awake, imagining taking him to Skye, to Rum, to Lundy, walking him to the cliff, then shoving him off. To see if his arrogance would help him to fly. To watch his body explode on the rocks below.

These are dark thoughts to have, especially now. I move to the dresser and switch on the radio. Inane chatter fills the silence, canned laughter. An advert for a tile company, then for a children's soft-play area down the road. All those children. Henry's children. The child I'd been once, too. Alone, always alone.

I will wear some make-up tonight, I think. I found an eyeliner pencil in my storage boxes. Amazingly, it still works, just. The powder was beyond saving, but my complexion is acceptable anyway. If this date goes well, I may walk into town tomorrow and treat myself to a few more items – lipstick or some eyeshadow, perhaps. Just a few things; I'm not one for vanity.

Alone, I think again, as I search for the eyeliner in my drawer. Could it ever be different? Yes, I tell myself firmly. Yes, it could.

'What do you think?' Bill asks, as he holds the glass door open for me.

The restaurant is dark. That's the first thing I notice. Ambient lighting, I think they call it. Fake candles flickering on the tables, swagged curtains blocking the view of the road outside.

'They score highly on Tripadvisor,' he continues, looking as nervous as I feel. It couldn't be more apparent that he's unused to such surroundings, a fact that makes him endearing.

A waitress scuttles over, waist nipped with a tight black skirt, a world-weary expression already in place. She looks impossibly young; then I realise she must be in her twenties, the age I was when I was first incarcerated. I wonder how this little scrap would cope with being trapped in a cell, day in, day out, and whether she'd survive it. It's doubtful. Few could bear it.

'Have you booked?' she asks, already flicking through the notepad on her podium.

Bill raps a finger on the pad. 'That's us. Seven on the dot.'

She forces a smile. 'Great. Come with me.'

I follow as she leads us to the back of the restaurant. It's a booth, no less. The irony doesn't escape me. It could almost be the table that Henry and I sat at, all those years ago. The same crimson seats, the same shine of the wood in the light. The music even sounds similar: low, tasteful, piano-led. The past just can't resist tormenting me.

'Everything all right?' Bill asks, as I slide onto the seat.

'Yes, it's all lovely.' I straighten my top. Perhaps black wasn't the best colour after all. It'll show any food that I accidentally spill down myself. It's difficult to meet Bill's eyes and his posture reminds me uncomfortably of Henry's for some reason. Maybe it's the proprietary elbow, taking up more space on the table than is necessary.

He leans back, and the illusion is broken. 'You're thinking deep thoughts again,' he tells me. 'I've got used to it now. You go somewhere, right inside your head, and you disappear almost completely.'

'I'm sorry. I'm too used to my own company. Sometimes I forget myself.'

'Don't apologise. Just promise to tell me if I'm upsetting you.'

'What do you mean?'

'I mean that sometimes, you look unhappy. We can't have the local life-saving hero unhappy now, can we?'

I force a laugh. 'Not that again.'

'I'm going to keep banging on about it. It's really something. Amber is even more convinced she recognises you now, though. She keeps squinting at your photo and muttering something about your eyes.'

Cold eyes. That's what the papers had said on more than one occasion, all those years ago. *Her cold, unfeeling eyes. No remorse. No emotion. Cold.* As though they could have ever known what was really going on behind them. I shiver, in spite of the warmth.

'You've gone again,' Bill comments, studying me hard.

The waitress interrupts, asks if we'd like any drinks. He orders a bottle of wine: the cheapest, I notice, not that it matters. We've both been open about our financial situations.

'I used to laugh with someone about how we'd sell our souls for a glass of Pinot Grigio,' I say, as the waitress brings the bottle over in its silver cooler. It was something Ditz and I said, a moment of camaraderie among all the tedium and unhappiness.

Bill pours me a glass, then fills his own. 'Why, was there a shortage or something?'

Another comment, destined to unravel me.

'I was teetotal for a while,' I say carefully. At least it's not a lie. Sobriety was enforced on me for twenty-five years, after all.

He nods. 'It's okay if you had troubles with alcohol in the past, you know. I certainly did. I only allow myself a few glasses at a time now. I know my limits.'

'What drove you to it?' I ask.

'You mean drinking?'

'All of it. The homelessness, the substance abuse – what happened?'

He eyes me for a while, then takes a drink from his glass. 'Tell you what,' he says slowly, 'I'll tell you, if you do the same for me. You can trust me, you know. I won't judge you; I'm in no position to judge anyone.'

Oh, but you would, I think, feeling sick at the thought, because I know it's true. Perhaps I can tell him small parts of my past, though – the elements that won't damage this fragile thing that's growing between us.

'Go on then,' I say.

'I was an idiot,' he says heavily. 'That's the main thing. I had a good job, running my own heating company. A nice house. A solid marriage and a happy little daughter, though she had her problems, bless her. But I messed it all up.'

'How?'

'Are you sure you want to hear this?' He shifts in his seat. 'I'd like to be honest about it all, but I'm worried you'll think less of me. To be honest, I've enjoyed basking in your approval. I don't want you to think I'm a horrible person.'

'I know what you mean,' I say, with feeling. 'You said you won't judge me, and I won't judge you. Go on.'

He takes a deep breath. 'I started feeling bored, I reckon. I'm ashamed to say it, but I began picking up girls in bars. I'd never see them again afterwards: they were never full-blown affairs. Just a series of dirty events that left me feeling disgusted at myself. Drugs, too. Anything to give me a lift, to add a bit of excitement. My wife found out. Kicked me out of the house, and she was right to do so. After that, I spent a long time on friends' sofas and in their spare rooms, until they got sick of me too.'

'Then the streets?' I guess.

'Not quite. My wife took me back for a little while. But can you believe it – I messed up again. What an idiot.' He looks up, jaw tense. 'I'm far wiser now. I've been to the very bottom and lost everything. I'll never be that idiot again.'

I reach over for his hand and squeeze it. 'I believe you.'

He doesn't reply, but there's a shine in his eyes that betrays his emotion. *He's not Henry*, I think, with a force that surprises me. Henry would never lay himself open like this. He was secretive as an oyster, and took delight in withholding as much of himself as possible.

'Now your turn,' Bill says, tapping my knuckles. 'You promised, remember?'

'What do you want to know?'

'Start with your childhood, then work up to now.'

I shake my head. 'That would take all night.'

'All right then. The abbreviated version. An entire history of Robin Smith, in five minutes. How does that sound?'

It sounds like a lie. It sounds like a theatrical production of a badly written character. I can perform it, just this once. But I need to remember the details, for later. I can't be caught out.

'I had a very normal childhood,' I tell him. Already, my words seem full of artifice. 'My mum and dad were standard, working class people. We had a nice house, and I went to school.'

He laughs. 'You're not giving much away, even now.'

'There's not much to tell. I told you before, I've lived a boring life. I went to work in an office—'

80

'What, as a typist? A receptionist?'

The assumption makes me bristle, but it's not worth getting into a conversation over. The less detail, the fewer questions, the better. 'I helped with the admin side of things,' I tell him. 'But I didn't have much money.'

He nods with understanding.

'I'm horrified to admit it,' I continue, warming to the tale, 'but I stole some money from the company. Quite a bit, actually. I was caught. The police were involved. It was all awful.'

He clamps a hand over his mouth. 'You were in prison?'

I take a deep breath. Sometimes, a softer version of the truth is easier to maintain than a total lie. 'I was,' I confirm, casting my eyes to the table. 'I'm sorry I didn't tell you sooner. I did a terrible thing, and I got put away for a long time.'

He frowns. 'The sentence for a crime like that isn't too long, is it?'

I curse inwardly. Has he realised I only just got released? Can I tell him it was years ago? My mind races ahead of itself, and I take a steadying sip of the wine.

'I'm so embarrassed,' I say, keeping my eyes to the table. 'That wasn't the only time, you see. I stole a second time, and got put back in prison again. But I was desperate for money. My parents had died by then and I had no help at all. Plus, there was a man who badly mistreated me.'

Bill sits up. 'I was wondering if a man was at the heart of this.'

A man is always at the heart of it. I raise my eyes to meet his. He seems concerned, not revolted. Nor does he look anything other than completely convinced by my story, thank goodness.

'I loved him,' I say simply. 'I trusted that he loved me back, but he only wanted to use me. I had nothing after that. So, I stole again. That time, I got a much harsher sentence.'

'Which prison were you in?'

I freeze. I can't tell him that. 'Do you mind if I don't say?' I say, wiping my eyes. 'I know we're being honest with each other, but I feel such shame about it all. And I was so unhappy there.'

He nods. 'I understand. Robin, I think you're brave to tell me. Many people wouldn't have, I know that. You're like me, I can tell. You own your mistakes, and you move on.'

'I try to. But it's hard. People are so horribly judgemental. They think they know you, but—'

'Oh, I know. Believe me, I know. As soon as people find out that I've been homeless, they look at me differently. Like I'm scum that should have been washed down the gutter years ago. They don't often take the time to find out about what happened.'

'They don't talk to you like a human being any more,' I say, raising my chin.

He beams, that same smile that makes me feel life could be okay, after all. 'You know what it's like,' he says, as though it's a revelation. 'You get it. Robin, I think someone was looking out for me, when the council gave me a home next to yours.'

I nod. 'I think the same.'

'We're birds of a feather, you and me.'

I raise my glass, and let it clink the side of his. 'Birds of a feather,' I agree. 'You're absolutely right.'

And that's how we'll stay, I add silently. Because I want him to be mine, I've decided. He likes me for who I am, and I mean to keep him now, regardless of what happens next. I need a companion, just as much as anyone else does.

CHAPTER 9

I am happy. Really, *truly* happy. I slept last night without any need for sleeping pills. No dreams either, only a feeling of refreshment and ease when I awoke. A *release*, as though something taut and tormenting inside me had been loosened. I can't remember feeling this good for a long time.

I spend the morning reading the latest *Nature's Home*, poring over one article about monogamy in seabirds, and thinking about Bill. Last night had been a courtship display, and he'd suitably impressed me, not just with his manners and easy speaking, but with his *attention*. I don't think I've ever had a man make me feel so listened to. Maybe we are albatrosses, who just found one another late in life. I'm aware this is fanciful, but who knows? Stranger things have happened.

The letterbox rattles just after lunch. It's a peculiar time; the postman usually does the rounds bright and early. I walk down the hallway, expecting to see a flyer or a brochure for a random company, ordered by the previous inhabitants of this house.

Instead, it's an envelope. Cream, not white, lying face down on the mat.

Bill, I think at first, but it doesn't seem his style. He'd knock on the door, ready for a chat. Someone else, then. My spine stiffens, alert and ready. It would seem that my body is ahead of my mind, which is still slowly catching up to the possibilities. I reach down and pick it up. It'll be nothing, I'm sure. A marketing ploy from a nearby estate agent. A note from a neighbour, sharing news about a local meet-up. Something innocent, surely. Surely.

There's one word on the front. A name, to be precise. Three simple letters, written in hard-pressed biro.

AVA.

A squeak escapes in the quiet. I realise it's me, childlike, fearful of unseen monsters. Only this monster is in my hand, small, yet larger than everything. *They've found me*, I think, suddenly unable to swallow. *I knew they would, it was only a matter of time.*

I drop it. It falls to the carpet, and for a moment I think my fingers are burning. I want to *unsee* it, to walk back to the kitchen, settle on the chair and return to my magazine. If I don't notice it, perhaps it won't be there. That's what Ditz told me she did when her boyfriend raised a fist: she squeezed her eyes shut to make it less real.

But we are scientists, Daddy's voice reminds me. *We gather available information, we examine the facts, we DO NOT shy away from the truth of the matter, no matter how—*

'Be quiet,' I mutter, driving my fingernails into my palms. I pick the envelope up again, nonetheless.

AVA.

I feel watched. Haunted, even. Maybe someone is spying on me right now, even as I pick at the flap to open it. My hands are shaking. I *knew* this would happen, that they would find me in the end. Henry may have had a hand in it, or his wife. All that rubbish that the prison officer said about being protected, the *stupidity* of changing my name, it's all for nothing.

I must get a grip. It's a letter.

It can't hurt me, unless they've put something inside. I sniff the paper, but of course, that's madness: if anything invisible was in there, it would have been released the second I opened it up. All that's inside is a piece of paper. Smallish. Neatly folded. Precise. That tells me something of what I'm dealing with.

Read it, Daddy whispers again, from deep inside me. *Know the obstacles, then identify how to conquer them.*

I unfold the paper. The violent lettering steals my breath, makes the world fuzzy for a second or two. They've gouged the paper, ploughing the pen-tip right through in places. They want me to feel their hatred, oozing from every line.

I KNOW YOU LIVE HERE. YOU SHOULD BE DEAD. YOU MURDERING, EVIL PIECE OF SCUM. YOU SHOULD HAVE BEEN EXECUTED. YOU SHOULD KILL YOURSELF NOW. YOU SHOULD BE MADE TO SUFFER FOR WHAT YOU DID. IF YOU DON'T DO IT SOMEONE ELSE WILL.

'What, no signature?' A pop of hysterical laughter snaps from me, sharp as gunfire. It sounds unnatural in the silence.

It's a woman who's written this. I sense it through the slash of each Y, the ragged curve of each C and S. Someone who has spent her life wishing ill on others. One who would have been burned at the stake for witchery, back in the day. She believes she can frighten me.

She has frightened me, a small voice says, hidden away inside. *Fear is an irrational concept, brought about by ignorance and lack of self-belief,* I hear Daddy chime in. *Once you challenge it, it cannot do damage.*

This letter, it's about more than hatred. It's a symbol of everything I could lose.

You're frightened that you'll lose him, Jean Marshall said, that day, when we argued by the woodland at the back of the house. She dared to be vicious, because Daddy wasn't around. Daddy had no idea about the incident, of course. Nor of what she was really like, what these sorts of women were capable of.

I was often frightened back then. Hiding under the bed, knees to chest, listening to them in bed, Daddy and her. I used to believe she was killing him as the mattress springs wailed and pitched, and didn't know whether to save him or leave her to it. I was frightened as a young adult too, of being alone. The sting of it wounded me, every time I saw Henry and his family, every time I watched them from behind the bus shelter opposite their house.

This is the past. This is not now, and I am *not* frightened. This letter will not best me. I was having a good day, one of the best I

85

can remember. This won't take that away from me, it won't make me feel all these terrible things. I should screw it up and throw it away with the rest of the rubbish. I should burn it. Or keep it, to remind myself that I'm never safe, but that I can conquer this. Perhaps it would be wise to show Margot. She should know that this identity programme hasn't worked, then perhaps I can reclaim my name. But that could have repercussions. The probation service might make me move again. I don't want to be uprooted a second time.

I need a drink. It's only just gone lunchtime, but I need one anyway. A large, soothing glass of wine, to stop myself from shaking. But my limbs aren't trembling with fear, not now. Instead, I'm shaking with pure, white-hot rage.

This will not beat me, I tell myself, while the voices inside me beg to differ.

This *will not* beat me.

I tuck the letter behind a plant pot on the kitchen windowsill, but its corner pokes out mockingly. I want it gone, but it could be useful as evidence in the future, if I decide to tell anyone about it. Perhaps someone can test it for prints, then legal action can be taken against the person who wrote it.

That's probably fantasy, of course. Dr Holland likes to remind me how important it is to separate facts from wishes. No one will do a thing about this letter, because I am worthless in the eyes of society. Worse than worthless, in fact, a burden. A negative mark on the balance sheet. Secretly, they'd probably all agree with the creature who wrote it and whisper among themselves that I should just put an end to it all, because there's no *point* to someone like me.

For the briefest of moments, I imagine what it would be like, to do as Ditz did. Clothes knotted tightly together to make a noose. A good, strong loop around the light fixture. One kick of the chair underneath and it would be done. I wouldn't be missed.

But then Bill would know. The papers would reveal it, the whole sordid story would be laid out again, and he'd read it, and he'd tell the journalists that he hadn't been aware of any of those awful things. And his smug daughter would nod, and declare that she'd suspected something all along. I freeze. Amber. Suspicious, narrow-eyed Amber. She's been odd with me since the first time we met. Could it have been her who wrote the letter? Bill told me that she kept going on about my familiar face. What if she's started snooping around online? Is this her way of torturing me with it? The timing is also unsettling, given that I went on a date with her father last night. I think back to my own childhood, how much I loathed sharing Daddy with Jean Marshall. Maybe Amber is the same – possessive and willing to do anything to keep her father focused on her, and only her.

Dr Holland would say this is paranoia. It is. It must be. This isn't a crime story, or some cheap thriller. Amber is a nasty piece of work, that's true, but would she go to these sorts of lengths?

Beware the ones that look innocent, Daddy once said, when we were ringing cormorants. *Those little chicks can poke holes in flesh with their beaks.*

Perhaps it's a bigger chick. Miranda. I remember her face, granite-cold and rigid, the hiss of her words as she sneered at me, calling me a monster. The other inmates stared at the time, then laughed about it later. Said that it was nothing more than I deserved.

No, it wouldn't be her. She's malicious enough to hate me, but this doesn't feel like her style. I'm overwrought. I shall have a bath, and force my mind to other things. It's a rational idea. My attitude is sensible, and I'm sure that Dr Holland would applaud me for it. However, even among the soft, glistening bubbles of the bath, I cannot stop the nagging sense that I've stumbled upon something true about Amber. I can't be sure, not yet. She will have covered her tracks, if it was her. Women are capable of so much more cunning than men give them credit for.

But if it is her, I shall find her out. I swear it.

CHAPTER 10

I've discovered a few old photographs, still in their shiny cardboard packet, buried deep in one of my old storage boxes. I vaguely remember putting them in there a long time ago. A selection that I kept because of their sentimental value. There's one of me, standing by a Christmas tree, swags of gaudy tinsel and baubles strung above my head. A festive event at Skye, if I remember rightly, held in the vestry of a church. Daddy and I sailed across to attend it. That was just after we'd first moved, when life was still one enormous adventure. I was a sweet child, I think. Hand clasped around a foil-wrapped gift, as though not quite sure whether it was for me or not. Another is of me standing beside a colony of gulls. Vast swathes of white and black, and rows of yellow beaks. I look a bit lost in this one. I wonder if that's when Jean Marshall appeared on the scene. She may well have been beside my father when the photo was taken, though I have no recollection of whether that was the case or not.

There are no photos of Henry, naturally. He never would have allowed it. But there is one of me at the office party. My expression makes me want to weep, not for nostalgia's sake, but for the fact that I didn't know how beautiful I was. Wide-eyed. Dignified and elegant in appearance. Soft. That softness still exists, somewhere. Bill saw something of it the other evening. He teased it out of me, bit by bit, rather than roughly grabbing for it, as Henry had.

Henry must have been at that office party too. It was before we were together, but still, he would have been present. Perhaps he was at the punch-bowl, or nibbling at the canapes. He always loved eating and drinking, satisfying his large appetites. Everyone adored him. I suppose you could describe him as one of those larger-than-life people, capable of magnetising others. They only saw the ready smile, only ever heard the cheery words. That wasn't who he really was; you could tell that from his interactions with his wife and children, and with me. Henry was selfish and cold, deep down.

In court, his lawyer told the jury that I'd stalked the family after our relationship was over. I have always resented the use of that word, *stalk*. It's predatory, threatening, and what I did was neither of those things. I simply needed to know why he'd done it. I wanted to get inside his head. Some of the papers said I'd developed an infatuation with Henry's son. With you. Others said I used you for revenge. Neither of these is correct, and I hope you know this, wherever you might be now. It was nothing perverted, and to claim it was is to corrupt everything that was good about our friendship. We were friends, despite what others said. I genuinely cared about you.

The first time we talked properly was in a supermarket, one of those monstrous warehouses devoted to food. It was recently built, as I remember, and brimming with people, keen to experience the super-abundance of produce on sale. You'd been sent to select a chocolate bar, you and your sister. She picked a Curly Wurly without hesitation. You took more time, sliding slowly down the aisle, surveying each shelf in turn, brow lowered in concentration.

I never usually approached people back then. I preferred to let them come to me; there was less risk of rejection that way. But your face was so very familiar – the streamlined jaw, the hint of dimple in one cheek, the sweep of hair over the forehead. You were Henry, only without the unkindness. A version of the creature he might have been, years before, before he corrupted himself. I asked if you remembered me from the museum, then told you I worked with your father. You nodded immediately and smiled, said that you'd been learning about migratory birds at school. You were such a warm, polite child. If I'd ever had children, they would have been like you.

After a while, your sister started tugging at your sleeve. You apologised, then said you had to go. I was tempted to ask you not to tell your father about our chat, but it would have been unfair. It wasn't your responsibility, after all. I'm sure the fact I was even there was unnerving enough for him, after he found out. He obviously presumed I'd just disappear, the moment he finished with me.

It would be nice to have a photo of you. They would all say how inappropriate it was, but it wouldn't be like that at all. I would look at it and remember how untainted you were, and how kind, when no one else was. How well we got on, and how you confided in me. They weren't good parents to you, I could tell, reading between the lines. You trusted me enough to give me those glimpses of how horrible Henry and Miranda were, and how little they deserved you.

Thank you for that. Even now, when I feel so troubled, the memory of it comforts me.

I gather my tissues and some lip balm, then check I've got my debit card in my purse. I shall go out, I have decided. I won't live in fear. If someone is watching this house, they can also watch me leave it, head held high. Then they'll get some idea of who they're dealing with.

My jacket. Do I need a jacket? I notice my hands have started to shake again, as I tug it out of the cupboard. It won't matter, I can easily stuff them into my pockets. My nerves won't be evident, I'll make sure of it.

I open the door. It's colder today, there's a bite to the air. Summer is definitely slipping away. The street is mercifully empty. Too empty, perhaps. Unnervingly silent. I can't even hear any birds singing. Come on, I tell myself. Stop being the frightened Robin. Remember who you really are. I step outside and lock the door behind me. So far, so good: nobody has rushed out to attack me, no screams of abuse are breaking the quiet.

You told her to do it, an inmate shouted, as they carried Ditz's body out of her cell. *You murdering butcher.* It wasn't like that at all, not that anyone cared. Everyone judges; they judge so easily and gleefully, without knowing any of the facts. Ditz was a lost cause, she would have had no life at all once she was released, but it wasn't me who put the makeshift noose around her neck. I didn't boot the chair from beneath her. That was her own doing, only hers. Still, that shout echoes through me. *You bitch.* Bitch. Female dog, snapping, howling. That wasn't me, they've all got it wrong. Plenty of other women are like that, but I'm not.

I'm in my stride now, handbag clasped tight under my arm, jacket zipped to my neck. Past the corner shop. Past the man with the baby strapped to his chest, who always seems to be here, along with his bellowing toddler. Down the alleyway that shortcuts to the main road. Out, next to grumbling cars. Fumes. Traffic lights, students chatting as they meander to lectures. They're all preoccupied in their own little worlds. No one can touch me; I exist in a glass case, protected by my thoughts. I am safe, I am safe. I will go to the shop, I will collect my pills from the pharmacy, I will visit a few more shops, then I will return again. It will be that simple.

The first shop is crowded, far too busy for comfort. People are milling about, choosing sandwiches, clutching packets of hair dye and sanitary towels. I hear noises, so many noises. The ceaseless thrum of chatter confuses me, a sneeze from somewhere close by makes me jump. Checkouts bleep and bleep, like hospital machines. I pick up a handbag-sized umbrella, useful for the coming autumn, then a bottle of shower gel. This is fine. I have managed this before and I can manage it again.

But what if someone screeches my name – Ava? Or calls me murderer? What if they—

They won't. It won't happen, because the person who wrote that letter is probably far away now, in their bland, modern box of a home, rapping their fake nails on the kitchen table. Some friend of Henry's, perhaps. Or a busybody vigilante type, who imagines it's their duty to destroy all ex-criminals, without finding out the exact nature of their past.

Or Amber. It could have been her. No. Why would she? Because she doesn't like me. She hates me.

'Excuse me, can I get to that shelf?'

I blink, mouth gaping like a fish. A woman, coated with heavy make-up, is pointing at something behind me. She looks embarrassed.

I recover myself, then step aside. 'Yes, of course. Sorry.'

'No worries, I go off in a dream world sometimes too.'

'Pardon?'

She shifts awkwardly. There's clearly something about my appearance that bothers her, and that makes my cheeks flame, especially when she gives me a harder, more guarded look. Could it be her? The poison-pen writer? Is this an elaborate ruse? Will she suddenly pull out a knife and thrust it through me?

'I'll just—' she says, her words faltering. Then she busies herself picking bottles off the shelf and studying them hard. I nod, though she's no longer looking. I need to collect my sleeping pills, find some painkillers, then go home. This is too much for me; I feel I'll crack into pieces if I stay here much longer. *Get the pills, get the pills*, I chant to myself. Nothing else matters. I want to sleep, to sleep as soon as possible, and forget all about this.

You didn't want to go to sleep, but I made it happen anyway. I meant well, I really, honestly did. You knew that, didn't you? I explained it all carefully to you. People need sleep, because otherwise they'll get ill. And you weren't well, not at that point, because you'd hurt yourself. You looked so much better after you nodded off, and I popped the throw over you to keep you warm. Your head didn't look nearly so—

That thought isn't welcome now. I should get back to thoughts of sleep instead, because sleep is kindness. It's the blanket that wraps us up, and makes everything bad go away.

I must get home. Now.

I swallow more pills than I mean to.

Then I sleep. Not the sleep of the haunted; there's no you, and there's no Ditz. No evil letters to worry over. There's only a vast, lonely expanse of nothing, darker than a winter sky on one of the islands, emptier than time itself. It's bliss, all that emptiness. The night stretches on and on. I vaguely hear banging from somewhere downstairs. It sounds like a hammer on wood. I can't open my eyes, and besides, the black is tugging me back. So I return to sleep again; there's no point resisting it.

It's dark when my eyelids flicker open. Not morning, then. I've no idea what time it could be. I've lost all sense of everything. Am I still here, or back in my cell? Am I a grown woman? A skittish thing in her twenties? A child, gripping tight to the duvet? It shouldn't be night-time, because when I took the pills, it was just gone five in the afternoon, and a normal dose keeps me asleep for at least twelve hours. The amount I took should have seen me right through until the following morning, if not further.

I sit up. My head feels clotted with cotton wool, my lips, cracked and dry. I'm a little queasy. I shouldn't have taken as many pills as I did; I knew that, even as I was swallowing them with water. It was more than I'd ever taken before. But I wanted my mind to be still, and that was the only way to make it happen.

I could have died, perhaps.

The irony of the thought doesn't escape me. The pills can kill. They may be small and innocent to look at, but they have the power to be deadly, especially in large quantities. They were even worse in my younger days, before the tighter regulations kicked in. So tiny, and yet so lethal. My gut twists suddenly, and I fold over like a pancake in a pan.

I only just make it to the toilet in time. Foul liquid pours from me, again and again. The sickness rises like a geyser, and I vomit, spraying through my fingers and onto the floor. All is heaving, it is primal somehow, and I feel violated by my own crude humanity. Sometime later, the waves of sickness abate. Finally, there is calm,

93

a sense of the storm having been weathered and survived. But still, the darkness confuses me. It could be ten at night or four in the morning, it's impossible to tell. Did I only sleep for ten hours or so, or have I managed to sleep far longer?

I flush the toilet, wipe the surrounding area, clean myself up as well as possible. Then I flick the switch in the hallway and head to the back room, to find my second-hand laptop. It displays the date, I remember. It'll tell me what day it is. Sure enough, the numbers at the bottom of the screen confirm what I suspected: I've lost a whole day, and been asleep for a frightening number of hours. There's something exhilarating about the knowledge that I cheated consciousness and stole more of that soothing, comforting darkness, but also something horrible in that it was out of my control. Anything could have happened during that time. I could have stopped breathing and not known a thing about it. Someone could have broken in, attacked me, sent me into nothingness forever.

I could be dead, I think again. Dead. And would I discover that you were waiting for me, on the other side? And Ditz? And others too, maybe?

These thoughts are unhealthy. My *mind* is unhealthy, perhaps. No, there's nothing wrong with me, aside from an understandable nervousness about the past. Firmly, I close the laptop. I need to sleep some more; the pills are still weighing me down. Besides, there's no benefit to being awake now, when the world is still so dark.

I wake. My curtains are rich with weak light: the sun, I realise, just a beat later. Morning at last. *And the pills didn't kill me!* I think, a giggle rising in my throat. I'm very much still here, regardless of what the rest of the world might want. Then the force of my headache slams against my skull as I sit, making me clutch my temples. Dehydration. It must be, after my violent upset stomach last night. I am hungry though, which is good. I can't have done too much damage to my body if I'm craving food.

As I go downstairs, I notice something on the doormat. For a moment, I think it's another envelope, another evil outpouring from the person who sent me the previous one. But it's a note this time, written in wavering, elongated letters, then pushed carefully through the letterbox.

Dear Robin,

I hope you're all right. I tried calling round this evening and there was no answer, then I tried at 10 o'clock and still no answer. I'm a bit worried. If you don't want to see me, I understand (though I thought we had a good night together), but can you let me know you're okay?

Your friend,
Bill

I smile. He cares about me, enough to worry that I might not be well, or that I may not care for him in return. It's intoxicating. Even if every other person is working against me, I feel that he will be there. A stoic, sturdy support through the storm. There's power to it, too. Relationships are never equal, and it's a thrill to be the one with the upper hand.

Food forgotten, I go back to my bedroom and get dressed, then quickly brush my teeth. I need to see him immediately, to let him know that I'm fine, and to make him aware that his concern is appreciated. He's a good man. Maybe one of only a handful left in the world.

The air is chillier than before, a noticeable briskness that reminds me of tumbling leaves, wellies in puddles. Migrating birds, too, flocking to warmer climes. I push through Bill's front gate, noticing the black bin bags in his front garden, the discarded plastic chair leaning against the wall. He most certainly needs a woman to help keep him organised; Amber is obviously failing at the task.

He answers almost immediately and breaks into a smile.

'I was worried about you,' he says, waving me inside. 'I know you said you didn't have any family, so I didn't think you'd have gone away for the night.'

His hallway is much the same as my own, only flipped in a mirror, with all doors leading to the right, not the left. The walls are grimier though, and there's a pervasive smell of damp. The place hasn't been as well looked after as my own.

He catches my expression and grimaces. 'It's not much, is it?' he says, as he walks to the kitchen. 'Still, it's a roof over my head. Amber's upstairs, shall I call for her to join us?'

'Oh, don't disturb her.' I perch on one of his stools, noting the mugs and plates covering the breakfast bar surface. His kitchen is an entirely different layout to mine, aside from the window, which matches.

'I've got some Battenberg cake, fancy some?'

'I'm all right, thank you.'

He grins. 'I can't resist a bit of cake, you know. I'm impressed by your willpower.'

'I haven't even had breakfast yet.'

'This late in the day? You keep strange hours, Robin. What were you up to last night?'

There's a hint of something in his face that I can't decipher. Is he suspicious of me? What would he have to be suspicious about? Unless of course Amber was the person who sent that letter, and she's now started to put ideas in his head.

He couldn't know already. He wouldn't be letting me sit here in his kitchen if he did, and certainly wouldn't be offering me cake. Cake is for friends, after all.

'Robin? Earth to Robin?'

I put on a quick smile. 'Sorry, I was miles away. I went to bed early last night, that's all.'

'Did you hear me knocking?'

'I took some pills to help me sleep.' I don't like admitting it, but I haven't the energy to come up with a lie.

He nods. 'I know how rough insomnia can be. Is that because of your time in prison?'

No, it started long before that, when I started dreaming of towering cliffs and those skuas circling above me, I think.

'Prison didn't help,' I say carefully.

A succession of light footsteps echo from the stairs. A few seconds later, Amber peers around the door, towel around her head, t-shirt hanging off one shoulder. I wonder how much of the conversation she heard, and whether she was listening from upstairs.

'The hot water's gone again,' she says, after giving me a curt nod. It's interesting, how she won't meet my gaze.

Bill groans. 'Not again. Honestly, if it's not one thing, it's another. I'll have another look at the boiler later, see if I can see what's going on.'

'I didn't know you were a plumbing expert,' I say with a too-high laugh.

'He's a man of many talents,' Amber says, reaching for a Coke from the fridge. 'Mum used to say he was a DIY whizz.'

I try not to flinch. It's clear she's trying to make me feel uncom-fortable, unwanted. What she doesn't realise is that I've spent a lifetime feeling that way. This is nothing new to me, and I'm perfectly able to meet the challenge. *Was it her?* I wonder, studying her expression. She's sly, underhand, and that fits with the profile of someone who'd write an anonymous note. But I have no solid evidence. I mustn't jump to conclusions, that's what Dr Holland would say.

'It must be useful to have a DIY expert around,' I say coolly, standing up. 'Thanks for the offer of cake, Bill, but I'll take a rain check today. I've got some things to do at home.'

'Maybe we could arrange another meet-up, what do you think?' he suggests quickly.

Amber rolls her eyes. She does it carefully, behind the fridge door, so her father won't see. Sneaky young madam that she is, she thinks she's got away with it.

I check myself, arranging my features in a more pleasant expression. 'We certainly could,' I say to Bill, deliberately turning away from his daughter. 'We had such a nice time at the restaurant, didn't we?'

A snort this time; low and easily mistaken for a cough, but I know it's Amber.

'I'll let myself out,' I say lightly. 'Let's catch up later on, yes?'

He gives me a wink. 'You betcha.'

Such a small gesture, but laden with flirtation. I'm surprised to like it as much as I do. Let's see who wins this war, I think, as I give Amber a final, contemptuous look. She's met her match with me, and if it was her that sent that letter, if she thinks that she can ruin what Bill and I have, then I will destroy her.

It's not as though I haven't done it before.

CHAPTER 11

'Did you have any friends when you were a child?' Dr Holland asks.

These sessions drain me. No, worse than that. They bore me to tears. I have no idea what they're expected to achieve, nor what I'm meant to gain from it.

'Why does that matter?'

'Perhaps you can gain greater understanding of your inter-actions with others as an adult, if you review how you were with others as a child?'

I frown. There was one girl on South Uist, Morag. Bright red hair and freckles, about as archetypally rural Scottish as could be imagined. Daddy left me at her house a few times, when he wanted to spend the day with Jean Marshall. Morag was bossy, I remember that. She told me that my dead mother would come back to haunt me. I wasn't bothered. My personal opinion was that Mother was too weak to make it back from death in any form, even a shadowy, ghostly one.

'I had friends,' I say slowly, picking at some lint on my skirt. 'But I preferred my own company.'

'Why was that?'

Because Morag tried to make me eat a torn-up bird's wing, I think, not that he needs to know that. We found it in the copse near her house, a tern's wing by the look of the feathers, mauled by a cat, perhaps. She held it up to the light, then, without warning, attempted to shove the bloodied end in my mouth. It smelt of wetness and rot.

I remember the metallic tang on my lips and the casual malevolence in her eyes. Cruelty came easily to her, which was certainly a lesson for me. Never believe in anyone, not even a supposed friend.

'It was just easier for me to be alone,' I tell him, eventually.

'Did you have any pets? To keep you company?'

'No. Daddy hated cats with a passion, and said dogs were too much trouble.'

I actually had a chick, once, back on Lundy, when I was very young. I found it in a nest, its mother perhaps out to sea, or else disappeared entirely. The parents did that, from time to time. Its sharp little beak took up its entire head: a diamond gash of redness, always screeching for food. I fed it some seeds, then put it in a shoe box in my wardrobe. For the next few days, it huddled itself in the corner, and shuddered each time I took it out. I suppose I must have tired of it after a while, as the next time I checked, it had died. Its body looked soft, but under the wispy feathers it was hard as stone.

'Do you think human company might have been something you craved as an adult?' Dr Holland asks, bringing me back to the present. 'As you didn't have much as a child?'

'No.'

He adjusts his legs, then eases forward. 'Let's talk about something else. The time you first met Ben Hulham.'

I can't prevent myself from starting, rearing back in my seat. 'Don't say his name,' I whisper. My fingers are gripping at my skirt, and I need to relax them. I *must* relax.

Ben. It was Henry who first introduced you to me in the museum, albeit reluctantly. His hand pressed aggressively against your shoulder, preventing you from coming too close. As though I was diseased, a thing to be nervous of.

I shake my head, again and again.

Dr Holland frowns. 'I understand that it's painful, but in order to move forward with your life, I think it's beneficial to—'

'It's not beneficial. Don't say it, I can't *bear* to hear it said aloud.'

'Can you articulate why his name is having this effect on you?'

Because no one knows the truth of it, I think. Dr Holland doesn't get to say your name; no one does. For a moment, I see you in the corner of the room, thin calves poking from school shorts, hands pushed into pockets. You're watching me, birdlike with curiosity, head on one side. But you're not there. I must remind myself of this very firmly, because to admit you're there would be to confess a sort of madness in myself. We are alone, the doctor and I. It's only us.

'Robin?' he says, quietly.

'Ava.'

'You know I can't call you that name.'

'Then you don't understand the power of a name. Not at all.'

He nods. 'And Ben's name is powerful to you, yes?'

'Stop saying it.'

'Robin, I'm noticing real tension in your posture right now. Do you need a break?'

I nod. 'I need to leave.'

'These sessions are part of your parole terms, so we should continue, but we can talk about—'

'What do you want from me?' I snap. I hadn't meant to; it won't do me any good. Already, he's scribbling notes in his pad. This will be fed back to Margot, to the rest of the people with control over me.

'I want to help you.'

'By saying his name?'

'By helping you to take important steps to move on from all of this. I think Ben Hulham's death still torments you, Robin. You wouldn't have such a violent reaction if it didn't. And that's a positive thing. It shows that you feel remorse for it.'

'I don't feel remorse, because I wasn't responsible!' I'm on my feet now, though I'm not sure how I got there.

'My intention isn't to upset you. Would you sit back down for me, Robin?'

I wish he would stop calling me that. This is going badly; I need to get out of here. The air is stifling, his central heating is far too intense, it's making me feel trapped. As though I'm trapped in an airless box in a cupboard, I think, wanting to laugh. He's making me helpless.

'We'll leave that topic for today, I think,' he says, as I sit down again. 'Perhaps we should discuss medication. We can—'

'That's not necessary.' The last thing I want is him probing into how many sleeping pills I take each night, and forcing me to explore alternative options. I remember Jean Marshall with her endless bottles of medicines. Pills of all shapes and sizes – not just vitamins, but ones for her heart too. I wouldn't want to end up like her. I stifle another giggle. It's shameful how I've lost control of myself today; I have to work hard to regain it.

Dr Holland sighs. 'I think it would help. We can review your current prescriptions and—'

'No. It's my right to say no, and I'm going to exercise that right.'

Exercise. Exorcise. Such similar words. I need to exorcise my mind, and quickly. Dr Holland only fills it with demons.

'Very well,' he says finally. 'We've got a few minutes left, so what would you like to discuss?'

'How about the weather?' I suggest. This time, the laughter erupts out of me, geyser-quick and violent.

He doesn't even smile, only makes another note.

As I walk home, I can't help but think of you, of course. The verdict was murder; Dr Holland seems to think that I need constant reminding of that. But that word oversimplifies the matter.

I don't deny that I killed you. But I do deny that I was to blame.

I remember the third time I saw you, after the conversation we'd had in the supermarket. You were coming out of school, with two other friends. I only happened to be there by chance; I was in the park over the road, eating a baguette and listening to the birds. There was nothing premeditated about it at all.

Your rucksack was slung over your shoulder, and your blazer still on, despite the warmth of the day. I liked that about you – your desire to be smart. So many of the other students had half-fixed ties around their necks, shirt collars gaping. You stood out as superior, a fellow intellectual, above the rest of the pack. I was proud of you. I didn't approach you, not then. I would have loved to have come over and said hello, but I knew your companions would have found it odd, a full-grown woman talking to a child. I didn't want to make you nervous, only to know more about you. To see if my suspicions were right, that you were a better person than your father.

You were. That quickly became apparent. I couldn't understand how such a maggot of a man could produce such a sweet-hearted, sensitive, clever boy. Your sister, on the other hand? She was cut from the same cloth as your mother. Sneery. Aloof. She even had the same large bottom. I had no interest in her whatsoever.

It was on the fourth or fifth occasion that I finally got my chance to make contact with you. You came out of the school gates alone, I remember that much. It was a bright, burning day, and the sun made your neatly combed hair gleam. I bumped into you, apologised, then feigned surprise. It took you a while to recollect where you'd seen me before. I suppose, out of context, adult faces can be confusing.

All it took was a mention of a rare bird in the park. You loved birds, and I loved that about you. You would have had so much fun on the islands with me, when I was a child. I suspect we would have been inseparable; two life-long friends, with the same interests and passions. A parakeet, I told you. It must have flown all the way from London, or perhaps it's an escaped pet. The temptation of the exotic proved too hard to resist, though you told me that you couldn't stay long, that your mother would be expecting you back for tea. We groaned at this together, and it was a moment of camaraderie, of shared experience, though I'd never been expected for tea in my life. She's always nagging at me, you told me some time later, and I put on a wry smile, replied that it must be tough.

There was no parakeet. Of course there wasn't; any adult would have seen through the lie in a heartbeat. I felt bad for letting you down, but I think you understood that it was important for us to meet, and to talk. You said you'd just been made class representative, that you'd been learning about the Holocaust in history. All these snippets of information – how eagerly you chirruped them out to me. You were starved of attention at home, that was clear.

That was the first time; the first proper time. There weren't many times after that, because Henry ruined everything. He was so adept at destroying beautiful things. But what little time we had together was special, and I'm certain you felt so too.

A splash of moisture lands on the bridge of my nose, making me jump. It's closely followed by another. I hear the roar of the rain approaching on the pavement behind me, before the fury of the shower hits me. I don't mind it. It's cleansing, and it rids me of all these memories for a while. Besides, I'm nearly home now. Let it soak me through, let it whip and bite at me. I need it. Finally, something to ground me back to nature, and to quieten my thoughts; thoughts put there by a cruel and negligent therapist.

I can survive this day, I think, looking upwards. I see myriad grey lines, shooting towards me, wetting my face. It's time I started doing it my way, and living in the way I know how.

At home, I peel off my clothes and throw them to the kitchen floor. Then I march up the stairs to the back room and find the necklace Henry gave me – that cheap, disgusting thing with the gull pendant hanging off it. It's easy to find, still resting in the top of a cardboard box. I seize it, then return downstairs. I have a hammer in one of my drawers, purchased along with a few other tools that I thought I might need on occasion.

The first blow is bliss. The gull leaps and jitters, making my breath catch in my throat. Some of its metal coating flakes off, and I hit it again and again; a flurry of swipes, each blow harder than the last. The pendant bends, warps, then breaks in two. The chain-links of the necklace crumple in on themselves, unable to withstand the onslaught.

'I hate you,' I hiss. I realise I am saying it over and over, an incantation that pours from the centre of me, quite of its own volition.

Hate. A short bark of a word, but capable of so much damage. Its abrupt power is intoxicating. But while satisfying, it's not enough. This hate hasn't been sated, not by a long way. Now it's the turn of that vile letter, which is still on the window ledge, behind the flowerpot. Tearing it is too tame. I want to watch it burn, to reach right through the words and let whoever wrote them feel my loathing for them.

There are matches under the sink. I strike one, then hold it to the corner of the paper. It takes immediately, turning the paper dirty brown, then black and brittle. Finally, a flame appears, flaring upwards. It's fascinating to watch, and at this moment, I understand arsonists completely. That caressing, sensual lick of heat is truly irresistible. The flames tickle my fingers and I drop the letter beneath the tap. A few moments longer and it's extinguished, now nothing more than a charred mess.

I will do that to whoever threatens me, I tell myself, aware that this is a sort of madness, that I've given into it completely, for the time being. But it feels good. Intoxicating, a victory over adversity. Powerful, even. They will not frighten me. Not the sender of the letter, not Dr Holland with his probing questions, not Amber either. I'm strong again.

Yes, I tell myself, as I start to wash away the mess in the sink. This is how it is, from now on. On the attack, not the defence.

I lie in the darkness, feeling the bedspread beneath me. It's pleasantly cool. I need coldness right now, to counteract the earlier burning, and the heat that still roars inside me.

We used to light fires a lot, Daddy and I. It was the only way to keep warm at times, particularly in the cottages with no central heating. Some of them had log-burners, and I loved their furnace intensity, the way the flames would blaze behind the glass door. I used to like holding my palm close to it, to see how long I could withstand the heat. Others were open fireplaces, with huge burning logs that sometimes popped and spat onto the slate flagstones. Daddy liked to read in front of those fires. Television was of no interest to him; he hated dramatised programmes and found the news too removed from his own sphere of interest. Jean Marshall often joined us too, feet tucked under her on the sofa, or laid out lengthways across it, ensuring there was no room left for me.

She passed Daddy a brochure once, for a boarding school in Glasgow. *It's got an excellent reputation,* she told him, without looking at me. *Ava would do so well there. She's a clever girl, she needs more than this.* If anyone else had suggested it, Daddy would have dismissed the idea immediately. But this was Jean, and she had a hold over him, which I never understood. So a week or so later, we took the ferry to the mainland, then drove for hours past sprawling lochs and rugged highlands, until the ground flattened, and buildings appeared on the horizon. The school was old, built of slate-grey bricks, with several pillars. Long corridors. Girls walking in straight lines, demure, anonymous. Jean marched ahead, talking to the liaison officer about educational opportunities, the prospect of university, a grand career. She nodded at Daddy, and to my horror, he nodded back, while dragging me alongside him.

Fortunately, I failed the entrance exam. It was so simple to do so, to mark a few wrong answers, but get enough right to fail convincingly. I couldn't help but enjoy Jean's look of bitter disappointment when they opened the results. She thought that she'd got rid of me. I think she realised then that it was never going to be that easy. She popped a few of her pills, then poured herself a glass of wine, and Daddy too. She didn't offer me anything, but that was fine with me. I wouldn't have accepted anyway.

Many decades later, Ditz suggested that Jean had been fond of me. This made me laugh so hard that I nearly choked on the water I was sipping at the time. It staggered me that after a life of relentless cruelty, Ditz could still believe that people were decent. That they had good intentions. I supposed it was down to that sister of hers: dearest Babs had made her think that women could be trusted. That was a joke, if ever there was one. *No one cares about people like us,* I told her. *Especially you, because you're insubstantial, insipid.* I remember her smile faltering. She wanted so hard to feel that the world wasn't a bad place, and to feel that she had a place in it. I believed it was my duty to set her right. Truth is important, after all.

Ditz may have hated me for it, may hate me still, wherever she is now. But I was correct. There is no goodness in humanity, and there was nothing of any worth to her, or others like her. Most people are parasites, set on draining everything dry until nothing remains.

The scourge of the planet, Daddy had once called the human race, after seeing a gathering of weathered plastic bottles in a rock pool one day. *They ruin everything.*

They deserve to be punished.

I am going for a walk this morning. Not my usual route into town, but the other way, towards the river. Before prison, I used to immerse myself in nature as much as possible, letting the scent of leaves and the rich, clean air do their work on me. After Henry left me, especially so; I needed it. Maybe it will help me now.

It's a blustery day. Already, a few brown leaves dot the ground, glued to the pavement with dampness. It doesn't bother me; I've got my scarf on, and I have already purchased a winter coat in readiness for the change of season. Not many other people are out. As I slip down the long alleyway that leads towards the river, I pass a few dog-walkers, who keep their heads down at the sight of me, and one elderly man shuffling along with his stick, but no one else. The peace is soothing. This is good. It was the right decision to make.

Today I am going to focus on looking forward, not back. I live in my memories a lot, I realise. It's not surprising, especially as Dr Holland seems so intent on keeping me in the past. Instead, I want to give myself goals, as I used to, before I met Henry. I want to learn a new hobby, to try something completely new. This will make me feel more positive, I think. I'm not sure what, though – maybe cross-stitching, or I could sign up for an online course and learn a new language. Margot told me there were learning apps that I could download for free, though I'm not quite sure yet what an app is. It's yet another modern thing designed to baffle me.

This is the first time that I've come down to the river. It's wide and fast-flowing, the water a dark dishwater beige. But it feels good to be here, the breeze sharp against my cheeks. I lean against a railing and watch a row of cormorants, drying their wings in the watery light. There are some mallards drifting in the reeds too, and a few herring gulls, perched on the other side. I spy a few cafés along the waterfront, a little way along, but I'll veer away from the company of others today, and stroll along the footpath. It's muddy, but it doesn't matter. I have my sensible shoes on.

As I progress, the river widens. It's an estuary, so this is unsurprising, but I hadn't predicted it would change its personality so quickly. After a while, I pause, slightly breathless, and enjoy the view. It's bleak, dominated by the cold-shine surface of the water, which blends almost seamlessly with the sky.

I'm meant for places like this, I think, inhaling deeply. Away from the rest of society. A thing of the earth, run through with stream water, sinewy with stone. This is me, who I really am. But of course, I can't stay rooted here forever, tempting though it feels right now. Also, there are clouds rolling in from the sea, dark and weighted with rain. I don't mind a downpour, but don't much fancy the long walk home while getting soaked. I turn back, head tucked down to avoid the sudden rush of cold wind on my neck. I will have a bath when I get home, I think. A welcome bit of warmth to counteract the chill.

The way back seems harder work somehow; perhaps the path runs at a slight incline. My breath shortens, and I'm aware of the sky darkening. There's yet another rainstorm on the way, I can tell. After a while, I realise there are footsteps behind me. They're some distance away, their sound only audible when carried on the breeze. I slow my pace and move to one side, a clear signal for whoever it is to pass. The steps seem to slow too. I risk a glance over my shoulder.

A figure in a black coat is some way behind me; presumably female, given the slenderness of the frame. They wear a wide-brimmed hat, pulled down over the face, with only a pale wedge of chin visible underneath. It's a strange hat to wear, here by the river, where the wind may pluck it off at any moment. Almost as if whoever is wearing it wants to conceal themselves as much as possible. My skin prickles, with cold or tension. Something is wrong, I feel it quite distinctly. I should know: I've been around wrongness for many years.

I face forward again and pick up my speed. It may be nothing, merely another walker enjoying the scenery but now keen to get home, just like me. The question is, why did they slow down when I did? And why is their hat tugged down so deliberately low? I'm being paranoid again. I mustn't allow myself to get as I did the other day, it's not good for me. But it can't hurt to test the situation. I deliberately quicken my walking again, even though it's far faster than I'd usually go. If it's nothing to worry about, I'll soon leave this other person far behind. For a while, it's impossible to tell, and I don't want to take another look, at least not yet. Daddy always said that the worst thing a bird could do when faced with a predator was to pause and display fear.

I hear another burst of footsteps carried on the wind. They're distant, but the fact I can hear them at all is worrying. The cafés by the river are in sight again now; I'm almost back to the alleyway that leads to my house. I just need to keep going until I'm safely locked behind my own front door. But the urge to know is too strong. I can't help it; I glance over my shoulder. The figure is still walking behind me. I could be imagining it, but they seem closer now. They've been keeping pace with me, that's for sure. Their hands are in their pockets, rummaging for something. A weapon, perhaps.

I'm being followed. *I'm being stalked.*

A gasp escapes me. This isn't right, it isn't *fair.* I refuse to be frightened by this; I'm not someone who deserves treatment of this nature. Who do they think they are, anyway? Are they attempting to act as a lone vigilante, on a fantasy revenge mission? It's not their right to determine whether I deserve punishment or not;

I've served my time, and in the eyes of the law I'm now a new person. I consider running, but fleeing will only make them think they've won. Instead, I stop walking, then turn to stare at them. They need to be made aware of who they're dealing with. They stop too, and mirror my posture – mockingly, I believe. Then they raise a hand, finger extended, and point in my direction. I can see a curl of lip beneath the hat-brim.

My gasp is stopped in my throat, my heart thuds harder against my ribs. I am found out, I am discovered. I don't know what to do, but I *must* think of something.

'Stop following me!' I shout, and am dismayed at how weak my voice sounds: mouselike, tremulous.

The breeze is stronger now, but I'm confident I hear a muffled laugh. It's a female, I'm sure. I see a wisp of hair, escaping from the hat, tugged backwards by the wind. Should I approach them? Seize their hat and *see* my stalker for who they really are? But their hand is still in their pocket; there may be a knife in there, ready to be pulled out, stabbed into my side like a butcher carving up a carcass.

'You're harassing the wrong person,' I say, so quietly that I can scarcely hear myself.

The figure lowers their hand, and again I hear a laugh. Then, without warning, they turn back the way they came, and walk quickly away. All I can do is stare, mouth gaping like a freshly caught fish. The person doesn't look back once, not even when they're a tiny mark of black in the distance. They don't need to, obviously. Their intention was to ruin my day, and they've succeeded.

Their hair was blonde, I think, remembering the wisp I'd seen, tumbling in the air. Now I think of it, I'm sure it was white blonde, the pale colour that some call angel hair.

It could have been Amber. It really could.

CHAPTER 12

I know, as I return home, that I am now a creature under threat.

Whoever it was following me, they're operating with serious intent. At the very least, they want to frighten me. At worst, they're out to cause harm. It's not as though there aren't people out there wishing to see me suffer; any of Henry's family or friends may be behind it. They might be working in tandem with Amber, getting her to spy on me, then report back. She's perfectly positioned to do so: who would suspect the innocent next-door neighbour, with no obvious connection to me?

I pour myself a glass of wine, even though it's not yet lunchtime. This mustn't become a habit, but I need something to steady my thoughts right now. I feel glassy, a transparent sheet that can be peered into, smashed to pieces if required. This isn't how I used to be. My nature is to be a featureless wall. Impenetrable. Strong. I need to get back to that, and quickly.

The wine does its work. After a time, I'm able to sit down at the kitchen table and breathe properly. I must think this through as a rational adult, not a panicking child. The letter was designed to inspire fear, and the person following me earlier was trying to frighten me. They want to *play*, to make me suffer as they believe I deserve to. This is good. I am getting inside their head, thinking as they do. That gives me power and an element of control, because I will be able to predict their next move. It *could* be Amber – the person's stature and hair colour were certainly the same. But equally, I must be pragmatic here. It may not be her. It might be Henry's daughter, for example. I have no idea what she would look like now, but she'd be in her thirties, and so she'd be a feasible option.

My glass is empty. Sadly the wine bottle is too, now, but it's probably for the best. I am in a perfect state of lucidity. My thoughts are clearer than they have been in months.

I shall conceal weapons around the house, just in case. I have a set of kitchen knives, even though I use only the smallest one for peeling vegetables, and the serrated one for bread. That's three or four weapons going spare. I have a couple of steak knives too. I shall put these in easy-to-reach locations around the house, so that I'm prepared if anyone does decide to get violent with me. The thought makes me want to laugh. I remember one of the women in the prison, a tousle-headed fiend with a cross-eyed glare, who fashioned a weapon by sharpening the end of a toothbrush. She managed to spear another inmate through the ribs. It just goes to show how enterprising humans can be, especially when trapped and with nothing to lose.

Ditz was scared for weeks after that incident. She was convinced that someone would come for her in the same way, because she'd informed on a drug dealer in the past. It was enjoyable to reassure her, to play the role of a caring parent. I held her close to me, and felt her twitching energy travel deep through me. Stroking her short hair seemed to relax her. It reminded me of how I used to calm birds, when Daddy was putting rings round their legs.

That's how I know I'm a good person. In those moments when she was desperate, and I pulled her towards me to make it better, I *was* a parent to her, when everyone else in her life had left her to rot in a cell. Even her precious sister couldn't take the pain away in there. It was an act of kindness to tell her the truth about her life, and what the people in it were really like. Evil. Self-serving. That's why I told her, over and over again, to stop feeling so much, to stop imagining that her existence had any purpose. Admittedly, I also wanted to silence her insufferable whining, because what good did it serve? Life after prison would have been miserable for her, that was irrefutable; so my words were compassionate, not cruel. Poor, weak Ditz.

It's a shame I don't have any more wine. I'll make myself a cup of coffee instead; that will make me more alert. Alert is exactly the state I need to be in, until all of this is over and done with.

There is now a knife by the door, balanced carefully in my little umbrella rack. One in the kitchen too, behind the microwave, and another in the lounge. That one's only a steak knife, as I think it's less likely I will be taken by surprise by an assailant there. I've placed one under my pillow, and a further one on the window ledge of the bathroom, concealed behind a bottle of bubble bath. Lastly, a little one in the spare room, behind the door. I am now armed and prepared, and this is reassuring.

Bill comes around just after three in the afternoon. He's made an effort with his appearance, a fact that doesn't escape my attention. His shirt is smart and tucked into his trousers. He's shaved too, though he's nicked himself slightly on the neck, just beside his scar.

'How are you?' he asks, strolling inside with easy familiarity. 'You left in a bit of a hurry the other day. I hope it wasn't anything I said?'

'Goodness me, no,' I tell him. I'm glad of his company, and the chance to have a normal conversation, rather than being left alone with my brooding thoughts.

'You weren't annoyed with my Amber, were you?'

I note the use of the word *my*. His precious darling. The woman who can do no wrong.

'Of course not,' I say, forcing a laugh. 'She's a lovely girl, so polite and friendly.'

He raises an eyebrow. 'Come now, Robin. I know what my daughter's like. She can be a bit curt at times, though her heart's in the right place. She just wants to make sure you're going to treat her old man right, that's all.'

Her *heart*. It's difficult not to scoff at the notion. She's a heartless little madam, in my opinion. 'I'm sure she's a very caring daughter,' I say, pointing out of the window. 'Shall we sit in the garden? Enjoy the last of the sunshine?'

There's enough warmth in the air for it to be a pleasure to step outside. The little lawn is speckled with leaves, the grass still shiny with moisture even though the sun has had all day to dry it out. Bill sits on an old metal chair, rusted but still functional. I gesture back to the kitchen.

'Coffee? Tea? Mug of hot chocolate?'

'Now you're talking. Hot choccie for me, please.'

I smile, then hurry back inside. A glance at the microwave tells me that the knife is concealed. That's good, I wouldn't want him to ask any difficult questions. I pile powder into each mug, mix it with milk for creaminess, then add steaming water. Bill takes it from me with a sigh of satisfaction.

'Is there anything better in life than this?' he says, waving a hand around. 'A warm drink in hand, and the sun's shining too.'

I think of the stalker by the river. The letter. Life could be a great deal better. They may even be watching me at the moment, peering through the crack in the gate that leads from my garden to the back alley, watching from one of the many windows that overlook us.

'It is a beautiful day,' I agree.

'And you're good company. What more could a man want?'

Men so often seem to want more, I think, remembering Henry. But of course, Bill isn't like that. He appreciates the simple things in life, much as I do. That's why we get on so well.

'What have you been up to, Robin?' he asks, after a time.

'This and that. I'm still sorting out my belongings. It's taking a long time.'

'It doesn't help when so many memories are tied up in them, eh?'

'That's very true.'

He studies me carefully. 'You mentioned a man, when we were at that restaurant. Was he your ex-husband?'

My mind freezes. What's the best answer in this scenario? A husband would mean a divorce; this may be brought up in future and used against me. If Bill asked me to marry him, for example, then they'd need to see divorce papers, and—

'Robin? Have I overstepped the mark again?'

'No, not at all. He wasn't my husband. But it was a long-term relationship. He cheated on me with another woman.'

Bill whistles. 'What a sod. Not that I can sit in judgement, as I made my fair share of mistakes in the past.'

'He was living a double life, the whole time we were together,' I tell him, warming to the story. 'This other woman was atrocious. She knew he was in love with me, but wanted him anyway.'

'If he was in love with you, why did he keep seeing her?'

Damn it. I hadn't meant to say that. I need to gather my thoughts, and quickly. 'He loved me, but loved sleeping with her,' I say softly, gazing out to the back of the garden.

'Now that is sad to hear.' Bill sips thoughtfully at his drink. 'I don't want to defend your ex-partner, but I can relate to it myself. I loved my ex-wife very much, but... you know. I looked for excitement elsewhere.'

'That's not very honourable of you.'

'I know. I'm deeply ashamed of it, especially as it caused so much pain. But I want you to know, Robin, that I've realised how appalling that behaviour is. Sometimes, a man needs to go as low as he can, to appreciate everything he had before. I went to the depths, and it gave me a new perspective. Maybe your ex-partner never had that chance.'

'If you mean that he led a pampered existence, without any hardship or worry, then you're absolutely right.'

He winces. 'I can tell I've hit a nerve here. Let's change the subject, shall we? It's too nice a day to talk about dark things like this. Speaking of which, I nearly forgot to tell you something important.'

'What's that?'

'Amber was so impressed by you saving that little girl's life, that she got in touch with the local paper. It took them a while to reply, you know what local rags are like, but—'

'She did what?' I slam my mug on the patio table, far harder than I meant to. Hot chocolate splashes over the metal fretwork and onto the ground below.

'Only because the article mentioned that people were wondering who you were. She thought it'd be nice to let them know, so you can get some recognition for it. Anyway, the reporter got back after a few days, saying that it'd be good to have a quick chat with you, and—'

'She had *no right* to do that.'

Bill's eyes widen. 'She meant no harm by it. She just felt it would make a sweet story for the paper. You know, local hero turns out to be Robin Smith, a new member of the community, who—'

'She shouldn't have done it. She absolutely shouldn't. I won't speak to anyone. Don't you dare tell them that—'

'Robin, please. Take a few deep breaths. I'm sorry if it's upset you. I thought you'd be flattered by the attention.'

'It's an invasion of my privacy.'

He sits back, lips pressed in thought, then nods. 'Okay, I can see it from your perspective. Amber just didn't think, that's all. She meant well by it.'

That's a joke, if ever there was one. Amber's clearly out to hurt me. I just need to work out how far she's willing to go, and how far she's gone already.

'Robin?' Bill's voice brings me back, gentle as a tugboat steering an ocean liner. 'I apologise if my daughter accidentally did the wrong thing. Please see the nice intention behind it, not the unwanted outcome.'

I have to show him that it doesn't matter, otherwise he'll start wondering why it bothers me so much. I must smile sweetly, shrug it off as something of no consequence. But it's hard to twist my mouth into the correct position; my rage is intent on keeping it tight and hard. Words will have to suffice instead.

'It's me who should apologise,' I say, in a bright, crisp voice. 'I'm such a private person that any sort of exposure bothers me. Of course I know Amber was only being kind; it's lovely of her to want to do that for me.'

'Would you consider talking to the reporter?' He shifts awkwardly in his seat. 'The thing is, I think Amber may have already mentioned where you live.'

Steady, I order myself firmly, though there's a temptation to march round there, seize Amber by the hair and shove her head into the nearest wall, again and again, until her face is nothing more than a bloody pulp.

'Does that mean I can expect a visit from a reporter at some point?' I ask, keeping the same false, shiny tone. If Bill had any sense at all, he'd hear the note of steel behind it, but men tend to be oblivious to such things.

'No, I don't think she's arranged anything – she wouldn't do that without your permission.' He holds up his hands in mock surrender. 'It'll only be a small thing anyway, not a double-page spread.'

My heart is hammering. I know I must squash my fury down or risk revealing something, an aspect of myself that would frighten Bill away. This is fine, it's nothing I can't handle. I've dealt with far worse. The interview with the papers will not go ahead, no one will read any further news stories about me, and there will be no more exposure. It's simple, when laid out in these terms.

'Of course,' I say, finally managing a smile. 'I understand. It's no big deal at all.'

He points a finger at me, cocking it like a gun. 'You're right, beautiful lady. But *you're* a big deal. Never forget your own worth, Ms Robin.'

His faux American drawl makes me laugh, genuinely this time. *He and I can work*, I think, as I feel myself calming quietly. *He's good for me. I just need to work out how to remove Amber from this equation.*

The solution will come to me in the end, I'm sure.

CHAPTER 13

I dream about the knife under my pillow. It slithers upwards, like a tendril of a plant, piercing through feathers, through cotton, into my head and out to the air. I feel nothing, but am pinned, helpless and afraid. And all the while, I hear the laughter of the inmates echoing along the corridor, sounding like a pack of desperate hyenas.

I wonder, when I wake, what it could have meant. Dreams are supposedly the keys to the inner workings of the mind. But I can't fathom this one out, only check that the knife is still where it was, nestled innocently between pillow and mattress.

I investigate each room before I make myself breakfast, to ensure no one has concealed themselves in the house. It's fortunate the property is small. Yet the shadows behind the doors seem longer, the air more watchful. Could someone have broken in while I slept? The pills always knock me out cold; I wouldn't necessarily hear anything. They could be in here now, waiting, sneering at my vulnerability.

The cupboards are mercifully empty though, the back of the sofa devoid of any hidden attacker. I even check in the laundry basket, in the cupboard under the sink. It's all clear; I am still safe.

Just after nine, the doorbell rings. I remembered Margot was visiting today, so it's not a surprise. I wonder if she feels as frustrated by this ritual as I do. She probably wants to quit work as soon as possible, to spend her days walking a dog or playing with grandchildren. Or maybe she yearns for promotion, but has been held back by her boss, who is undoubtedly male. For a moment, I feel pity for her, but only for a moment. She's my jailer, after all, even if I'm supposedly free.

'Hasn't it turned cold?' she says, entering the house without being invited. 'I even thought about wearing gloves today.'

I agree that it's indeed cooler than it was, and follow her dutifully into the kitchen. She scans the countertops, then the table. I wonder if she's looking for the usual plate of biscuits.

'So,' she says, settling on one of the stools. 'Jobs. I've got a few things to run through with you on that front, so we'll—'

'Hang on, is this about me finding employment?' I ask, sitting opposite her.

'Yes, we discussed it last time, didn't we? I'm sure we did, though to be honest, my mind's all over the place at the moment.'

'I'm a bit old for work, aren't I?'

'Nonsense. You're nowhere near that yet.' She snorts. 'At the rate the retirement age is being pushed back, none of us will ever be. We'll all be working until we're dead, you mark my words.'

'I don't feel ready to take on a job,' I say bluntly.

She gives me a look. 'You don't have much choice, I'm afraid. *My* job is to make sure you're contributing to society as quickly as possible. The government can't afford to support you on benefits forever, you know.'

I understand exactly what she's driving at. Why should the country want to support me, after all? It's already written me off as evil. In an ideal world, most people would probably want to see me dead, rather than living off the state.

It should have been you that died, not him, Miranda snarled at me, in the prison visiting room. *You monster.* Monster. Butcher Bird. They're wrong, all of them. But now isn't the time to let these memories overcome me.

'Very well,' I say. 'But I'm not good with people. Please don't make me do something where I have to be exposed to others.'

She sits back, arms resting on her expansive chest. 'Why don't you like talking to people, Robin?'

119

Ava, I think, instinctively. It's *Ava* who doesn't like speaking to others. This Robin is a fiction, after all.

'I'm nervous that I'll be recognised,' I tell her. 'I don't like to think about what will happen if it gets out that I… that, you know.'

'Well, you can't go on living your life in fear. You look very different now, so it's highly unlikely anyone will know who you really are.'

Who I really am. It makes me want to laugh out loud. They all *think* they've got a grasp on me. Child-killer. Jealous, jilted woman. Remorseless and cold. But they haven't at all. No one can see what's in my heart, the real creature that lives and breathes through me.

'What if I told you that someone already *does* know who I am?'

She frowns. 'Is that what you *are* saying, Robin? Because if it is, we have to launch a formal procedure. It'd be a nightmare, to be honest; anonymity orders are hellish to obtain. We'd certainly have to relocate you.'

I think of Bill. I don't want to be moved away from him, not now that we've become close. Whoever the stalker is, I'll handle it my way. I've coped with worse in the past. Quickly, I shake my head.

'I was talking theoretically,' I tell her. 'I wanted to know what would happen if that situation occurred.'

She continues to view me with suspicion. 'Let's not worry about that for now,' she says. 'Today, I want to give you some goals, which you'll need to have completed by next week. Okay? See it as a fun exercise, and your path to getting back in the real world.'

'What did you have in mind?'

'Firstly, a visit to the Jobcentre.' She pushes a leaflet towards me. 'I've even booked you a meeting, look. All the details are here.'

I keep my eyes away from the leaflet. I will read through it later. It's too much to take in right now.

'I also want you to enrol on an online course,' she continues. 'Learn something new. It's a great opportunity, and the scheme's available to all ex-inmates.' Another leaflet joins the first, right under my nose.

'Can it be something I'm interested in?' I ask.

'Absolutely. See it as a new hobby.'

Now that *is* something better. A fresh focus for me. That's something I can do.

I nod, and give her a smile. 'Leave the homework with me.'

'You're going to get an A-star in it, right?'

I think of Bill, winking at me, encouraging me to move forward, to try new things, to break free from this meagre existence. 'You betcha,' I say, and cock my finger like a gun in her direction.

She smiles and nods, satisfied. As for the interview at the Jobcentre? We shall see.

As I ready myself for bed, I see you in the corner of the room.

It's been a while since I saw you so clearly; in fact, since I've been out of prison, you've mostly restricted yourself to my dreams. To see you in my waking hours – that's considerably worse.

You look well, as you often seem to in these visions. Skinny and long-limbed, but also brimming with youthful strength, that power fostered by home-cooked food and fresh air.

Then your face pales, far more than it should. Your lips turn white, then swiftly blue. Your eyes glaze over, and I'm vaguely aware of my voice, murmuring *no, please no* in the quietest whisper. Because I don't want this, I can't bear to *see* this again: you as you were on that day, when everything went so wrong.

I can feel your accusation still, even after all this time. The bitter, weary anger of what could have been, had things not happened as they did. How you would have been a man of nearly forty now, with children of your own. You'd have had a successful career, a detached house with a driveway, probably. Spectacles and slightly thinning hair, but that same, welcoming, calming expression. You would have been loved by so many.

I am so, so sorry, I whisper. Not that it matters; you can't hear me. Or if you can, you hate me too much to acknowledge my regret.

The bitterness of it gnaws at me, erodes pieces of me each and every day. Can't you see that? I would give anything to reverse it all, to never have invited you back to mine, though it was all innocent, don't you realise? The shouting, the shove, which was such a gentle shove really; none of that should have happened. It wasn't my fault: you should look to your father, your mother – they're the ones to blame. They weren't there for you. You told me that, you know you did.

I'm pleading with a shadow of you. Such a futile, pathetic thing to do, because you're not really here, you haven't been for a long time.

You vanish slowly, responding to my thoughts. It's more a fading than a disappearance, like a dissipating dawn mist. I wipe my eyes and take a deep, shuddering breath. That's what they don't understand. I never, ever meant to hurt you. Other people, yes, maybe. I have it in me; I know what I'm capable of. But you? No. I'd always thought so highly of you, and it's agony to see you like that, over and over again. Part of me wishes you'd come back. I mean *really* come back, so I can talk to you properly. We always had such good talks, you and I. Do you remember those times we strolled along together from school, before Henry found out about our friendship? It was just a couple of casual strolls, maybe three or four at most. All of them entirely harmless, innocent and true. You found me easy to talk to. After those initial awkward greetings, you settled into a conversation, content in the knowledge that I meant you no harm and that I was genuinely interested in what you had to say. You obviously didn't get listened to much at home.

I don't recollect exactly what we talked about. It was so long ago, after all. Birds, sometimes. You loved hearing about the islands, and asked questions about what it was like, not to have to go to school, to spend whole days tramping through long grass and staring at the sea. You used to say that Miranda preferred your little sister to you, that she'd take her shopping, bring her small gifts, praise her for her schoolwork. It must have been so hard for you, to have a mother like that. She was the monster, not me.

Whenever I observed her entering or leaving the house, she always had a designer handbag draped over one arm, or else was laden down with shopping. She liked to spend, that much was evident, and she always had the same sour, superior expression. It was detestable to look at, and it must have been so awful for you to live with.

Sometimes I asked about your father too. It was clear that he pressurised you to be something you weren't. That's what men like him are like, after all. They're always trying to bend people to their will. Then, once they've got the desired results, they drop them like a sack of stones. He would have done that to you, I'm sure. He was a terrible father.

I never took you all the way home, as it was too risky and would have looked suspicious. Henry found out about us nonetheless. That particular confrontation was very unpleasant, though at least he had the good sense not to have it in front of you. He threatened a restraining order, as though I'd been the one tormenting him, and not the other way around.

You're obsessed, he spat at me.

I wasn't. That's the part he never understood. I was furious, not obsessed, full of rage at what he'd done, and how he'd got away with it.

I suppose I could just have told Miranda about us and had done with it. But I suspect she wouldn't have believed me. She would have instinctively sided with him, even though she must have known what he was like. After all, he was the one paying for all those designer handbags. Maybe she thought it was best not to bite the hand that petted her so indulgently.

I would have liked a designer handbag or two. A holiday to Tenerife, or whatever fancy island they went to that summer. Not because I liked material goods; I was always above that sort of thing. More because I knew that Henry valued them, and that the more he spent on someone, the more it signified that he held them dear.

Oh, but I am confusing things here. I *didn't* want Henry, so logic dictates that I never wanted those things. I never did. I was content in my tiny flat, with its narrow kitchen, its mould-rimmed bath, its built-in cupboard with one door hanging loose. It was my home, and it displayed all too clearly how I rejected the capitalist dream. I was far better than that; like my father, I was able to live on very little in the pursuit of something better. I hope you realised that, back then, on those after-school walks we used to share, before Henry took it all away from us. We were companions, weren't we? And I had such great respect for your opinions, the breathless, untainted way you viewed the world. I hope this counts for something, wherever you are now.

There is excrement in my front garden, among the loose pebbles. I notice it on my way out to the local shop, and it sours my mood immediately. For a few minutes, I toy with the notion that it was placed there maliciously, that this is the next stage of the hate campaign against me. But then I consider it more carefully. It has the look of a cat's turd, thin and coiling, and there are several cats prowling around the neighbourhood. Innocent, then. Nothing to be alarmed by.

I detest cats. I respect their composure, the confidence of their strut, but their sneaky, cunning nature is repellent. If you're a predator, why conceal the fact? Why pretend to be demure, when you're a savage killer? Daddy used to say that he'd shoot every one of them if he had the chance, for their murderous ways. As it was, he took a few people to task over their cats, insisting they attach bells to their collars, to at least give the birds fair warning.

I fetch a wad of kitchen towel and scoop the offending dung up. It gives beneath my fingers, spongelike and soft. I cannot help but gasp with disgust, before throwing it into the wheelie bin.

'Cat shat in your garden?'

I spin around, prepared to see a mocking face and finally confront the person who's been stalking me so surreptitiously. It's Amber. She's smiling, but with a hint of mockery. *She is my enemy*, I think, and yes, it could be her, she could be the one making my life a misery. Like the cat, she's sly, underhand. She doesn't have the courage to show her true nature.

'I believe it was a cat, yes,' I reply tightly.

'Funny, they don't seem to poo on Dad's.'

'Well, they never did on mine until today.'

'I wonder why?'

I won't rise to it, I refuse to. Instead, I shrug, nod curtly, then head back to the front door. She sidles along the dividing wall, then, to my horror, reaches for my arm.

I want to recoil. No, I want to grasp her in return, throw her aside for daring to touch me. How dare she do such a thing? How *dare* she?

'Dad said you weren't too keen to speak to the reporter,' she says, oblivious to my anger. Her fingers are spiderlike: delicate yet insistent.

'No,' I confirm, as I shake her fingers from me. 'I shan't be talking to them.'

'Why is it a problem?'

'I don't want it to be a big deal. I hardly rescued the little girl at all, she merely ran past me and I reached out and—'

'You seem nervous, Robin. Are you all right?'

Little cow. She's toying with me, and that false look of concern doesn't hide it at all.

'I'm perfectly all right,' I retort. 'I just don't like having my privacy invaded. I like to keep to myself.'

She holds both hands up in mock surrender.

'Gosh, sorry. I hadn't realised it would offend you.'

'It hasn't offended me at all.'

Suddenly, she grins. It's sharklike, there's no other way to describe it. 'Why don't you leave it to me? I can smooth this all over, without you getting involved at all.'

'Well, the main thing is that I don't wish to be disturbed.'

'Yes, that's fine. But I still think you should be recognised for your brave act.'

She's openly ridiculing me, I think, fists curling by my sides. Her sweet expression wouldn't fool anybody.

The smile drops suddenly, and she moves in closer. 'Robin,' she says, in a voice not much above a whisper. 'Dad told me about your past. You know, the whole *prison* thing.'

I stiffen. A hurricane of thoughts fight for supremacy, deep within me. *Why did he tell her? How did he dare to do such a thing, after I trusted him? How much does she know? Is she taunting me? What is she thinking?*

'Robin? Look, I didn't mean to intrude. I can tell from your face that you aren't happy with something I've said. Sometimes I find it tricky to communicate and it's always been a problem for me—'

I have no idea what she's talking about, but she *has* intruded; she has smashed through what few defences I had, and she's determined to ruin me, it's obvious. It's *her*. I know it now, with total certainty.

'Was it you the other day?' I hiss.

She steps back. 'When? What day?'

'Down by the river. It was you, wasn't it? And the letter.'

'I honestly have no idea what you're talking about, Robin. By the river?'

'Don't play innocent with me.'

'I'll get Dad, shall I?' She points at the house. 'He's better at dealing with this sort of thing than me.'

'No – you started this, you can damned well finish it.' I reach over and seize her wrist, perhaps too tightly, but I can't stop myself; my rage is too swollen, too immense to contain. It's *her, it's her*, and I want to bring her to her knees. She can beg me to stop, and I—

'Robin, please let go, you're hurting me.'

She has angel hair. Her eyes are wide, like Ditz's used to be. Suddenly, she *is* Ditz, pleading, asking me to stop saying all those horrible things, and telling me that she can't cope, that she'll *do* something if I carry on, that she'll— I release my grip. My fingers are tingling. I know I lost control. This is what the doctor said in the prison, that I had to master myself if I was going to function out here in the real world. My face burns. My lips are trembling. I need to make this right, and quickly.

'I apologise,' I say. 'But I think you're deliberately trying to make my life difficult, and it's been hard enough. I won't tolerate it.'

She shakes her head, still clutching at her wrist. 'I admit, I wondered at first about your intentions regarding my father, but—'

'You must not snoop into my private affairs. And you must stop this nastiness towards me. Whatever you believe I did in the past, you're wrong, and if you're in cahoots with Henry, you tell him that I didn't do it to get at him. You tell him that, yes?'

'I don't know what you're talking about. Who's Henry?'

I've said too much. I need to go inside. I need some pills, some wine, anything to stop my thoughts racing.

'Just ignore me,' I whisper, and swiftly walk inside. I hear her say something else, but it's muffled by the sound of the door slamming. I hadn't meant to slam it. I hadn't meant for any of that to happen.

God, what have I done? I hurt her, for goodness' sake. I didn't mean to, although she deserved it, because what she did was wicked. But I stooped to her level; I attacked, when I should have walked away. I should always take the higher ground, and seek out the advantage.

I think of the skua. Circling above, always circling. The sudden dive, the snatch of beak, the tearing, the screaming of the other birds. It has a cruel poetry to it, an allure that's hard to ignore. But I'm not like that, I'm *not*. What Daddy shouted at me after the Jean Marshall situation, it wasn't true. I'm not without feeling, and I do take emotions into consideration, I do.

It's lucky I went to the shop earlier and purchased two bottles of wine for the week. They will serve their purpose for now. They'll stop me from thinking, maybe stop me from breathing if I take some sleeping pills with them. I need quiet, a settling within, because my thoughts are stormy and wild.

If I take too many pills, I'll be just like you. Silent and still, forever more.

I shouldn't think about that, I really shouldn't.

CHAPTER 14

I thought a trip to the park would clear my pounding headache. However, I've been sitting on this bench for over half an hour now, and I still feel horrendous. Dried out. Blood thumping too hard through my temples. A bottle and a half of wine was too much, admittedly. But it served its purpose at the time, so I suppose I mustn't complain.

I'm technically not permitted to be here, as there's a playground at one side, and the terms of my release state that I'm not allowed to be in areas where children are. Schools are another no-go zone. This is a difficult rule to uphold, if I'm honest. There are schools everywhere; every neighbourhood seems to burst with them. Children, children everywhere, nor any drop of peace. Procreation seems to be more of a priority than ever these days. No one will know I'm here, though. It's not as if Margot has the time to watch me, nor would she want to if she could. No one really cares that much; they merely set the rules to emphasise to society that they're doing the right thing. It's all for show. Also, I resent the suggestion that I'm a threat to children. Not that anyone cares about my resentment, or even pretends to.

I've brought a sandwich with me, but the air is too chilly to sit here comfortably. I feel out of place, unable to settle on the hard slats beneath me. The bench reminds me of the ones that used to line the prison rec room – that same unyielding, cheaply painted wood. Designed for maximum awkwardness, the main purpose being to move the seated person along as quickly as possible. It's been a while since I've been in a park, though. One of the last conversations I had with Jean Marshall was in a park much like this one, only more overgrown, with a view of the bay below. It's funny how memories can be triggered just by a place, or a smell or taste. I'd entirely forgotten it until now.

Why did she take me there? The details aren't clear, but then I was young. Perhaps Daddy had taken a trip to the mainland for a meeting. He did that on occasion, and he wasn't always comfortable with leaving me at home on my own. Or maybe she offered to take me as some sort of grotesque bonding exercise. Who knows? The only thing I can be certain of is that her intentions were selfish, cruel or both. I recollect that we sat on a bench, after I'd had a half-hearted go on the swings and the slide. She gave me a thermos with some watery hot chocolate inside. It must have been winter: I was wearing my thick coat, which was too small for me, with worn patches at the elbows.

I sense you're not comfortable with me, she said. *We should be friends, not enemies. I'm not here to steal your father away from you. I know you still miss your mother.*

I think we must have talked about other things too, but I don't know what. All I remember is seeing that horsey face of hers staring down at me – the long, sallow cheeks, the prominent front teeth. I was repelled.

My health isn't so good, she told me, and I thought of those pills of hers, all lined up in bottles on the kitchen windowsill. *I could do with less stress, if I'm honest, Ava. Let's try a little harder, shall we?*

I don't know what I said in return, though the memory of her breath is still strong: how it gusted warmly in my face, laced with stale toast and a hint of peppermint. I must have recoiled, and she probably noticed, storing it up in her bank of things to hold against me. Did she really imagine that I'd be taken in by her performance, her pretence at kindness? If she did, she was more stupid than I'd taken her for.

A mother is approaching with her boy, which snaps me out of my thoughts. He looks about three or four. It is fine for me to be here, they are entering *my* space, not the other way around, as I was here first. I won't be made to feel guilty about my presence. The boy's coat is covered in mud, and his knees too. He glares at me as he draws nearer. Already so suspicious, at such a young age. People are born unpleasant, perhaps; it has very little to do with nurture.

I get up and straighten my skirt. This hasn't been an enjoyable experience, but it served to give me some clarity, and to clear the fug of my hangover a little. It also got me out of the house, which was a blessing, as I am afraid Bill may have tried to visit. Not the friendly, welcoming Bill I've become attached to, but the angry father instead, furious that I've upset his precious daughter by shouting at her. I don't want to see that Bill, I want him to calm down first, if indeed he is upset at all. I can't guess what he's thinking and I don't like that. Amber is set on coming between us, and she's succeeding, I sense that. But I must go home at some point, I can't linger outside all day. I must be brave, yet again.

Every day, a new need for courage. It's exhausting, it really is.

I have an email, sent yesterday according to the date at the top. I must get in the habit of checking more regularly, especially as this one is from Margot. Familiarising myself with technology is one of the things she asked me to do, and I should prove my willingness to obey her. It's necessary, after all, to ensure she keeps ticking all those boxes.

I scan the screen quickly. It's about the appointment at the Jobcentre tomorrow at ten in the morning. I need to wear smart clothes and treat it as a formal interview, as apparently that's expected of me. It all feels so ridiculous. Who would want to hire me? Even if I hadn't got a criminal record, I'm a woman in my fifties, without any formal qualifications, though my life experience should really count for something. Still, it's not as though I actually *want* a job, so I suppose it's a good thing that

I'm unemployable. What a situation to be in. Relying on the benefits of the state, when I wish for nothing more than to *leave* the state, to hide away on a remote island and become entirely self-sufficient. It would be simpler all round if they just let me go. Bill would be good at cultivating vegetables on a lonely island, I think. And fixing things. He has a capable way with him, a sense of efficiency and unflappable patience. He'd survive perfectly well on one of the islands of the Outer Hebrides, and I believe he'd be good at caring for others too. Such as me, even.

I sigh, then shut the laptop down. When I applied for the job at Society for Bird Preservation, I was so confident of my rightness for the role. To be fair, being Daddy's daughter helped a lot. They were full of condolences at the interview, rattling on and on about what a loss he was to the birding world, and how his research had influenced so many others.

I presume they thought that at least *some* of his genius must have rubbed off on me. They weren't nearly so effusive a few years later, when they told me to leave. Then, I faced a row of impassive faces, each refusing to meet my eye. *You know you can't stay here*, one said. *It's easier if you resign, rather than having to go through the process associated with gross misconduct.* Henry wasn't dragged into any such meeting, wasn't told he'd committed any misconduct, gross or otherwise. He kept his job, because he was higher up than me, and a man, of course. Men are permitted to do such things; women are not.

He cost me everything, that man. But I can't allow myself to give in to the hatred, not again. I wonder if Margot reports anything back to him. Does he have a right to know what I'm doing, and whether I'm managing well outside prison? Perhaps the victims are given special access to this information. If so, I bet he's enjoying a good laugh at my expense, at my solitary, sad little life. I'd love him to know about Bill, and to know that I haven't been beaten, not by a long way.

This is perhaps paranoia again. I don't know for sure that Margot is in touch with him. I'm getting ahead of myself, making assumptions based on feeling, not fact. As Dr Holland says, I need to scrutinise situations with a rational eye. Why would she bother? There would be no advantage to it. Still, I can't help but wonder.

I shut the laptop softly, then place it back on the floor. This room needs a desk to give it some sort of real purpose. I wonder if my benefits money would stretch to that; I've already used the furniture grant on the other items in the house. People out there would hate to think that their taxes are being used to support me. Even thinking about their vitriol makes me shudder. But I would ask them, what is the alternative? Throw me out of prison to live on the streets? That would make an ex-inmate turn back to crime in a heartbeat, as what other option would they have? If threatened, even a saint would go on the attack. It's a natural response. *I looked at this situation with a rational eye, Dr Holland,* I think, with a rueful smile. *But I don't feel it helped much. Because the fact is, everyone loathes people like me. They want me dead, really.*

It's a sobering thought, and not one I care to dwell on. I am *here.* I am alive. I may yet contribute something positive to this world, but I won't be able to if I am given no chance to. I can make a difference. I *can.* I can make Bill happy, for starters, and that is worth something. I just need to make sure that Amber hasn't ruined everything first.

The nights are drawing in earlier now. It's just gone six, and the sky is already on its way to dark. I admire the sunset from the kitchen window, a vivid pink and orange, smearing the horizon. Shepherd's delight, Mother would have said. Good weather tomorrow.

I notice movement behind the wall at the back of the garden. It's the top part of a head, silhouetted by the light, which isn't uncommon; people walk by all the time. But it lingers for far too long. Motionless, waiting. Why would someone stop there? There's nothing in the alleyway, other than burst bags of rubbish and a sagging mattress, slumped against the bricks. My skin prickles. Is someone watching my house? Perhaps they're staring at me right now, drinking in the sight of my expression, savouring my anxiety. It could be Amber out there; all she'd have to do is slip out of her father's back gate. I squint, trying to detect hair colour, some sort of identifying feature.

The head moves along. Another few seconds, and it's out of sight.

It isn't good for me, all this brooding and worrying. I shall take a walk. Under the cover of darkness, I can be anonymous and walk freely without risk of being seen. If someone is lying in wait at the back of the house, they won't see me slip out of the front door. Besides, it's a spectacular sky. I shall enjoy it, because it's my right to. No one can stop me, especially not Amber.

I have no evidence it's her. I *must* keep remembering this.

As I leave the house, I notice Bill's curtains have been pulled across unusually early. He tends to leave them open, oblivious to people peering into his living room, but not today. I wonder why. To block me out? No, that's silly. Or has Amber now crept back home? Is she behind that curtain, telling him that he needs to be careful, as there's a murderer next door and— Not that word, I don't like that word. It is too diminishing; it doesn't represent the truth at all. Accidental killing is not the same as murder, and that's a fact. But what if she's told him? Or even just revealed the fight we had yesterday? What if I left bruises on her wrist? I didn't mean to, but I accept that I gripped her too hard. Her silly, fragile little arms might bruise easily for all I know, and she may have shown them to him, saying *look what that woman did to me, you have to stay away from her, she's pure evil, she's—*

I have no evidence that this happened, so I must stop these thoughts. The curtains may be closed for a perfectly good reason. I see one of them twitch, just as I walk past, but it could have been my imagination. It was a very subtle movement, a mere hitching at the centre.

The street lamps light up above me, a series of flickerings up the road, until they come into their full glow. It's a shame; I rather liked the gloaming charcoal of the early evening. Now, there are puddles of light scattered over the uneven pavement like spilled

133

paint. It's very quiet out here. Surprising, for a city. You'd have thought there'd be at least one person coming back from work, or a single car, searching for a space to park.

I don't like it. I feel watched.

I look over my shoulder, anticipating a stretch of empty pavement behind me. But there *is* someone there, further down the road. I note the long black coat. The hat, pulled down over the eyes. I'm not being watched. I'm being hunted. Quickly, I face forward again, keep my eyes up, fighting to contain my panic.

It's the same person as before. They're certainly slender enough. It could be Amber, it really could. Her posture is brittle, aggressive as a bantam cockerel, but nervy too. Worse still, she has the advantage, as she's between me and the safety of my front door. Maybe that's deliberate. How did she manage to get from the back alley so quickly? Presumably she can move fast; she has that sort of frame – wiry, built for stealth and speed.

It might not be her. It could be someone else, someone paid by Henry and Miranda, who hid behind a car, ducking out of sight until I passed them. They could have been watching my house all day, for all I know. I need to know for sure; this uncertainty is crippling me, making me fearful and hesitant, when I must be decisive, swift to act.

I can hear footsteps now: that must mean whoever it is has quickened their pace. Without pausing to think, I speed up too, then strain to listen, but my breath is coming fast, and too loud. I steal a glance behind me.

They've gone. No, I'm wrong, they've crossed over the other side of the road, and stopped moving. Or have they? They're standing in between two lamps, where the light is muddled. I can't hear them walking any more. I need to focus on getting back, and quickly. If they were to stab me out here, no one would notice. I'd bleed out on the street long before someone came along. Thankfully, it's not too far, especially when I pick up my pace. I refuse to look up – I don't want to give them the invitation to attack. I push through my front gate, shove the key into the lock, then step through into the warmth, slamming the door behind me. Then I tiptoe into the living room, sliding slowly across the walls, and wait by the window in the dark.

I can't see anyone. A minute or so passes. A car drives past, headlights glaring. After five minutes, a person marches along the road, but they're male, far broader in the shoulders than the figure I saw. Whoever it was, they've either given up or gone back to their place of hiding, if indeed they were following me in the first place. I hate not knowing. If it was Amber, she must have gone elsewhere, not home; I would have seen her otherwise. Of course, she could have gone the back way, down the alleyway. She could be outside my house now, maybe on the phone to Henry, asking for further instructions. It *feels* possible, even as I think it. Whatever the case, there's little point in me remaining by the window. I pull the curtains, shutting out the night, then switch the light on.

My thoughts are racing. Amber is the only logical explanation – it's all starting to add up. If it is Amber, she won't win this war, and neither will Henry. Maybe they're having an affair? Bill mentioned that Amber's relationship had broken up; it's feasible that she could have started seeing Henry instead, and that he's using her to get to me.

It all makes sense, laid out like that. I'm frightened at how easily the pieces seem to be falling into place. But I need time to mull it over carefully. Amber's playing a long game here, I can tell. So I shall have to as well, though that's not a problem. Patience is a skill of mine. I had twenty-five years to master it in prison, after all.

I don't like being woken by the alarm, but needs must. At least my head feels clearer; the dregs of the hangover are now entirely out of my system. I only took one sleeping pill last night too, even though drifting off was virtually impossible thanks to Amber. I won't let her take over my thoughts. I need to focus on the task at hand: my appointment at the Jobcentre.

I select a skirt and shirt. Not my best clothing: I want to look presentable, but not too eager. I won't have them thinking

I'm desperate and giving me any old job. My hair is a little lank; I should really have washed it last night, but I was too distracted. It'll have to do. The day is sunny, just as the stunning sunset last night had indicated. I debate taking a jacket, then pull it out of the understairs cupboard. Better to be safe than sorry. It's just a short walk. I'm almost certain my stalker won't be out here now, and anyway, the street has an entirely different personality during the daylight hours. It's energetic, exuding the force of all those people, busy behind their front doors. I am safe, for now.

The Jobcentre is on the edge of town, which makes it easier to reach. It's a brutal, concrete building, set by a busy roundabout. Ugly, like every other building that serves the public, but at least there's no artifice to it. It's a case of getting down to business, right from the moment it hits the eye. I push through the door and walk straight into a wall of warmth. My hair crackles and shifts under the blast of the heater above me, before settling as I move towards the reception desk. There are four other people seated on the chairs lining the wall, all with identical expressions of boredom.

'I've got an interview,' I say, smoothing my hair down. 'Ten o'clock.'

'Name?' The receptionist doesn't even bother looking up, her eyes fixed instead to her computer screen. She looks about fifteen, scrawny, collarbone jutting above her neckline. What a career for one so young; it's certainly a swift way to get cynical about the world.

'Robin Smith.'

She frowns, then gestures to the seats, even though they're all taken. 'Wait there,' she mumbles. 'You'll be called through shortly.'

I stand by the wall. One of the men waves towards his seat with a raised eyebrow, and I shake my head, though the gesture is appreciated. At least some people still have manners.

Time stretches to the point of breaking. The hands of the clock on the wall opposite seem to be stuck in place, and the ticking swiftly becomes an annoyance. Gradually, like ducklings diving into a pond, each of the men is called. More people arrive, filling the space with their glum demeanours. It's a busy place, but not a happy one. There's no sense of positivity here, only resigned acceptance.

Finally, a large, stubbled face pokes around the corner. 'Robin Smith?'

I raise my hand, obedient as a child, then follow him through. It's the first door on the left, and the room is spartan, windowless. There's a single plastic chair one side of the desk, a slightly fancier leatherette swivel chair on the other. A laptop, some papers, and that's all. The man takes a seat, then sighs.

'So, you want JSA?' he says, already rapping on his keyboard.

'JSA?'

'Jobseeker's Allowance. Most do.'

'Oh, I suppose so. But I was sent here to find work.'

He moves the laptop's mouse around, squinting hard at the screen. Then he frowns.

'I see,' he says, then sneaks a glance at me. 'You've got a criminal record. That makes the process trickier.'

'I suppose I have to declare it to the employer?'

'You certainly do. And it looks like that'll always be the case for you, because of the length of your sentence. It was a long one, wasn't it?'

I don't like his tone: it's taken on a sneering quality. He's already made assumptions, and I'm willing to bet they're mostly incorrect.

'So I suppose I won't be able to get a job, then?' I say, fighting hard to keep the hope from my voice.

'Well, we may as well try, eh?' He taps at his keyboard, massaging his face with the air of someone who'd much rather be down the pub, drinking himself into oblivion. 'We've got a few options you could apply for. There's a job with a local cleaning company here. They're only a few roads down from you, so the location is good.'

'I don't think I'd make a very good cleaner.'

'In this instance, there might not be much choice. You'll need to apply, otherwise you won't be eligible for JSA. Didn't your parole officer tell you about how it works?'

Margot may have mentioned it in the past. She goes on rather a lot, and sometimes I shut off. I shrug.

'I'll print the details off,' he says, clicking his mouse. 'Let's try this one too. A florist in Falmouth Street, looking for a retail assistant. You look like you might be into flowers.'

'I'm not sure where you got that impression from.'

He passes the print-out to me, then leans back in his chair. 'To get JSA, you'll need to apply, then go for an interview. You've also got to agree to actively seek work. No cheating the system, as trust me, we've seen it all before.'

'I'm not a cheat.'

Again, that look. The look that says no, you're far, far worse than that. He purses his lips, then nods.

'I'm sure we'll get you sorted in the end, Robin.'

I swallow. This is obviously going to be a more odious process than I'd imagined, and it's yet another thing to worry about. They'll all keep pushing me until I break, I realise. But I won't let that happen, not now, not after everything I've endured. If they think they can scare me – with their stalking, their sneering, their judgement – they've got another thing coming.

CHAPTER 15

As I near my house, I see someone standing by the front door, peering in through the glass. They're not female, which is a relief. It can't be the postman, as the clothes aren't right. Then I see the shining head and the slight stoop: Bill, then, and I can guess what he wants.

It's not a threat, I remind myself, straightening my top, smoothing my hair. Bill likes me. He doesn't want to hurt me. He turns, sees me approaching, then raises a hand. It's difficult to interpret the gesture: perhaps I'm being paranoid again, but it doesn't seem as jovial as it usually is.

'Good morning, Robin,' he says, as I push the gate open. 'I wondered if you were out.'

'I had an interview,' I say. 'Is everything all right?'

He sticks his hands into his trouser pockets: a defensive motion, if ever there was one. My stomach clenches in response.

'Well now,' he says reluctantly. 'I wanted to have a chat with you about something.'

Here we go. Amber has succeeded in corrupting our relationship, it's obvious. His eyes are guarded, where before they were open, welcoming. Likewise, his shoulders are tense, his arms too.

'Do you want to come in?' I offer.

'If you wouldn't mind, that'd be good.'

I unlock the door, throw my handbag on the stairs, then wave him through to the kitchen.

'What's up?' I ask, as I set about making some tea. I'm aware that I'm bustling more than usual, moving from here to there like a restless fly. It's better that than meeting his eye; I'm worried about what I'll see there.

'Amber said she and you had a bit of a scene.'

A bit of a scene. He's referring to when I grabbed her. If only he knew what she was capable of; the real scenes have been her attempts to frighten me. But I can't let that show in my expression. I need to be cunning and deceitful, as she is. It's time to fight fire with fire. I take a deep breath, then turn around to face him.

'I'd like to apologise,' I say, smooth as silk. 'I acted out of character. It was just that she was pressurising me about the journalist, and—'

'Yes, she mentioned that. She was upset, you know. Amber doesn't do well in confrontational situations, and she's already been through a lot with that ex-boyfriend of hers.'

It's always Amber first, every time. What about my needs? Doesn't he care about how I feel?

'I didn't intend to upset her,' I say, slowly. 'I was too curt, I know. She caught me on a bad day.'

Finally, his expression softens. 'I wondered if it was something like that. I said as much to her, but she's got it in her head that you don't like her. She's always had problems with this, ever since school, you can—'

'Sure, I understand.' I don't, actually, and I have no desire to know what her problems are, but he doesn't need to know that. Best that he believes I care.

The kettle switch clicks, and I pour the water. The tea needs to be strong and milky, as that's how he likes it, I've noticed. See, I've observed these things and remembered them, because I'm thoughtful. I'm not just manipulating his emotions, like his daughter.

'Get a nice brew inside you,' I say soothingly, sitting down at the table with him.

He grins, then clinks his mug against mine. 'Thank you for being understanding, Robin. I was worried, you know. About there being bad feeling between you and my Amber. I don't want there to be. I'm fond of you, and I'd like you to get along with her.'

He's fond of me, I think, concealing a smile. He likes me, he's just openly stated it.

'I'm fond of you too,' I say. 'And I absolutely guarantee that I have no bad feelings towards your daughter.'

'That's wonderful to hear.'

'We should go out again sometime, don't you think?'

He looks up, the steam from the tea making him blink. 'We should, yes. What about a walk this afternoon, down to the river? We may as well enjoy the last of the season's sunshine.'

I stiffen. 'Why down there?'

'It's a lovely spot, so why not?'

There's nothing to it, I tell myself. No connection; it's merely a pleasant stroll. But it makes me wonder if, after Amber returned from stalking me by the river the other day, she mentioned it, and now it's in his mind. No, that's too far-fetched. I need to focus on the facts here: Bill just wants a scenic place to spend some time together, and that's a positive thing.

'I'd like that,' I reply eventually.

He gives me a sideways look, and a strange smile.

'I'd love to know what you're thinking, sometimes. You get a faraway look, and I can't read you at all.'

I return his smile, while thinking *trust me, you wouldn't want to know at all*. Some things are better never spoken aloud, and that's the truth.

Is it silly to put on make-up for a walk? My hand hovers over my little box of cosmetics, before finally dropping back to my side. It is. Bill is an observant man, and he'll notice if I make that effort. But then, would that be a bad thing? He'd know how highly I regarded him, then. That would bring him closer to me. I go to the sock drawer instead and pull out an extra pair. My feet get cold easily, even though we're not in winter yet.

Then I sense you. Standing in the corner, as you were the other day, watching me carefully.

'Not now,' I mutter, sitting on the bed, keeping my eyes on the carpet. 'I'm due to go out in a moment, and I don't need it.'

You're still there. I look up, and gasp. My hand flies to my mouth.

You're scarcely more than a skeleton: dirty bones, empty-eyed skull. But it's obviously you – the posture, the tilt of the head. There are clumps of moss on your hip bone, and on one of your feet. Earth packed into the crevices. It will fall out, surely, if you move, then leave marks on my floor. *I've just hoovered in here*, I think, gasping at the inappropriateness of the thought. Laughter bubbles in my throat, or is it a sob? I can't tell the difference.

You never look like this usually. I hate it, I *hate* it, because I know this is what you are now, what you really are. Lying in that coffin, cold and silent and untouched for decades.

'Please, *stop it*,' I beg, in a voice that's scarcely more than a whisper. I can't bear to look at you, but I can't turn away, not least because I can see tears shining in the empty hollows of your sockets, even though that's not possible; none of this is. You cannot be crying. You're dead, you died so many years ago.

I wish you'd leave me alone. I wish you'd stay. I want you to *listen*, to properly listen to me and then be gone for good, because this can't continue. I want you to torment your father like this, your mother too. Not me. I don't deserve it any more, I really don't.

You do, a small voice whispers. Yours? Mine? I don't know any more. I look down, then up again. To my relief, you've gone.

I'm shaking. Not just my hands, but all over: a full-body tremor. It's hard to regain control of myself, though I know I must. Bill will be here soon, and he can't see me like this. He'll ask questions, and I haven't gathered enough composure to provide the right answers.

Is it because I'm about to go for a walk? Is that it? You hold it against me, because of that walk we went on together? The last one, before you came to mine? I didn't know. You must believe me, because I'm not lying. I was upset, I'm not saying I wasn't. Your father had been *very* rude to me, and the letter from the solicitor was the final straw. But when I found you that day, on the way into town to meet your friends, I had no concept of what would happen. I'd just planned for us to have a chat, to spend some quality time together, to give you a chance to offload about your parents again, if you wanted to. I was like a sister, a replacement mother, even. You enjoyed talking to me, I know it. The glamour of having an older friend, especially one who was female, obviously appealed to you. If I'd known what would happen, I would have walked away the moment I saw you. Because it's ruined my life, too. You're gone, which is terrible, but I'm still here, and every day is a punishment. Just existing is a torment at times.

I'm alone, I remind myself. I'm almost too scared to examine the carpet in the corner, for fear that I'll find dirt there, some evidence that it really happened. But it's spotless, as usual. It was another hallucination. I need to recall what the doctors in the prison told me to do when I experience one. Breathe deeply. Remember it isn't real. If possible, move away from the area, to somewhere safer.

Safe. That's a joke. Still, I will go to the living room and wait there, until Bill knocks for me. I never see you in that room, so I know it will be okay.

'Are you all right?' Bill asks, standing on the doormat. 'You look flustered.'

'Do I?'

'Yeah. A bit spooked, actually.'

I wish I'd had longer to compose myself. I've spent the last few minutes sitting in the living room with my eyes closed, terrified that I'll see something I don't want to. *Spooked* is an interesting choice of word, given the circumstances. I suppose I am haunted, in a way.

'I'm fine,' I lie, nodding to the door. 'Shall we?'

'Straight to business, eh? Come on then, let's go.'

I lock the door, and we meander companionably down the street. It's a relief to be out of the house, and the fresh air revives me. It was just a hallucination, I reassure myself. There was nothing in the corner of my room – no mouldering skeletons, no you. Out here, it's far easier to believe that.

'So, what shall we talk about?' I ask, as we head down the alleyway. I need to take my mind off things.

'The weather? That's the British thing, isn't it? Or else politics?'

'God, no. I've no time for politicians.'

He chuckles. 'Nor me. They've never done me any favours in the past.'

'They're not doing me many favours now.'

'What do you mean?'

I consider it before answering. 'When you come out of prison, it just feels like a series of hoops to jump through. I don't feel that anyone really cares.'

He eyes me shrewdly. 'Is that because ex-prisoners aren't seen as very sympathetic characters? If you'll pardon me saying?'

'Yes, you're probably right. And I suppose I should be grateful that they've given me somewhere to live, benefits, a new identity, and—'

The words. The words. I falter, mouth open. I *knew it*, I knew I would accidentally say something in the end, and that it would be horribly incriminating. I don't know what to do – what should I do? Laugh. That's it, pretend it was a joke. I giggle in an experimental manner, then glance over at him.

'New identity, eh?' he repeats, eyebrow raised.

'Just a little joke of mine. Probably not very funny. I used to tell people that I'd love to change my name, as I hated this one so much. Coming out of prison would have been the perfect time to choose something new.'

'But your name *is* Robin, yes?'

'Yes. Of course it is.'

Get a grip, I order myself. I'm usually more guarded than this, but the shock of what happened earlier has made me careless.

144

I stretch my lips into a reassuring smile and force the tension from my posture.

He visibly relaxes as we continue walking. 'I'm glad it really is Robin,' he says eventually. 'I can't imagine you as anything else. You're such a *Robin* person. The name suits you to a tee.'

That's depressing to hear. I *hate* the name. Everything about it is banal and insignificant.

'I'd have preferred something a little grander,' I tell him.

'I never had you down as grand. I like that you're nice and normal.'

Nice and normal. I'm shocked that he sees me this way. Though maybe that's not what he means. He probably means kind. Gentle. Easy to talk to. He can tell I'm not like everyone else, and I'm certain that's what he finds attractive about me.

We continue along the path until we come out at the river. I scan the landscape, but my stalker, thankfully, isn't in sight. Of course they're not; if it was Amber, she'd hardly be following when her father was with me. She's shrewder than that.

'How about a nice coffee and cake in one of the cafés?' Bill says, pointing. 'My treat.'

'Go on then,' I say, as he leads the way. I dodged a bullet earlier, so I have cause to celebrate.

After the coffee, we walk for a long time, longer than I realise. We talk about light-hearted things, which is a relief. Nothing more is said about Amber, or the past. We converse as ordinary couples do, with laughter, with the occasional disagreement over minor points. Bill's views of the world differ in some ways from mine. His opinion on women's place in society is positively archaic, for example. But overall, we are a good match. It feels *right*. We finally return to my house, just as the sun is setting. The air is biting more fiercely now, ready for the chill of night.

'Would you like to come in?' I ask, then feel myself blush. It sounds like more than an innocent invitation, which wasn't what I'd intended.

He grins, leaning against the doorframe like an old Western cowboy in a bar. 'That depends what you're offering.'

'I can do us a mug of something warm, or I have some wine? Or perhaps it's too early to drink?'

'It's never too early, Robin. Go on, then. Let's heat ourselves up with a glass of the good stuff.'

I feel odd, entering the house again. It feels different somehow. The angles seem to have shifted by a degree or two, leaving walls slightly out of alignment and floors somewhat skewed. I know that this is just a trick of the mind, but still, it's disorientating. Discomforting, even. I feel like something bad is about to happen, which is just silliness. I am safe in here. Everything is as it should be.

Bill strolls into the living room and makes himself comfortable, while I fetch the bottle of wine from the kitchen. It unsettles me further, seeing him sprawl on my sofa. He takes up a lot of room, and there's something a bit presumptuous about it. Perhaps it unnerves me because it reminds me of Henry, of how he used to saunter into my flat like it was his, not mine. He used to leave mud on the carpet, teacup-rings on my side tables, urine on the toilet seat that he never bothered to close after using.

Bill isn't Henry. Bill is a sweet man, who would treat my house, and *me*, with respect. I sit down beside him, knees pressed neatly together, then set about pouring the wine.

He reaches for his glass, then raises it.

'To you, Robin. If that *is* your real name.'

I freeze. 'It is. You know it is.'

'Just checking, as you said earlier—'

'That was just a joke.'

'Well, *whatever* you're called, I'm raising a toast to you. You're a tonic for an old boy like me.'

'Likewise,' I say, clinking his glass. We drink, maintaining eye contact, until I finally look down. Bill can be rather intense.

'You're an attractive woman, you know that?' he says, after a while.

His conversational tone throws me somewhat. I laugh, then quickly take another sip of wine. 'That might have been true when

I was younger,' I reply, 'but I'm old and grey now. I sometimes miss what I was.'

'We all feel like that. If you could have seen me when I was in my prime! No woman could resist me.'

His mouth is hitched at the corner, so I presume he's joking.

'I was never like that,' I say quietly. 'I didn't really notice when men gave me attention, if they ever did.'

'Oh, I bet they did.'

'I'm not sure. I was pretty, but also very shy. The only man who ever really paid me notice was—' I stop quickly, aware of how close I was to saying his name. Had I given him a false name, when we'd been talking about him in the restaurant? Damn it, I can't recollect. I'll have to avoid any name for now, just to be on the safe side.

'Do you ever see your ex-partner?' he asks, leaning back into the cushions.

'No. Goodness, no. He's still with the woman he left me for, as far as I know.'

'That's hard for you. Pardon me for saying, but I thought you said he just liked sleeping with her? Was it more than that, then?'

Had I said that? My mind races through previous conversations. It's entirely possible. But what if he's trying to trick me, to get me to reveal my lie?

'He had a sordid affair with her, then when I booted him out, he fell into her arms,' I say finally. That seems ambiguous enough; no major details there to worry about.

'I see.'

His expression is worrying. He doesn't seem totally convinced, and this bothers me. He mustn't be given any reason to start prying into my private affairs; it would be catastrophic.

'So this man,' he carries on, studying me intently, 'what did he look like? I'm wondering if you have a type.'

I laugh. 'I don't think I do.'

He leans in. 'Everyone's got a type.'

'I like people who are nice.'

'Do you think I'm nice?'

I feel panicked. I feel exhilarated. He's moving in closer. He's going to kiss me, and I want him to, but I don't. I protest his invasion of my personal space, but I'm drawn to his weathered cheeks, the flash of his grin. I want to touch him. I don't want to. It would be a violation, and no man may—

His lips are on mine. They're harder than I thought they would be. Like stone. Insistent, applying pressure to my own, forcing them apart.

I should be enjoying this. I am, perhaps, just a little. I am desired, and that is intoxicating. This is power: I have a hold over him, and that has value. But his tongue is now inside my mouth, and it feels more probing than erotic. A slug, squeezing through a crack in the floorboards. A damp catkin. I touch it with my own, and fight the urge to recoil. His kiss is wet. That may be my doing too, I have no control over my saliva. What should I do? Should my tongue be curling around his, in some sort of muscly, dripping dance? Should it be darting in and out, as his is now doing? And where should my hands be? One is still clutching the wine glass, but there's nowhere I can safely put it without it spilling.

Finally, he pulls away. I breathe, deeply.

He licks his lips, then gives me a wink. 'I've been wanting to kiss you for a while.'

'It was… pleasant,' I say weakly.

'I'm going to be a gentleman, though,' he continues, helping himself to another glass of wine. 'I expect nothing more, and I won't ever force you. I enjoy your company, Robin, and I want you to feel comfortable with me.'

Henry never would have said that, I realise, relaxing slightly. Bill is concerned about how I feel. He is attracted to me, and has base needs, as all men do. But he is controlling his urges, for my sake. He is a good man.

'Thank you,' I say simply. 'I really do like you very much, Bill.'

'Now you've made an old boy very happy.'

I smile, wanting to lean in against him, and have those strong arms around me. But I also want him to leave. I need some peace now, time to process my thoughts. But a dark part of me whispers that his leaving now would mean the hallucinations will come back. I push the thought to one side. It has no place, not here, not at this time.

CHAPTER 16

I've slept badly. Not because of any nightmares this time, thank goodness. Rather, my head was full of thoughts. Images of fleeing this city, ignoring the stupid rules of my parole, and catching a train as far north as possible. Taking Bill with me, finding a tiny cottage somewhere, nestled on a distant island. Darker thoughts, too. Wondering how long I can go on convincingly lying, before someone finds me out. It's a tremendous pressure. I must have drifted off at some point just before dawn. I remember it starting to get light, that's for certain. When my phone starts ringing, I initially think it's the alarm bell – that clanging, insistent noise that woke us up each morning in prison.

Whoever is calling me, they're persistent. I let it ring out, then fret. It could have been the Jobcentre, or Dr Holland. Or Margot. Which reminds me, I still need to complete the application for Jobseeker's Allowance and start applying for actual jobs.

The phone rings again, about fifteen minutes after the first time. This time I answer it.

'Hello? Is that Robin Smith?'

The voice is female, but too young to be Margot. Strange. Could it be my stalker, ready to take their harassment to the next level? I look around the living room, remember that I have the knife in here, plus others concealed about the house. I am well protected.

'I'm Robin,' I say carefully. 'How may I help?'

'Fantastic, I'm glad I've got the right number. Your neighbour, Amber, let us know your address, so I took the liberty of finding a way to contact you. I hope this is okay?'

'I'm sorry,' I say, blinking. 'What's this about?'

'I'm Madeleine Mason, from the *Echo*?'

'An Echo?'

'*The Echo*. The local newspaper. I don't want to keep you long, it's just we're running a piece on the dangerous nature of the roads in the city centre, and we'd love a few statements from you, about how you saved that young girl's life. I understand the car actually veered right up onto the pavement?'

So. A stalker of a different type, then. I should have known the situation wouldn't just fade away.

'I don't think I can help you,' I say.

'We'd only like a few quotes from you, just to highlight how risky it is for people. It might encourage the council to do something about it.'

'I can't help.'

'Oh.' She pauses. I can imagine what she looks like: slender, prissy little pencil skirt, red fingernails, which she's probably biting right now. 'Well,' she continues, in a slightly colder tone, 'we'll be mentioning the incident again, as quite a few people witnessed it. Would it be possible for you to send me a recent photo of yourself?'

'Absolutely not.'

'Or is there one online that I can use?'

'No, and I'll thank you not to snoop around for one.'

She tuts. The little minx actually dared to tut at me, for daring to stick up for myself and my right to privacy. It's fortunate she's not here in front of me, otherwise I'd have grabbed her by the ponytail, as I'm willing to bet she'd have one, and smacked her face into the nearest wall. How *dare she* invade my life in such a way? It's disgusting, how little respect people show each other these days.

'Thank you for your time,' she says stiffly, after a while.

I hang up without answering.

The incident has put me in a bad mood. I didn't *want* to be in a bad mood, as today should be a good day. Bill kissed me yesterday, and I'm sure that's what I wanted, and I should be happy. Now I feel hunted again.

I've kept the curtains drawn. I don't want people looking in on me. What if that nosy little madam, Madeleine, or whatever her name is, comes along to take a photo of me, when I'm sitting watching television? What if Amber decides to spend the morning observing me through the window, without me knowing? Besides, it's not such a nice day. The rain is heavy and persistent. It has a defeated air, as though it simply cannot be bothered to stop.

I consider going back to bed. But that would mean taking more sleeping pills, and I don't want to dip into my supplies unnecessarily, even the weaker over-the-counter varieties. The packets and bottles are lined in a reassuring wall on the cabinet shelf, a fortress of comforting oblivion whenever I need it, and I rather like having them there, after they were so restricted in prison. Dr Holland offered to review my medication, but that would mean giving control to him, permitting him to say what I take and when. I prefer to remain the one in charge. It's my body, after all.

Jean Marshall's medicine-taking was out of control. The sheer volume of pills she took was vaguely repulsive, and the rattling of those bottles used to drive me mad. Every morning, she'd shake one of this sort, two of another onto the work surface, then scoop them up and glug them down with her water, like a thirsty animal. Daddy used to tell her off for not counting them carefully, sometimes. Once, he even said *I lost one partner, I don't wish to lose another*. As though mother's death had been a careless mislaying, rather than an end to a life. I took an interest when he said that. I was sitting in the living area at the time, reading a comic I'd found in the back of my wardrobe, presumably left there by the previous inhabitants. And I peeped over the back of the sofa, to see him kiss her neck. A peck, nothing too passionate.

She saw me looking, and smiled.

God, she really wanted me to be gone. Few people can understand what it feels like, as a child, to be unwanted. Of course, Daddy would have been different if she hadn't shown up on the scene. He used to talk to me occasionally, back then, to convey his wisdom. I used to follow him as he worked, and he'd tell me all he knew. I was his protégée, and I could have gone on to achieve great things, I'm sure. But then Jean Marshall arrived and spoiled it all. Jean of the too-big teeth. Jean of the whinnying laugh. Jean of the waxed jackets and sensible wellingtons. Jean of the many, many pills.

I took a few of them out, one day, when she and Daddy were off talking to some visiting scientists, giving them the tour of the main bird colonies on the island. I laid them on the table, then dropped them, one by one, into a glass of water. There was a chalky residue at the bottom, especially after I'd put ten of them in. But if you sipped the water, it was hard to taste. In tea or coffee, it would have been unnoticeable.

Her heart pills. They were the most interesting. They were only small. Such tiny things, but so important for maintaining life. I think I would have liked to have studied science, when I was younger. I had an aptitude for slow, patient testing, which was quite unusual in so small a child.

The following day is better, though it is still raining. A day alone helped, yesterday. Sometimes, all it takes is some solitude, and total silence. This clears the head and permits thoughts to be carefully organised once more. I feel better. Regrettably, it's a Dr Holland day, but needs must, for the sake of my parole terms. Fortunately, I have an umbrella. The rain will not get me, and even if it does, what of it? It's only moisture, after all.

Already, my feet seem to know the route to his office, without me thinking too hard. I dance around puddles and avoid the edge of the pavement when cars veer too close. The last thing I want is to be splashed by a careless driver.

Dr Holland is still adjusting his tie as he answers the door. It makes me wonder if he has only just got dressed. If so, what was he doing before this? Indulging in a leisurely breakfast? Watching some dreadful daytime television programme? Having a sly dram of whisky to settle his nerves? Any of those could be possible.

'How are you today, Robin?' he asks, as I follow him to the counselling room.

'Good, thank you.'

'In spite of this weather?' He waves at the window. 'Isn't it dreary? Please, have a seat.'

I wait patiently as he settles himself, then reaches for his notes. He takes a few minutes to scan them – something he really should have done before I arrive, I think. There's no excuse for lack of preparation, even if you're dealing with someone you think is worthless.

'Last session was quite emotional, wasn't it?' he says, looking up. 'We covered some tough ground, which may have been painful, but nonetheless, it may be beneficial in the long term.'

'To be honest, I don't see how,' I say. It's incredible how easily this man puts me on edge, fool though he is. 'I'm aware of what happened in the past. It tortures me daily. Talking about it only rakes it all up again.'

Dr Holland nods. 'It's understandable that you'd feel like that. However, when we bury our feelings within ourselves, they often come out in unexpected and harmful ways. That's what we want to avoid. This is a safe place for you to discuss things, Robin.'

'I'm not sure I feel safe.'

'Well, that's a shame to hear. Please know that I'm here to help you successfully reintegrate with society.'

'I feel like I'm achieving that. I'm looking for work. I've even got a boyfriend.'

'Goodness me, that's news.' He frowns. 'How have you found it, being in a relationship?'

I smile. 'Very good, thank you. He's a nice man, very open and friendly.'

'That's an interesting choice of words. Are you open with him, about your past?'

'I've told him lots of things about myself.'

'Including what you were put in prison for?'

'Not yet.'

'Not yet.' He writes something down. 'I presume this is the man we've talked about before, the one you went on a date with. How will you manage this relationship with regards to your past?'

This is a difficult question to answer. I shift in my seat. 'I don't think my past actions define me. I'm who I am, regardless of all that.'

'These are very passive words, Robin. Again, I'd urge you to consider taking more ownership of these actions. You may well have deep regrets, but nonetheless, we have to acknowledge that—'

'I'm sure I'll come to some arrangement in my own time.'

'That's good to hear. If you'd like to talk through some strategies about how to approach the task, then we can—'

'No, that isn't necessary at this stage.' I place my hands neatly in my lap. 'The relationship is in its early stages.'

'Fair enough. It's probably easier to consider it sooner rather than later, though. Some food for thought, perhaps?'

I don't want his *food for thought*. I'm perfectly capable of thinking for myself. But I nod anyway. It's what he wants to see: that I'm behaving myself and swallowing his nonsense like a good girl.

'Could we discuss my medication?' I say, keen to change the subject.

'In terms of the options available?'

'No, just my current sleeping pills. Would you be able to prescribe a higher dosage, just for a short while? I've been having trouble sleeping again.'

He taps his pen on his pad. 'They're only meant to be a temporary measure. It'd be more helpful if we examine the root causes, or try some alternative therapies.'

We? As far as I'm aware, he won't be doing any of this with me. But I smile and nod.

'That sounds wonderful, but could I just have some more pills for now, to help me catch up on my sleep?'

'When did you last take them?'

'I had a break recently,' I lie.

He sighs. It's clear he's not sure whether to believe me or not, but doesn't have the energy to contradict my claim.

'I'll issue a final prescription to get you through this period of sleeplessness, then we'll need to explore other options. Also, I need to make you aware that there are risks associated, such as confusion, difficulty breathing, there have even been rare cases of death through overdose—'

'That's the same with all medications, isn't it?'

He smiles ruefully. 'I suppose so.'

'So you'll prescribe them for me?'

'Yes, I can do that.'

'Good,' I say, easing back in the chair.

He studies me, opens his mouth, then closes it again and starts scribbling notes on his pad. I don't know what he's writing, and nor do I care. The main thing is that he's being useful, for once.

It's been a productive day, I feel. Dr Holland prescribed me the medication I requested, and I found a pharmacy, on the road next to my own, which gave me the drugs without a murmur. What a wonderful society we live in, where these things are so easy. For a moment, it makes me believe that people *do* care, after all. Certainly they seem happy enough to shove hundreds of pills at you to numb the pain, with no questions asked. I suppose a deadened, emotionless person is easier to cope with than a sick, unpredictable one.

I add the bottle to my collection in the bathroom cabinet. They look like freedom, lined up in a neat row, and it's satisfying to know that they're there.

When Ditz used to talk about ending it all, I recommended pills to her. I even explained how to make them more palatable, by crushing them down and mixing them with water. Everyone knows they're the more peaceful way out, far more so than dangling on a rope. It was foolish of her not to listen, or rather, to choose to hear what she wanted to hear. Still, that's not my problem, and it never was.

I've had personal experience with pills, and I knew what I was talking about. Ditz remained blissfully ignorant of the exact nature of my past, so it was like writing tales on a blank piece of paper. An easy flow of words for a remarkably simple woman who was happy to swallow anything down. *Butcher Bird*, they called me, afterwards. *You killed her, you murdering bitch.* They were wrong. I didn't touch her: her death was self-inflicted, nothing more, nothing less. She wouldn't have survived in the real world, anyway, she was too weak. I tried to toughen her up, tried to support her as any caring-friend would, but it had all been futile.

The guards gave me a grilling after they removed Ditz's body from the cell. Even the doctor questioned me. He said he had to, and that if I had anything to share about it, I must do so. I had nothing to confess, and wasn't really sure what he was driving at. Did they imagine I'd materialised through Ditz's cell wall like a ghoul, and strung her up myself?

The other inmates have made comments, he muttered. All those hard-faced inmates. Grassing was considered the ultimate sin – unless, of course, they were the ones grassing on *me*. I didn't care; none of them had any value.

My thoughts have drifted again. When I was younger, I had such tight control of them. They were pebbles in my hand, that I could roll as I liked, then clasp my palm shut when I wished them gone. Now my thoughts have crumbled to grains of sand; always shifting, hard to keep control of.

The day has become dark, without me even noticing. That means the shadows are longer in the corners of the rooms, and it's probably time to turn the lights on. I don't want to see things that aren't there. I wonder whether Bill knocked earlier, while I was out. I think he must have done. He's falling in love with me, and that's how it's done, isn't it? The gallant lover pursues his maiden with ardent devotion; or that's what the movies tell us, and the books, too. I want him to have tried. That means he desires me, and he regards me as a person of worth. But as for the kissing? I'm not so sure. I've never known how I feel about physical

157

contact. I don't like to think about it much; it seems so ungainly and fumbling – a sweaty mass of writing arms and legs, a smelly exchange of various body fluids. But a kiss is a romantic thing, and it symbolises a lot. So I suppose, from a symbolic perspective, I'd like him to do it again. He will want to take things further, of course, because all men do. A kiss is never enough; it's merely the thumbs-up of approval that they need to proceed.

Henry sometimes didn't even need that. There were times, when we were intimate, where he didn't kiss me at all. When I don't think he even looked me in the eye.

See? There are the sand-like thoughts again, drifting through the past, gathering messily in the corners of my mind. All those dark and unvisited corners: they're the real problem. I need a brain that's vast and airy as a piece of open land. Less of the darkness and shadows. I should go to bed soon, before my thoughts blacken with the day. Today has been productive, and nothing bad has happened. That's a positive thing, and these are small mercies that I must be grateful for.

CHAPTER 17

In the morning, I set about completing my Jobseeker's Allowance form. It feels something of an achievement, to be able to do these things, especially given how complicated the laptop is. A single click of the mouse seems to take me to all sorts of places I don't want to go.

Now comes the process of applying for jobs. The print-outs I was given aren't particularly appealing. I cannot imagine myself standing behind a shop counter, day after day. Nor scuttling around someone's house like a nervous crab, duster and polish in hand. These are tasks better suited to others, not me. However, the Jobseeker's Allowance form clearly states that I must actively seek employment, and that people will be checking. I suppose I just have to hope that my criminal record will put them off.

I fill in two application forms, quite badly, if I do say so myself. Of course I know how to spell *acumen*, but it looks so much less attractive when I spell it with an *o* instead. In fact, there is something quite satisfying about this task. So much so, that it takes me a while to register that the doorbell is ringing. It must be Bill; I'm not expecting anyone else today. I quickly check myself in a mirror before going downstairs.

Immediately, I can tell that there are two people at the door, not one. A taller figure, and a narrower, shorter one. It's Bill, that's for sure, but less fortuitously, it's also Amber. Damn. They must have noticed me in the hallway, so there's no way to avoid opening the door to them. I stand for a moment, frozen, because they look so much like the police did that day. One big, one small. One male, one female. Their voices penetrating the door, *Ava, we can see you, and you need to open the door now. Ava, we will have to use force to enter if you don't. Ava. Ava.*

Me. Ava. I am Ava, not Robin. I can handle this.

I twist the lock, then pull the door open. They are both wearing black, a set of uniforms marking them as a duo, leaving me as the isolated one. But he's mine now, I think, meeting Amber's gaze. Not hers any more. I've got him.

'Hello, Robin,' Bill says, with his usual grin. 'Amber and I were about to go into town for lunch, did you fancy joining us?'

'Goodness, is it that time already?' I take in both of them: he's positively gleaming in the autumn light, she's flushed with reluctance. He's roped her into this, forced her to play nice for the sake of his happiness. I can tell how much the role pains her, that of the dutiful daughter. She's a vicious sort, through and through.

'There's a new café on Sidwell Street, and it serves a cracking full English. What do you say?'

I shake my head. 'I can't, I'm afraid. I'm job-hunting.'

'Are you?' Bill frowns. 'They've been nagging you, have they?'

I give him a wink. 'You know what they're like.'

'But you want to contribute to society, don't you?' Amber interjects. 'That's all they're trying to do, get you to give back, rather than taking.'

There she goes again, with her snooty, judgemental assumptions about me. Bill reaches for her arm and gives it a reassuring pat. 'You're right, I need to get back into the game. I just need to start respecting society again, rather than seeing it as the enemy.'

'I think you respect society very well,' I say.

'But the government can't just give money to people who can work,' Amber says.

'Do you work?' I ask her. 'What job is it that you do?'

Bill gives a low cough. 'Amber's between jobs at the moment; she's taking some time out. But anyway, if I can't persuade you to join us, can I come over later? How about a nice takeaway?'

'Oh, I don't want to encroach on your evening,' I say, looking directly at Amber.

She shakes her head. 'I'm out tonight, at a yoga class down by the quay.'

Is it just me, or did she say that very deliberately? After all, that's near the place where I saw the figure stalking me for the first time. She's got that peculiar half-smile now, the one that suggests she's toying with me.

'Yoga, how lovely,' I say, without any sincerity whatsoever. 'And such a pleasant location, down by the river. Do you go walking there often? I love to take a stroll down there.'

Her jaw twitches. I saw it, a revealing sign that she understood my meaning. So it *was* her. I have it, I have the evidence. How dare she try to frighten me, and why has Henry set her up to this? How did he locate her in the first place? He's a resourceful man; I suppose he found out where I lived, then got in touch with Amber and told her how she could punish me. That means that she must know what happened and—

'Robin?' Bill says, waving a hand in front of my eyes. 'You were off in a dream world again, like always.'

'I was, sorry.' I smile at him, avoiding looking at his lips. It reminds me too much of that kiss, which now feels licentious, just wrong in so many ways.

'Shall I come over tonight then?' He wraps an arm around Amber's shoulder. 'Tell you what, I'll buy some grub in town; something we can just fling in the oven. Then we're not taking the mickey with our benefits, right?'

'That sounds like a good idea.'

He reaches forward. His hand is on my arm, then suddenly his mouth is against my cheek. I note the warm breath. A slight hint of coffee that departs as soon as he retreats. It was tender. Nothing more, no expectation at all. Best of all, it shows Amber that I am not to be trifled with. She won't get rid of me so easily. I just have to work out how much she knows, and how I can keep her quiet.

'I'll be over about six, does that sound good?' he says, already turning to leave.

'That sounds marvellous.'

Amber raises a hand. 'Bye, Robin,' she says. I may have imagined it, but I'm fairly sure she put special emphasis on that name, maybe to show that she knows it's not real. Silly girl. She's taken on the wrong woman.

I can't shut the door fast enough. My heart is pounding, I hadn't realised how hard until now. The pieces of the puzzle are starting to fall together, and now I have my evidence that Amber is my stalker. The big question is *why*. What has Henry offered her? Is he paying her for this? Or maybe he's used his charm to get her to do what he wants. It may be as I suspected before; he may be sleeping with her, using her as he's used others. I don't like not knowing. There's still a chance that Amber may be working independently, of course. She may just have it in for me. She's certainly vicious enough to start a vendetta, just for the sheer fun of it. Or perhaps she found out who I really am, and has taken it on herself to punish me, like a vigilante.

That must be my next step: to find out exactly what she knows and what her motivation is. I shall pump Bill for information tonight, subtly, so he won't detect what I'm doing. I have a hold on him, and I can use that to my advantage. I can make him more mine than he already is, then steal him away from her clasp.

It's a plan. This is war, then. Amber won't see what's coming, because she's badly underestimated me. I'd wish her good luck, as she'll need it. But actually, I want her to have the worst luck in the world, over and over again.

It's time for my battle-mask. Lipstick, even though I'm not terribly skilled in applying it. A touch of rouge, or blusher, as the label on the plastic tub tells me it's called. Hair freshly styled into waves. It looks almost as it used to, silky and full. I could be a young woman again, when viewed from the right angle.

I suck in my stomach, hold it, and study myself reflectively in the mirror. My figure is good. Slightly crepe-papery about the abdomen and thighs, and there's some loose flesh bulging over the top of my pants. But it is not an undesirable figure, especially given my age. A lack of children has no doubt helped, enabling my skin to maintain some elasticity. I cup my breasts, just for a moment. They're fuller than they were, and they hang lower. But they will serve. Men love to fondle them, to slobber. Henry used to bite. He reminded me of an eagle, ripping into a freshly caught rabbit. Not Henry, not now. I don't want to think about him. But, if my instincts are right, maybe soon. I will find him again, and he will be forced to face me like a man, not a coward.

I suppose there is you to consider. I sometimes forget that – all the bitterness and misery that Henry must have gone through, after you'd gone. But then I need to remember it was his fault, and anyway, I don't want to think about you either, because then you may appear in the corner of the room, and I don't want that. I don't.

I shall wear this black blouse, with the top button undone. It is alluring, it suggests something more. A skirt, knee-length, without tights. It has to be said, I look good. Ten minutes to go. Time for a quick drink to loosen myself, to make me feel less like a coiled spring. Glancing in the mirror, I see a darker, more knowing woman than I am used to. But there is also something of the sacrifice in me. I am a lamb, laying herself down for the greater good.

It's been a long time, and I am scared. I won't dwell on that right now. A glass of wine, then.

He's a few minutes late, but that doesn't matter. I feel disorientated; it must be to do with the speed with which I drank the wine. Deep breaths. All will be well, and the evening will unravel exactly as it's meant to.

He's wearing a denim shirt and a pair of casual slacks. I like that he's rolled his sleeves up: it emphasises the curve of his forearms, and the strength within them.

'I come bearing food,' he says, holding a tote bag aloft. 'Some sort of Chinese meal. All we need to do is bang it in the oven for thirty minutes.'

'Sounds perfect.' I usher him through, noting the glance of approval that he gives me. He can see I've made an effort, and it pleases him. This is good.

The next few minutes are spent in mindless chit-chat, while I unwrap the food and pour us both a glass of wine. *Another* glass in my case. I mustn't drink too much, or I risk ruining everything. I must keep my purpose in mind. He leans against the countertop, watching me. I feel his eyes on my backside as I bend over. Then on my legs as I stand again. His admiration is warming, yet alarming, but I can handle it. I've done this in the past; I know how to bend people to my will.

'So, did you have a nice time with Amber?' I ask, putting the oven gloves down.

He nods. 'We ended up going to a vegetarian place. It was all right. She's into these eco-friendly diets. I suppose it's a good thing, really.'

'She's a committed girl,' I say, picking up my glass, then waving towards the lounge. We need comfort, right now. I want him to be relaxed, and I want him to open up to my questions, so I know what I'm up against.

'Amber fixes on certain ideas, sometimes,' he says, easing into the sofa. 'You know what it's like. It can make it hard for her to form relationships with others.'

I don't really know what he's talking about, but smile understandingly anyway. That's what he needs from me at the moment. Sweet, pliant little Robin. Trustworthy through to her bones. I think of your bones for a second. How they looked, when you were standing in the corner. Moss-coated. Ancient. *It's not the time*.

'Did you know that a journalist called me the other day?' I say, changing the subject.

'Did they? Amber said she'd dropped all of that.'

'It would seem not.' I pat his leg, leave my hand there a fraction too long. 'It wasn't a problem, don't worry. I doubt they'll call again. It's not as though it was *that* interesting a story, anyway.'

'Well, the local news takes any story it can get, doesn't it?' He grimaces. 'Amber meant no harm though, you do understand, don't you?'

'Oh, of course. I think she's a lovely girl.' I take a deep breath, then get to the grist of the matter. There's no time like the present, and only a lie will catch the truth. 'I heard her on the phone the other day, talking to someone called Henry,' I lie smoothly. 'Is that a new man of hers?'

He frowns. 'I don't think so. Henry? She's never mentioned anyone with that name.'

Would he tell me if she had? Yes, I think he would. He definitely has no idea about my past, that's obvious. 'Don't say I said anything,' I continue, leaning closer. 'But the conversation she was having seemed quite intense. Are you sure she's not seeing anyone?'

'I'm almost certain. She'd tell me. She's very honest.'

No, she's not, I think. You have no idea. Still, it seems that if she's liaising with Henry, she's being sly about it. Perhaps he got in touch via email or something. Social media? I don't understand all these modern ways of communicating.

'I thought I saw her the other day,' I add, sipping at my drink. 'Down by the river, wearing a wide-brimmed hat. Could that have been Amber?'

Again, the frown. 'She's got a knitted hat,' he says, scratching his forehead. 'But she only started wearing that again yesterday. It hasn't been cold enough yet for hats, really. I reckon it must have been someone else, Robin.'

I force a laugh. 'Oh, that's embarrassing then, as I waved to the person, thinking it was her.'

'I think you were mistaken.'

I wasn't. I know it was her. She's obviously good at covering her tracks.

'Does she spend a lot of time on the internet?' I ask. She's finding information out from *somewhere*, it's just a matter of—

'You're asking some funny questions,' he says, giving me a sideways look. 'What's troubling you? Are you worried about my daughter? Is that it?'

I haven't been as subtle as I wanted to be. What a fool I am; I've blundered in like a stampeding elephant, and that's not the way to get answers. The wine is to blame; it's clouded my judgement.

'She's said a few strange things to me,' I say slowly. 'I'm a bit worried about her state of mind. She sometimes seems a bit delusional.'

There, that should cover it. If she starts throwing accusations, I can buy more time by saying she's imagined the whole thing.

'Oh, she's definitely not that,' he replies. 'Don't you worry. She's forthright, she'll tell it like it is, but she's not got any mental health problems. It's nice that you're worried, though. She'd be touched.'

'You mustn't say I said anything.'

'Of course not.' He places his hand around my shoulder. 'You're looking very beautiful tonight, Robin. Can I flatter myself that you got dressed up for me?'

'If I can flatter *myself* that you did the same for me?'

'I did, I don't deny it. This is my special shirt, which I only wear for special people.'

I force myself to touch the top button. 'It suits you.'

'I'm glad you think so.'

And there it is, his lips on mine again; quite without warning. This time is better. I am more numbed by the alcohol, and I am able to place my glass down on the coffee table without risk of spillage. He's more forceful this time: the tongue is in play straight away. Less wet this time though, which is something. It's almost pleasant. Almost. I could let myself drift into it, as others do, perhaps.

His hand is on my waist. It tenses me, reminds me of those other times I was grabbed and thrown around as carelessly as a rag. But he's less frantic than Henry was. His fingers have an assurance, as they caress my skin through the fabric of the blouse. They move upwards, then touch the underside of my breast. I inhale sharply and he takes it as a signal of pleasure, I can tell. Perhaps it is. I don't know what I'm feeling, only that we have fifteen minutes until the food needs to come out of the oven, and that is a good thing, as it limits him.

'Robin, I really do like you,' he whispers into my ear. Then he starts kissing my neck, which is better. I like the feel of his breath as it travels down to my collarbone.

His intentions are clear now. I have given him the green light, and he feels confident enough to race towards the finish. I dare to glance down and see a bulge at the front of his trousers. *I did that*, I think, with something like pride. He would want me to touch it. I'm not sure if I want to. I need to stop overthinking things, and start *doing*, like every other person on this planet seems to. I must act normal, because that is what's expected.

His fingers drop suddenly, slide beneath my skirt with serpent speed. I am taken unawares, the walls of my defence smashed through before I have a chance to react. His hand is between my thighs, prising them apart. Suddenly, he withdraws.

'Am I going too fast?' he asks, eyes alight with concern. 'You must tell me, Robin. Sometimes I find it hard to read you.'

I don't know how to answer. I need him to be on my side, completely, and the way to achieve that is to make him love me, to make myself indispensable above all else. A small part of me wants it too; that feel of someone on top of me. It's the animal part of me, buried deep down. It frightens me.

'Can you give me a few minutes?' I ask.

'God, yes. Yes, of course. We don't have to do *anything* if you don't want to.'

'Maybe we should eat first.' I try a small smile. 'It might relax me a bit.'

He pulls me towards him, affectionately now, without passion. 'Listen,' he says, kissing the top of my head, 'you take as long as you want. I'm not going anywhere.'

He's not going anywhere, I think, with a thrill of excitement. I really have got him now.

The meal is bland and watery, but it's sustenance. It helps to channel my thoughts somewhat, to stop my mind from racing. We eat at the kitchen table, tell jokes, talk about our favourite places to go walking when we were younger. He's fortunate; he's always been free to wander, whereas I've spent half my life trapped in a cell. But I don't want to think of prison just now, not when it all feels so companionable again. His face is softened by the light of the table lamp, and I am at leisure to examine the sharp shape of his cheekbones, the smattering of stubble on his chin and beneath his nose. He is a handsome man. Even his baldness is masculine: firm and protective somehow. I can do this, I'm sure. It won't be too much of a hardship, and the benefits will outweigh the drawbacks.

We finish at the same time, and both pat our stomachs. This makes me laugh. We are already so attuned to one another's movements, like two dancers on a stage. I realise, at that moment, that I am ready. I want to be wanted again. It's been too long, and my experience of love to this day has been limited to abuse. It will be now, and I must give him the sign to make it happen.

My hand wanders to his. My fingers stroke at his thumb, then down to his wrist.

'Why don't you come upstairs?' I ask.

He blinks. 'What, you mean—'

'Yes, I mean it. Do you want to?'

He doesn't need asking twice.

CHAPTER 18

Bill spends the night with me, though I hadn't asked him to do so. Sleep, as a result, is elusive, a few snatched moments here and there, before the *cluck* of his ticking breath awakens me again. His presence is reassuring yet intrusive. A hillock of shoulder where before there was only flatness, and that rhythmic rise and fall, like a slow earthquake, shuddering through the bed.

Still, it gives me a chance to process what has happened. I feel deflowered, but that's only to be expected. The sex was a strange event, slow and caring to begin with, stroking, pressing, languid. Then he entered me, and it was all over quickly. It was as though I lost him in that moment, as he surrendered to the storm inside himself. I went from woman to receptacle in an instant. Nonetheless, this is what power feels like. It's that intoxicating moment when you know that you have them, trapped in the cage that you've so carefully constructed. They can be moulded, manipulated, and their hearts become a possession, to be used as desired.

Ditz was the same, though the relationship was more like that of a mother and daughter. And you, you were like it too. How you looked up to me, and wanted me to make life better for you. I would have done. I *could* have done; it was in my power to make it happen.

On that day, when you walked back to mine, you were so keen to see the baby starling I'd found. Your mother would never let you bring a bird into the house, you said. She called the garden birds vermin with wings, or some such nonsense. How Henry could have married such a person was beyond my understanding.

We discussed its name. *Gerald*, you suggested, for some reason or another. *Topher. Star.* Star. Shining bright. A little life, for you to hold and admire. That seemed apt.

You hesitated outside the door, but that was because you were a sensible boy. After all, we hadn't known one another that long, and you mentioned that your parents might be concerned. I praised your good sense, then told you that I couldn't bring the chick outdoors to show you: it was too vulnerable, too easily frightened. You understood, and followed me inside. It was that easy. No, not easy. Right. It felt right. You were like a little chick yourself, and you needed caring for.

If you were shocked by the meagre size of my flat, you were polite enough not to show it. I made you a drink first – blackcurrant squash. You didn't realise, but I'd bought it especially for you, because I'd seen you drinking it a few times, through your living room window. You declined the cake; you weren't a fan of raisins, apparently.

The little starling started chirruping loudly when I opened the box. I placed him in your open palms and you laughed and told me that the feathers were tickling you. I asked if Henry had ever let you hold a little bird. You gave me a strange look, which I took to mean no.

It went well, up to that point. We played a few card games, and I taught you Gin Rummy. I was planning to make you some dinner, just as a good mother would. My mother used to cook up such bland, tasteless fare. I'd bought some spaghetti, good quality minced meat, basil and parmesan. A hearty meal for a growing boy, something to sustain you, to put some weight on those delicate bones of yours. I did it out of honest, innocent affection, I swear. There was nothing corrupt or cruel in it. I only wanted to make you happy. But then you asked to go home, and that spoiled everything.

I did not like the expression on your face. You changed quickly from peaceful compliance to suspicion, sharpness. It hurt me, if I'm honest. I'd given you no reason to mistrust me, but then, you were your father's son. Henry's blood ran through you, whether I liked it or not. I reminded you that your mother had never given you the attention that I did, and that it was gratitude you should be feeling, not anger. You called me an offensive name at that point. It was so out of character, I didn't know what to do. I was so disappointed. I felt I didn't really know you at all, that you were yet another person who was letting me down. One could argue that it was your fault. But you were only a boy. No one was to blame, no one at all. It was just one of those awful, terrible things.

No one was to blame. No one.

Bill stirs in his sleep. For a moment, it sounds childlike, like you, and I cry out. I have to cover my mouth, for fear that I'll look over and you'll be there, staring sightlessly, with lips turning blue.

God, I never meant it to happen. I never, ever—

Bill's eyes have opened. He looks confused, rolls onto his back, then stretches.

'I wondered where I was, for a second,' he says, still stuffed with sleep.

'So did I,' I reply.

He chuckles. 'You're a funny one, Robin.'

In one fluid movement, he's over on my side of the bed, sliding one arm beneath me, and another over my shoulder. I am enveloped, suffocated somewhat under the pressure of his body. However, it's a welcome distraction from my thoughts.

'Last night was very special,' he says softly. His breath is pungent and dense; the digestive juices from that Chinese meal, no doubt. 'It's been a long time. I hope I wasn't a disappointment.'

'You weren't,' I say, and it's not completely a lie. How could I be disappointed when I had no expectations in the first place?

He kisses me. I wish he wouldn't, I find it difficult to breathe. Thankfully, he keeps his tongue to himself this time, but his hands immediately crawl beneath the duvet, hunting out my bare flesh. It's clear what he wants, but I know from experience that giving in puts me in a weaker position. So I pull away, then soften the gesture with a laugh.

'You're insatiable,' I tell him, slapping his arm. 'You wait there, I'll make us both some breakfast.'

'I can think of something else I'd prefer,' he says, reaching for me.

I evade his grip, nimbly flinging the duvet away and catching a glimpse of his exposed penis in the process, already swollen with anticipation. Triumph washes through me – because there is the sign, the physical symbol of my control. *I'll get you to hate your daughter*, I think.

'Would you like eggs and bacon?' I ask, slipping into my dressing gown.

He has the good sense not to push it, though I detect a hint of churlishness in the curve of his lips. The poor boy has been denied his toy, for now.

'A fried egg sarnie would be a treat,' he says, sitting up. 'If you're sure you wouldn't rather—'

'All in good time,' I interrupt, and saunter out of the room. Let him wait. The gate has been opened, now all that remains is to walk him slowly through it, and to let me lock it tightly behind him. Fried egg sandwich it is, then. I shan't think of you, and you must stop creeping through my thoughts; you've had control over them for too long. Now I need to think about taking revenge for myself, for the years that were stolen from me. Perhaps for you too, because you would still be alive if your father had treated me better.

There. That's an end to the thoughts, for they won't serve me well this morning. Not today, not today.

Bill finally leaves just before lunch, despite my repeated hints that it should be sooner. The house seems to relax as soon as the door closes behind him, and I can breathe again. It's been a productive night, but the effort involved has been exhausting. I need to sleep, and for my head to be empty.

No pills are required for this sleep: it falls fast upon me, like a blanket dropped from a great height. I sprawl across the entirety of the mattress, and for a while, know only the wasteland of nothingness.

When I come to, it's already getting dark outside. It must be five or six in the evening, I'd guess. The sky has that dusty, washed-out look to it, that signifies the approach of the moon. I smell of Bill, and of something grubbier and more illicit. It's definitely time for a bath, and to wash the filth of it all from me.

As I run the water, the scent of the bubble bath fills the air. Lavender, tuberose; all those naturally intoxicating scents. The bubbles feel luxurious against my skin as I ease in, the heat blushing me to pinkness. I sink downwards, patting myself clean, and wash all remnants of last night from me. Finally, I am me again. The water has cooled to a gentler warmth, and the bubbles have attached themselves to my stomach, my arms, my thighs. I reach downwards, and let my fingers linger for a moment or two. This body is capable of marvellous things; it is a tool of the greatest importance. I shouldn't forget that. There's more to me than just my mind.

As I touch myself, Henry's face rises before me. The way he used to raise his eyebrow, to suggest something unspoken: a message for me, and me alone. I was special to him, I was a lover, not just a woman to play with. He cared about me, he must have done. It was *her*, Miranda, who couldn't bear to share him. Despite the fact that I had nothing, and she, everything.

I pull my hand away, then reach for the plug. It's time to get out anyway.

There's no chance of me sleeping now, not after my long nap earlier. I will take some more pills later, but for now I shall familiarise myself more with the internet. It is a wonder of the modern world, after all, and I don't want to be one of those older women who can't keep up with things. I open up the browser window, as the instructor taught us to do in prison. We didn't have much access there, of course, only to the material they approved, which was mostly learning resources, all far too basic for me. It is a miracle that I can type whatever I choose into this little white box, and it will find it for me. I type in Bill's name, but there are too many other Bills. Bills on Facebook, Bills that work for legal firms in London. A big, dark-haired Bill who plays for a rugby team in Yorkshire. Such a bewildering number of people, all united by the chance event of their parents liking the same short little title: *Bill*. Bill, also money. Also the mouth of a bird. So much meaning in just four letters.

I look for Amber too, but again, there's too much. It doesn't help that her name is the same as a lump of fossilised resin. Pretty, but murky and deceitful. That's about right. Then I dare to look for Henry, though I worry that there will be ways for the government to access my searches. It wouldn't surprise me if they could do that; they seem to be able to do anything these days.

I find him with ease. Or I find what he was, anyway. There are several newspaper articles about us, or what happened. One from the *Mail*, complete with a mugshot of me: the one I hate most, as my lips are in a snarl. It was a cry of terror, for the record, but the photographer managed to twist it, to make it look cruel. These hateful articles tell me nothing that I don't already know. Anyway, this isn't Henry now; this is the Henry who existed all those years ago. I want to find out what he's doing at this moment, where he lives, who he lives with. This isn't for me. Hastily, I close the internet window. It's a relief to be able to do it so easily, yet I spend a minute or so staring at the screen, frightened that it will suddenly pop up again, like a ghost that can't be exorcised. But it's gone, it's all definitely out of sight, and I am safe again.

I shouldn't have looked. I was expressly told never to try to find him. It's not even as if I want to see him, not after what he did. But I yearn to have that knowledge of his life. To see whether his hair has turned grey, or fallen out entirely. To view those shoulders, that torso, and to assess whether they've become wasted, or plump with too much good eating. What would he do if he saw me? Would he be shocked at my appearance, or impressed by how well I've kept my figure?

Actually, he probably knows what I look like now. There are no restrictions on his access to information. He may be aware of my address; this would certainly be the case if he's working with Amber to bring me down. He might even have passed the house, laughed at how meagre it is. Seen Bill, even, and wondered how I could be satisfied with *that*, when I'd had someone like him. There's also a chance that he regularly meets Amber around here, and that they've talked extensively about me. If he's retained his looks, it wouldn't surprise me if he'd seduced her. There are certain women who are attracted to older men.

As I stand, I check behind the door. The knife is still there, where I left it. As is the one under my pillow. Henry can't get me, or at least, not easily. Neither can anyone else.

It would appear that I have an interview. Or so this email informs me anyway. A woman called Samira, from the florist's, is asking if I could come in either today or tomorrow. This is a catastrophe. I don't want to work in a florist's. I don't like flowers very much, and I certainly don't like people. But I know that Margot will have received this email too, as I had to include her contact details. She'll know if I don't reply, and then my Jobseeker's Allowance won't be approved.

I finish the rest of my toast, even though I rather burned it, then hastily type out a reply that today will be fine, that I can pop in after lunch. Maybe it *will* be fine. I may get on with this Samira very well, and we might end up as friends. I am able to have friends, I'm sure, contrary to what others have said in the past.

I see Bill's head, bobbing around over the garden fence. It is a cheery beacon, an egg-like dome with the sunlight glinting off the top. I shall tell him my news and ensure I am in his thoughts today. The last thing I would want is for his interest to wane.

'Good morning,' I call, as I slip out of the back door.

His eyes pop up over the fence, creased at the corners.

'It's nearly good afternoon,' he replies. 'Haven't you seen the time?'

'I've only just had breakfast.'

'You're living the dream, you are.'

'Guess what? I've got a job interview today.'

His eyes crinkle more. 'That's interesting. How do you feel about it?'

'I'm going to go along with an open mind.'

He raises his hand, giving me a half-visible thumbs-up. 'Good for you. It's nice that they don't mind your criminal record.'

'Well, I'm not really a criminal in the strictest sense of the word.'

'I think they'd see it differently.'

I frown. The patronising quality of his tone is grating. As if he'd understand what it was like. He's never stood in my shoes, never had to walk the difficult path that I have.

'I'll explain to them that I was wrongfully accused,' I say, putting my hands on my hips.

His eyebrow raises. 'But you weren't, were you? You told me you'd stolen that money.'

Damn it. I've forgotten again; I have to remind myself of this daily, or risk arousing his suspicion. 'Yes, that's right,' I say quickly, then panic that the words sound unnatural.

'That *was* what you said, wasn't it? Or have I misremembered?'

'No, that's right.'

I don't like the silence; this wasn't how I wanted the conversation to go at all. It was meant to be flirtatious, not laden with angst.

'Well, good luck,' he says eventually. 'I'm sure they'll hire you.'

Ask to come over later, I think, shifting from one foot to the other. Come on, it's the perfect opportunity.

'I was just fixing this rose,' he says instead, prodding at the plant. 'It isn't climbing right.'

'They never do what you want them to.'

'That's true. You think you know a rose, then it goes off on a totally different route. Complicated flowers, they really are.'

'But beautiful.'

'And thorny.' He shakes his finger ruefully. A spot of blood shines on its tip.

'Did you want to come over this evening?' I blurt, just as my feet turn to leave.

'Can't, I'm afraid. Amber and I are going to see that film in the cinema.'

And are you going to invite me? I wait. He slept with me, for goodness' sake, the least he can do is take me to the movies. Or is this how it is? He's had his fill and now he's moving on? All this nonsense about wanting me and Amber to get along: that was *before* he got sex. Now he doesn't care about me at all.

'Fine,' I say, and walk away.

I hear him mumble something after me, some line about catching up another time, but I ignore it. Let him suffer a little. If he thinks he can treat me as an obedient little pet, to be stroked one minute then disregarded the next, he's entirely wrong.

Samira is efficient. I can tell that straight away, from her severe grey dress to her steadfast, impassive gaze. Her shop is similarly effective: white walls, flowers lined up in neat pots, buckets of wrapped bouquets all neatly stacked.

I position myself by the counter, push my hands into my pockets, then withdraw them again. This is ridiculous. I have no customer service skills, and no interest in this job whatsoever. It's just another meaningless task to be performed, so the authorities can congratulate themselves on supporting me, out here in the real world. But in spite of this, I want to make a good impression. I don't want to be dismissed as yet another unemployed no-hoper.

I wait as she finishes writing a note on her pad. Finally, she pushes it to one side.

'I'm with you now,' she says. There's a hint of a smile somewhere, but it certainly doesn't reach as far as her lips. 'So, you're Robin Smith, and you're currently seeking employment. You say you don't have any experience of working with flowers.'

'None whatsoever.'

She folds her arms. 'Which begs the question, why did you apply in the first place?'

'I had to. The Jobcentre forced me.'

She laughs, explosively and with enjoyment. I hear the London in that sound, the harsh gravel of her natural voice, concealed behind a polished veneer.

'You're certainly honest.'

'To a fault, yes.'

'You've got a criminal record.'

I nod. She's got to it quicker than I anticipated, but that's not surprising. She's clearly a woman who doesn't beat around the bush.

'I'm technically permitted to ask what you were imprisoned for,' she says, meeting my eyes. 'As you'll be working with the general public. So, do you care to share?'

'I was wrongly accused of murder,' I say, as levelly as possible. 'But I'd rather not go into details, as it may compromise my current situation.'

'I see. That's problematic.'

'I can see why you'd think that.'

'It's a shame,' she says, after a while. 'You seem sensible. I like sensible people. The last woman I had used to flap all the time – it drove me mad.'

'Maybe you should judge me on how I am now, rather than what they say I did in the past.'

Again, a pause. 'Yes,' she says slowly. 'But it's murder, isn't it? That's the big one. If you were to go berserk in here, kill one of my customers, people would point the finger at me, say I never should have hired you. Do you see my problem?'

'I never went berserk.'

'I'm sure you didn't. But still.'

'So that's a no, then?'

She nods. 'I think it will have to be. A word of advice: when you're applying in the future, you may want to disclose the nature of your conviction. It saves wasting people's time.'

'I'm sorry if you feel your time was wasted.'

'Don't mention it. Good luck, by the way.'

Good luck. Is she mocking me? Her serious expression suggests not, but there's a lilt to the words that suggests she thinks I'm deluded.

This is how it's going to be, though. On the one hand, I will never be employed again, which is good, as I don't like being around others. But on the other hand, it shows clearly how I will always be judged for this. It will never let me go. You will never let me go.

This is your real revenge, not prison.

CHAPTER 19

There is no point sitting here brooding. Yet that's what I'm doing, in the darkness, on the sofa.

I am angry. Dr Holland said it was important to acknowledge my feelings, so here they are, an ugly spill of emotion. I am angry at that woman in the florist's, for making me feel as though I am worthless. I am angry at Bill, because he's out right now, watching a film with that horrible daughter of his, when he should be here making me feel better. I am angry at Amber, of course. Her manipulation. Her sly stalking. Her attempt to break me, perhaps in collusion with Henry.

I'm angry at myself, too. In prison I said to myself night after night that I would never drop my guard again, that a situation like Henry wouldn't occur a second time. Yet here I am now, giddy as a stupid girl, even though I hadn't wanted to do that thing with Bill. I didn't like the feel of his hands over me, in me, nor the wet squish of his lips. I didn't like that tongue, soaking and probing. The greed of it, the violation of everything that is me: I hated it, but I did it because it was necessary. I should have realised that he, like every other man, would just take what he wanted, then discard the rest.

Earlier, I found the knife I'd left in the lounge, picked it up and placed it on my lap. It wasn't as satisfying to have it there as I thought it would be. I pressed the tip into my arm, to test its sharpness. It produced blood, but only after significant pressure.

The cut throbs, and that's useful at the moment. It provides something for me to focus on. No, a knife isn't my idea of a good weapon. To do damage with it, you'd have to get close. Force would be needed, a lot if you were aiming for the chest, as presumably the ribcage would offer some resistance. There would be blood too, of course, and it would be messy. A knife is clearly an instrument of passion, one for those who act with the heart, not the head. Daddy used to call the kitchen knife the butcher's friend. Butcher. Butcher Bird. He butchered lots of birds with it too, chicken mostly, for us to eat. To think of that knife is to remember it sliding through mottled, plucked skin. To see the pearl-pink flesh inside, and the sinew of muscle, pulled to tightness.

Turkey, too, at Christmas. God, how I hated those Christmases with Jean Marshall. I only endured three, which wasn't so bad, I suppose. The third was shortly after they announced they were getting married. She wanted to let Daddy's organisation know, but he was worried. It wasn't as if they'd been very open about their relationship to that point, anyway; they'd panicked too much that it might compromise their careers.

She never used to let us put tinsel up. It was tacky, she said, a product of consumerism. Instead, it was always sprigs of holly. Pine branches across fireplaces, strung over doorframes. The strong scent of damp tree pervading whatever cottage we were in at the time. Admittedly, her decorations weren't offensive. But she was insufferably proud of them, always insisting that Daddy took photos of her posing underneath a clump of mistletoe like a flirtatious teenager.

That third Christmas was memorable. Or at least the day after it was. That's when Jean Marshall's health took a turn for the worse.

I hold the knife up, so the edge glints in the glow of the street light outside. Killing someone with this *would* be murder, there's no doubt of that. An active deed of aggression, violent, unpleasant and sudden. Slipping a few too many pills into someone's mulled wine is rather different, I feel. It's also important to take intent into consideration. If someone doesn't necessarily mean to kill someone, but it happens anyway, then this cannot be construed as murder. Nor if they acted in an experimental manner, more in line with research than emotion.

I'd mainly wanted to see what would happen if she took too many of those damned pills of hers. I wanted to shut her up, to see her pass out on the sofa and leave the place in silence again. I was young; I had no real understanding of the fact that too many pills could result in heart failure.

I did feel some remorse afterwards. But then I am almost certain that she would have got me in the end, if I hadn't got there first. When I remember those days, I recollect worrying events. Standing beside her on the cliffside and feeling her hand pressing suddenly on my back. Ready to shove hard, maybe; it wouldn't have surprised me. She wanted me out of the picture and was probably willing to do whatever it took to make it happen.

Daddy was devastated, naturally. But then he knew she had a heart problem, and the doctor even confirmed what he suspected already: that it could have happened at any time.

Pills or no pills. There's a chance her death had nothing to do with them at all.

It was a bad night; there's no use pretending otherwise. I spent a large portion of it in the bathroom, sitting on the floor, head leaning against the wall. It was the only place I could get cool; the whole house seemed ablaze in those dark small hours, and the sweat poured off me. I feel a little feverish still, so perhaps I am sickening for something.

I have become quite attached to my laptop. It serves as a little window to the outside world, which is preferable to actually venturing out myself. I am gaining ground with the internet too, testing out new things to search for. The news channels really are very sensationalist these days, and it makes me wonder what is real and what isn't. Maybe it doesn't matter any more; it's all just a matter of perspective anyway.

Perhaps I should search for more jobs to show the Jobcentre how willing I am to make an effort, even though I'm clearly unemployable. However, I'm reluctant to expose myself to such scrutiny, time and time again. The more people who know what I was imprisoned for, the more likely it is that someone will start piecing things together.

A letter lands on the doormat at some point after lunch. I can even guess what size the envelope is, just from the telltale noise of the thump. It's not the postman's usual time for delivery, which immediately sets me on edge. Another poisonous letter is not what I need right now. If it's *her* again, I shall go round there now, squeeze her cheeks until her mouth opens, then stuff the paper into her throat.

There's no address on the front, but the name reads *Robin*, not Ava. Handwritten. Non-threatening in appearance. I force myself to take a breath, gain some control. These over-reactive responses aren't helpful. I rip into the envelope and tug out a card: a long-eared puppy, holding a bunch of daisies. It's cheaply made, and the image is quite frankly rather stomach-churning. Still, I open it up.

Want to do something later? Drink down the pub? Love Bill xxx

Why didn't he just knock on the door? That's his usual style, after all – brisk and straightforward. This card smacks of silly play-ground flirtation. But two can play this game. I head back to the kitchen and pull out my notepad.

That depends if you're buying. Robin xx

Hastily, I slip outside, nip around the gate, then slide the folded note through his letterbox. There's a stirring from within as I do so, from somewhere further down the hallway. I quickly dart back into my house, smirking.

A few minutes later, the doorbell rings. I let him sweat for a while. I still haven't forgiven him for last night, and it'll do him good to realise he's not indispensable. Finally, I pull it open.

'Fancy seeing you here,' I say, fairly coolly.

He bows, then leans forward and kisses me on the cheek. 'Of course I'll be buying. As long as you don't order champagne.'

'But that's what I like to drink.'

'Well, you'll have to be very nice to me if you want that sort of treatment.'

It's hard not to grimace. We sound like two characters in a poorly written romance novel. 'How was the film last night?' I ask, leaning against the doorframe, denying him entry.

'I nodded off halfway through. Amber wasn't too impressed.'

'That good, eh? You should have asked me to come with you.'

He raises an eyebrow. 'I figured you and Amber might be better off kept apart for a while. You don't seem to get on so well, and she said…'

'What did she say?'

'Nothing, it's not even worth mentioning. Now, shall we go to the White Horse tonight? They do a good range of ales.'

What did she say? I think again, studying his face. I want to know. If she's been bad-mouthing me, or even worse, starting to sow the seeds of doubt in his mind, leaving clues about my past, I need to be informed about it.

'Amber is such a *nice* girl,' I say. The sarcasm drips from every word, and his frown shows he notices.

'Let's not start with anything like that,' he says, folding his arms. 'I'd rather focus on that night we spent together.'

'Would you now?'

'Wouldn't you? You seemed to enjoy it.'

I'd mewled like a tortured kitten, because that's what men expect. If he was taken in by that, he really wasn't terribly observant. Presumably he was concentrating too hard on reaching his own sweaty climax.

Pull the right face, I remind myself. Bill is a kind man, he deserves it. I smile coyly, but feel like a tramp while I'm doing it. I'm too old for this sort of thing; not that I was ever that good at it in the first place.

'Shall I knock at seven, then?' he says. 'We can walk down together.'

'Make it six. I like to be home early.'

He winks. 'I like your thinking.'

184

God, I hadn't meant it that way. And just like that, I've set myself up for another night of intercourse. I'd much rather have the opportunity to sleep; I can hardly keep my eyes open.

'See you later, then,' I say, just as something crashes behind me. A deafening, unnatural sound, brutal enough to make me jump.

Disjointed thoughts jostle in my mind, while I fight to make sense of it. *Something broken. Threat. Butcher Bird. It's her, they've found me, they're coming for me.* Bill stares at me, mouth open, and I realise my own mouth is mirroring his expression.

'What the devil was that?' he asks, jerking into motion, already pacing down the hallway.

I only blink stupidly like a startled owl. It had been glass breaking. A lot of it. But that isn't possible – I don't *have* a lot of glass… unless it was the window.

Someone has thrown something through my window, perhaps to try to hit me. An explosive device? A rock, designed to smash my skull open? I don't want to think about skulls being shattered, not now, otherwise it may invoke hallucinations of you, and— *Stop it,* I tell myself.

I follow Bill into the kitchen, steeling myself. It's worse than I imagined. The entire floor, the sink, the countertop, everything is covered with glittering glass. The window is a ragged hole, letting in the wind. And there's a brick in the middle of it all. A *brick*, for God's sake, with a note tied around it.

Bill reaches for it. I do too. Our hands meet in a collision of knuckles.

'Let me have it,' I hiss. 'It's mine.'

'Robin, I was only trying to—'

'Don't look at it.'

He leans back on his haunches, then whistles. 'Who's Eva? Or Ava, or whatever it says?'

I'm undone. I feel myself unravel like thread from a spool, unwinding onto the floor, joining the glass. There's blood on me: I must have cut my finger. Hastily, I smear it over the note – anything to rub out that name. He mustn't see, he *can't*.

'It said *Eve*,' I tell him quickly, pulling the brick away. 'It's a nickname.'

'A nickname? You mean you know who did this?'

Think fast – think *faster*. I need the answers to flow like a stream; they mustn't be stagnating in this silence, otherwise he will start to suspect. He *already* suspects, I can see it all over his face.

'It's my ex-partner,' I tell him quickly. 'He wants me back, and he keeps attacking me.'

Bill frowns. 'But you said the other day that—'

'I know, I was lying. I'm sorry, I just didn't want you to get caught up in all of this.'

He waves at the window. 'We can't let him get away with this. I'll call the police.'

'No!' I grab his arm. He cries out; it was harder than I'd meant it to be.

'Robin, we can't leave it like this. The guy is a nutcase. You might be in danger.'

I wonder who threw it. Amber, it must have been, over the back wall of the garden. She knew that her father would be here too, and that he'd read the name on the note. I will kill her. I swear to God, I will end her life for good, the malicious, poisonous—

'Robin?' Bill taps me tentatively on the shoulder. 'I don't like this at all. I'm worried. Can I read the note?'

'No, absolutely not.'

'Show me. I can help.'

'No.'

I should start crying. That will make him softer again, less alert to the inconsistencies. But I've never been one for crocodile tears, and besides, my rage is too overpowering. I want to curl my hands around Amber's stupid scrawny neck, not sit here sobbing like a schoolgirl.

'Bill, it's best that you go,' I say, still clutching the brick behind my back. I want to see what the note says, I want to read what cowardly thing Henry or Amber has to say to me. But I can't do it with him watching.

'I can't leave you like this; look at the place. You must call the—'

'I'll call them later, I promise,' I lie. 'I just need some time to take this in. Please understand.'

'Can I at least help you to sweep up the—'

'No, honestly. Come over at six. I'll be much better by then.'

I don't like the look in his eyes at all. There's confusion there, but something worse too. He senses that something isn't adding up, and his mind is already working it through, trying to identify exactly what feels wrong.

He stands, shaking some glass off his shoe. 'If you're sure that's what you want?' he says, in a guarded voice.

'Yes, I'm sure. But I appreciate your concern, I really do.'

He waits a moment longer, then leaves. The front door clicks shut, and finally I can breathe again. He's not happy about the situation, but that's to be expected. I'll deal with him later, when I've had the chance to take this in.

The note is carelessly attached to the brick with an elastic band. It's similar to the ones that our postman uses, yellow and thick. Another sign that it's probably Amber. Block printed letters. No giveaway as far as handwriting goes.

AVA

> YOUR SECRET WILL COME OUT YOU MURDRER I
> WILL EXPOSE YOU TO THE PAPERS. I WILL MAKE SURE
> EVERYONE KNOWS WHO YOU ARE. I KNOW WHAT YOU
> HAVE BEEN DOING AS I AM WATCHING YOU.

Short and sweet. The misspelling of the word *murderer* strikes a discordant note; I hadn't pegged Amber as the ignorant sort. But that mention of the papers: that's her for sure. She must have waited until her father announced he was popping over to see me, then stolen outside to the garden, slipped out of the back gate, and lobbed the brick over. My garden is tiny, so it wouldn't have required much effort for it to reach. I'm sure she was triumphant when the glass shattered. The grin was no doubt still fixed in place as she raced back inside, heart beating with excitement. I wonder if she giggled, imagining the horror on my face, the desperate way I attempted to hide the brick from her father.

I've sunk to the floor, without even noticing. My legs are in shards of glass, and so is my free hand. The other still clutches the note. Funny, I hadn't noticed the sharpness until now, or the pain. I am pierced all over by her cruelty.

I won't tell Margot about this. Not yet, anyway. I need to gather my thoughts and think carefully about the consequences of my actions. That's what Dr Holland always recommends.

Amber will be dealt with, though, and Henry too. That's for certain. I've had enough of this bullying, this psychological torture. I've served the time, I've done my penance. I've spent years rotting away in a cell, listening to simple-minded cretins like Ditz whine on about life. Now it's time to stop playing the vulnerable bird-chick, and become the predator. I stand, then brush my legs down. Glass tinkles to the floor, harpsichord-high and fluting. There is blood on my skin, speckled and shining. It's all rather beautiful, in a strange, skewed way.

Thank you, I think, as the pain provides me with focus. It is a gift, and I shall use it well.

CHAPTER 20

'You swept it all up, then,' Bill says, hovering awkwardly by the kitchen door.

I nod and smile. He has no idea how long it took me to clear everything, how I scrubbed and scraped at each surface to ensure no pieces of glass remained. The hole in the window is blocked with my old atlas, folded outwards and taped into place. It's the best idea I could come up with at short notice.

He shakes his head, staring around the room in horror. 'I still can't believe someone did that to you.'

'It's terrible, isn't it?'

'It's worse than that, it's frightening.' He pauses, then glances at me. 'When I told Amber about it, she asked if it was someone called Henry.'

I can't hide my shock in time. It's there, for him to see, in the tension of my muscles, the sharp exhale of breath. 'How does she know Henry?' I ask, words slithering out before I can stop them.

Bill frowns. 'She doesn't. She said you once accused her of helping him to get at you, though. Is Henry your ex-partner, then? I can see from your face that he is.'

'No, that's not right,' I mutter, holding my head. The room feels like it's underwater, muffled and more muted.

'Who is Henry? Robin?'

Get it together. I am tumbling apart, and if I carry on, he will ask Amber more questions and she will finally tell him everything.

She's going to anyway, but this will speed things up and I'll lose my chance to gain the upper hand.

'His name is Harry,' I blurt. Even as I say it, it sounds unutterably wrong, but he mustn't know Henry's real name, it's far too risky. 'Amber misheard me. I didn't mean to accuse her that day, I wasn't thinking straight. You see, I'd received a letter from him, and—'

'What does that have to do with Amber, though?'

'Henry – Harry, I mean – he likes pretty girls. I thought he might use someone like Amber to get to me.'

He frowns. 'That's strange logic, Robin, if you don't mind me saying.'

'No, it really isn't. That's how his mind works. He psychologically abuses me. If he knows we're together, then he'll use whatever he can to pull us apart.'

He flinches. At which part? The notion of us being separated? Or at the idea of us being together in the first place? Have I got ahead of myself? This is torture, it really is. I never thought he would be like this; I thought we'd go to the pub, have a drink, then forget about all the nastiness. Why did he have to bring up Henry? Or rather, why did Amber have to? If she's trying to break me, she's doing an admirable job, I have to give her that.

'I think perhaps we shouldn't go out tonight,' he says slowly, fiddling with his shirt cuff. 'You look overwrought.'

'Don't you want to?'

'It's not that I don't want to, it's that you seem upset. And that's not surprising. I still think you should get in touch with the police.'

'There's no point,' I say heavily. 'But if you don't want to take me out, that's fine. I can't force you.'

The silence between us is a gulf, full of private thoughts. He's studying the atlas at the window, rather than looking at me, and his body language screams discomfort. I don't like where this is leading.

'Look,' I say, forcing myself to be calm. 'It's been a tough day. But I'd love a drink, if you're still up for it.'

He opens his mouth. Closes it again. Then, finally, takes a deep breath. 'I think we'd best give it a miss.'

'But why?'

'I don't know. I've got concerns, Robin.'

So there it is. The admission. He has concerns. He was happy enough to put those concerns to one side while he was having sex with me, but now they're suddenly important. He's just the same as Henry – just as worthless, just as selfish.

'What are those concerns, exactly?' I say, each word a stalactite, hanging in the air. I wish the words were glass, like those shards on the floor, then they could cut him to pieces.

'Let's talk tomorrow, when you've had a chance to have a good sleep. And honestly, if you want me to call the police for you now, I will. I don't want you feeling unsafe.'

'No, I don't want to talk tomorrow. What concerns?'

'Let's leave it. Forget I mentioned it.'

'Tell me.'

'Only that you're a hard woman to fathom out. And some of the things you say; well, they seem a bit—'

'A bit what?'

'I don't know. Let's—'

'A bit *what?*'

He shakes his head. 'I feel like there's someone else, hiding in the Robin I've grown fond of. Don't take this the wrong way, but have you seen a doctor recently? It might help to have someone to talk things over with. It's clear that your ex-partner did some real damage, and not just to your window.'

'Are you trying to say there's something wrong with me?'

'No. Not at all. Only that sometimes, you remind me of a man I used to know, when I lived on the streets. He was a good fellow, friendly enough, but he'd suddenly flip and turn in on himself, say things that didn't add up with what he'd said before.'

'My God, and you're saying I'm like that?'

He blushes. 'No, not nearly so bad. He was obviously mentally ill. But I don't know, I worry about you sometimes. That's all.

Sometimes you remind me of Amber – she finds it difficult to manage her emotions, too.'

'For goodness' sake, I haven't got anything wrong with me and I am *nothing* like your daughter.'

My fists are curling, though I don't mean them to. I mustn't show this rage, though I want to hurt him so badly right now. To get that knife that I've hidden, to violate him with it, as he violated me. I *let* him, and all for nothing, because look at how he sees me! A thing to be pitied, to be wary of, even. He has taken my substance, the very heart of me, and twisted it into something revolting.

'See, that's another issue,' he says, warming to the topic now. Clearly he's been wanting to get this off his chest for a while. 'You're always having a go at Amber. She can't help how she is, you know. She's a brilliant, good-hearted woman and I don't like how you insinuate that she's otherwise.'

'Because she's been horrendous towards me, that's why!'

'But she hasn't! I've been there with you most of the time. She's just being Amber. A bit abrupt, but perfectly friendly. She even tried to help you with that newspaper article, as she thought it'd boost your confidence.'

'She had no right to presume I wanted such a thing.'

He holds his hands out, shielding himself from me. 'Let's not fight,' he says eventually, in a softer tone. 'We've been good friends up until now. I'd like that to continue.'

'Friends? Is that what we are? Do you normally *fuck* your friends?'

'Robin, that's ugly, and very unlike you. You're usually so ladylike.'

'You've got me all wrong.'

'Maybe so.' He shifts on the spot. 'I'm going to go home now. We can talk more tomorrow, when you're less upset.'

'Bill, don't go, please.' One last try. I have to stop him, otherwise this is all at an end, and everything will have been for nothing. I rush over, drape my arms around his neck and pull his face towards me. He resists the kiss, lips stonelike, resolutely closed, and moves me firmly backwards, like a father reprimanding a child. It is horrifying in its finality.

'You get some sleep,' he says firmly. 'And if you feel worried in the night, please call the police. They're the best people to help, you know.'

Are they? I remember the police at my door, all those years ago, how they manhandled me once they'd found you, how they pressed my head down to get me into the back of their car. And how the neighbours stared, all of them craning over their balconies to get a better view. It was one of them who phoned, I'm certain of it, who heard the noise and immediately jumped to the wrong conclusions, tainting them against me, right from the start. People are sickening, and that means Bill too: he's no better than the rest of them. I reach towards him, but he's already moving down the hallway, opening the door. A last rueful glance over his shoulder, and he's out, and all the while, I stare like a slack-mouthed simpleton. Like Ditz would have done, or some other sheep-eyed fool with no intelligence.

I am alone again, then. Just as I always seem to be, in the end.

'You seem very agitated today, Robin, if you don't mind me saying,' Dr Holland says.

I hardly hear him. To be honest, I'm not even sure how I got here; my feet found their own way, quite independently of my conscious thoughts. My hair is damp, my trousers too. It must have been raining.

'May I ask a question?' I say frankly.

He looks startled, but nods.

'How long must we continue this farce?'

'Farce? Robin, these are important—'

'That's not even my real name. I am who I am; I can't be moulded into someone else.'

He takes a deep breath, then crosses one leg over the other. 'Robin,' he says patiently, 'nobody is attempting to strip you of your identity.'

'That's *exactly* what you're doing. You've given me this ridiculous name, Margot's trying to make me find an unsuitable job even though I'm unemployable, you've stuck me in a house that I wouldn't choose to live in if someone paid me, and—'

'Please, let me stop you there, as I sense this is adding fuel to the fire. Let's look at those points from a different angle, shall we? Your new name protects you. Having a job would give you something to focus on. And you have been given a roof over your head, when the other alternative was fending for yourself on the streets. Some might say these are gifts, Robin, not curses.'

I think of Bill, lying in a doorway somewhere, sleeping bag pulled up to his unshaven chin. Dr Holland is frustratingly correct; I couldn't have coped with living like that, and I suppose I should be grateful that the state pays for my accommodation. But the reality of this existence is appalling; it's hardly living at all. I'm under attack, I'm at the mercy of a spiteful woman next door who's hell-bent on destroying me, and—

'Robin? What do you think about what I've just said?'

I bring my gaze back to his. 'I'm sure you're right.'

He nods, satisfied. 'As for being unemployable, my notes say you've only attended one job interview so far. There may well be the perfect career out there, just waiting for you to find it.'

'My perfect career? I don't care about any of that. I just want to move away.'

'Okay, let's talk more about that. Where to?'

'Anywhere. As far away from other people as possible.'

'But what about the boyfriend you mentioned in our last session?'

I'd forgotten I'd talked about Bill last time I was here. I shake my head. 'It didn't work out.'

'Is that why you're feeling angry today?'

'No, it has nothing to do with it. The man wasn't worth much, that's all.'

'What makes you say that?'

'Because he's a user, just like every other male.'

He scribbles something down in his notepad. Sometimes I yearn to reach across and rip that damned thing to pieces, then force-feed him the paper, all in one screwed-up bunch. It would probably choke him, which admittedly wouldn't be an easy death. I've never seen anyone choke before, but I can envisage what it would be like. The dawning realisation that the obstruction won't budge. The frantic, unproductive swallow reflex. Eyes bulging. Hands flailing. Garbled words, wheezed out under a flagging oxygen supply.

He coughs, oblivious to my thoughts. 'Do you really believe that, Robin?'

'Believe what?'

'That every man is inherently out to use you?'

I scowl. 'Aren't they?'

'I can't tell you the answer to that.'

No, I think. Because you're a man, and you all stick together.

He makes a few more notes, then looks up. 'We need to discuss your medication, and how it's been going. Do you feel that you're sleeping better now?'

Yes, because sleep is all that matters. My emotions, my mind – that's all secondary. I resist the urge to scream at him, to open my mouth and let the fury fly out, and instead nod dutifully. 'It's been much better.'

'That's good, that's what we want to hear. Obviously I can't prescribe you any more, but—'

'Yes, I know.'

'And your general mood? I've noted that you seem tense today. What have you noticed about yourself?'

'Nothing.'

'Hmm.' Again, that appraising look – the one that makes me want to punch him, hard. 'Robin, I think we might call this session to a halt today.'

'But we've still got seven minutes to go.'

'I'm aware of that. But I sense it won't be productive, unless of course you have anything you'd like to discuss?'

How about how utterly useless you are? I think. How about how I believe the world would be a better place without you, and others like you, in it?

'I think I'd like to refer you for further assessment,' Dr Holland says finally, fingers tapping a slow rhythm on his thigh.

'Why?'

'It's for your benefit, to ensure we're offering the very best care possible, both for you and those around you.'

'You're not treating those around me.'

'Yes, but they may be impacted by… You know what I mean. It's part of the rehabilitation programme.'

I wonder if he's spoken to Amber. Maybe even Bill. That would make sense, that they'd get in touch with those who live next door to an ex-inmate. Why hadn't I thought of it before? Even as the words filter through me, the enormity of the realisation hits, like a boulder dropped in water.

Bill perhaps already knew. Amber already knew. They were stooges, put there to monitor me, to see how I was behaving.

That doesn't make sense. Bill wouldn't have slept with me, that would be construed as unprofessional. But what if that's how they do it these days, in a clandestine manner? For all I know, offering sexual services is part of the programme, ensuring the inmate is kept content and is thus less likely to hurt others. How ironic, if that were the case. No. No. But… maybe. I don't know what to believe.

'Robin? You've gone very quiet.' Dr Holland's voice is clamorous as a castanet, piercing through my private thoughts.

'I would like to leave now,' I say quietly.

CHAPTER 21

I keep seeing you today – you and Ditz. Why must you appear together? Why do you sometimes become blended in my mind?

This morning, when I woke, you were at the foot of my bed. Pale, ghastly pale, but at least with skin and flesh on you. There were tear-stains on your cheeks, which proves it's all just a hallucination, because in life, you hadn't looked like that when you cried. You were blotchier then, puffy as a sightless mole, calling out over and over.

Ditz is hanging in my wardrobe. I see the top of her head, poking out over the top of my rail, then the rest of her when I yank the clothes aside. She looks demented, neck broken, mouth slack as a thirsty dog. I know she's not there, but that doesn't help the matter. Especially when she starts to laugh.

I wonder if anyone misses her. She only ever talked about her sister, but perhaps there was a man who meant more than others. A distant cousin who sometimes still gives her some thought. An old teacher even, who remembers the young Ditz as a wide-eyed, frightened girl, capable of nothing of any importance. I doubt it. She was a true nobody, which is why when she talked about dying I told her it was probably for the best. Why would you linger in a world like this one? I may have told her to end it all too many times. But I was doing her a favour, really. She had no purpose in life.

What's my purpose? I wonder. But I won't let myself think along those lines. I'm not her; I wouldn't even consider doing something so cowardly.

I see you out of the corner of my eye, throughout the day. When I open the fridge, I spy you in the gap in the door, watching me. When I go upstairs, I sense your footsteps close behind, slow and steady as a tap dripping. You are dogging me relentlessly, trying to tell me something. I'm not sure I'll ever understand what you want.

That day when you were at my house, after you'd tired of the baby starling and had enough of the card games, you asked me to take you home. I told you to wait, because I wanted to get to know you a bit better. This wasn't unreasonable, and that's why my voice rose in volume. I was only trying to make you see that. You *owed* me, don't you see? For your father's crimes. I wanted some sort of explanation from you, a reason for what he did, and why he chose to destroy me.

I offered to play more games with you. I had chess, Ludo, and the deck of cards of course. I would have happily cooked dinner for you. I was a good cook; I'd taught myself from scratch. But you became ill-mannered and that was so unexpected. You became like him: brutish, curt, hurtful. You called me names, then tore my hands from your shoulders like they repelled you. I was only trying to calm you down. Ironically, I was worried that you'd hurt yourself. You were so fragile, in so many ways. We *had words*. That's what my father always called it, when he told me off. And I'll admit, when you started to cry, it nearly broke me. You were so small, in that moment. A thin, neglected chick, desolate and calling for help.

I should have let you go. I *would* have, don't you see? If you hadn't said you'd tell them, if you hadn't said those other horrible things, I would have pulled open the front door and let you walk out. That was always my intention. But you called me *mental* and said I had something wrong with me. How could you say that? It was so unfair, especially after all I did for you.

I reached for you again, though you batted at my hand with weak, feathery blows that I took as a sign of your despair. How like me you were; how alone, in the midst of your family. How ignored, how uncherished. I pulled your head to my chest and pressed you to me, tenderly as any mother would. But you resisted. Even then, when I was showing you such kindness despite your brutality, you pushed me away.

You should have been mine. Everything would have been so different if you'd come from me and not Miranda. A different life would have enveloped us then: me at the oven, cooking your dinner. You sitting at the table, pencil in mouth, scribbling sums for your homework. Henry, calling a cheery *hello*, hanging his coat up, smiling at the sight of us both. I shared this with you, I think. I don't know – the memories are knotted together like tangleweed, some belonging in other places, others perhaps not real at all.

You shoved me away, and I asked, over and over, what I'd done wrong. I tugged you back from the hallway, but not to hurt you. Only to protect you from yourself. All the while, it was about you, never me. I may have pulled you too hard. I did. I know I did. It astonished me, how strong my slender arms were at that moment. You fell backwards, out of my grip. It was a fall, not a push, despite what the lawyer said. How birdlike your voice was. The desolate cry of a creature tumbling from a great height, when really it was such a short way to the floor.

Your head connected with the corner of the coffee table. Nasty cheap thing, all angles and hard edges. It was a soft, giving sound, like a brick dropped in wet concrete. And your eyes went on staring at me, even as your body started to convulse.

Everyone said afterwards it was deliberate, but it wasn't. You know this is true, because you were there. It was entirely your own fault. Not that I was angry. I knelt down, cradling your head. That's the thing with head wounds: they bleed terribly, so they often look far worse than they really are.

The court was more concerned with the sleeping pills, of course. They came up a lot, in the case against me. It wasn't surprising. I can see how it must have looked. But I only meant to keep you calm, while I worked out what to do for the best. You were so frightened. You were panicking at the sight of all the blood, and the pills, they always calmed me down, don't you see? I believed they'd do the same for you. I only gave you more to make them work more quickly. They certainly worked quickly, but not in the way I planned. At the time, their effectiveness seemed like grim justice, repayment for your cruel rejection of me. Now, I realise it was your revenge. It marked the start of my suffering for many years to come.

You guzzled that blackcurrant squash down like a puppy, and the pills with it, though some slopped down your top, and some onto my carpet, too. It was the shuddering that was the problem; I wasn't able to keep you still. Your eyes rolled to white about a minute afterwards, and I believed you were at peace, though your blood kept on leaking. So much, for such a thin, narrow boy. It made a mess of your hair, my carpet, my hands. I wept, not that the court believed that either. After you became still, you were perfect as a newborn. So quiet, so calm. I stroked your forehead again and again, and hummed a tune to you, hoping you'd hear it.

It wasn't my fault, it was only one random event after another. That's life, isn't it? It throws us this way and that, and we have no say in any of it.

I can't think about it – it's agony to do so – but it's impossible not to, when you follow me around. You are here now, fitting and shaking as you did then. All that froth at the corners of your mouth – I never knew it was possible for a human to produce so much. The crying is worse, though. The begging. The caught sob in the back of the throat, the way your hands stretched upwards in the last moments, as though trying to grasp something out of reach. I'd give anything to make those memories go away.

The prosecution accused me of *watching without mercy*. How dared they judge me, when they hadn't been there to see what happened? There was no greater mercy than the way I thumped your back, trying to make you vomit the drink up. I even poked my fingers down your throat, but you kept flopping backwards, then your teeth bit down, hard and sharp.

Please. I can't think of it, I can't. I don't want to get to the part where I knew you were – when I knew I'd—

When I laid you back on the floor, and that awful *sigh* escaped from your lips, like everything was just sliding away, and—

I'm crying. Oh God, look at me, I can't stop. This heaving, it's tearing through me, it will break me apart, I know it will. And I hear Ditz's laughter. I think this is what she wants, to see me shatter into pieces. Jean is here too, somewhere, watchful and waiting. They are here, they are *all* here, and they want me dead: Bill, Amber, Henry, Miranda, they all want me dead, but still I live. In spite of them all, *still I live.*

I sink to the floor. Down. Down.

It's dark but I don't care. The darkness is better in some ways, because I only *sense* you then, instead of having to see you. There are other people in the house, I swear. Jean is lurking above me somewhere, in the attic perhaps, searching for her pills. Her feet are dragging across the floorboards, she can't walk properly, she's clutching her chest and she's confused, she doesn't know what's happening to her.

Daddy is somewhere else, but he's facing away, no doubt focused on other more important things. He always had his eyes fixed on birds, or Jean; anything but me. What a disappointment I must have been to him, such a drab, uninteresting daughter. Is he laughing now? Or is it crying? No, he never wept. Even at Jean's funeral, he remained impassive, and not a tear was shed, not even when they lowered her coffin into the ground. One of the ropes loosened too quickly and the upper corner hit the earth with an ungainly thump. Her head must have lolled and rolled inside, like a badly thrown bowling ball.

There are women all around me too, endless rows of women, banging at their metal doors. Screaming obscenities. Wailing, howling, shrieking things like *your fault, you did it, Butcher Bird, you're the one to blame, you should die, you should do it now.* Those corridors, with their rows of locked doors, they went on forever, into the darkness, always the darkness. My arms are around my head to block them. My body has adopted a rhythm of its own. Back and forth, back and forth, like a rocking horse. It's incantatory, it takes them further away, like a protective shield. I'm in my mother's arms; she's stroking my hair without saying a word. She never needed to say anything, it was just *her*, her soft breath, the warmth of her cheek on mine. But Daddy said she was a mouse, that she was feeble, that she had no thoughts of her own. She held him back, he was unable to do his research while she was there, and so—

And so. Rock forward.

And so. Rock back.

I cannot focus. My mind whirls, it rushes me with it, I am swept in memories, emotions, opinions. Words spatter through me, some needle-sharp, others fuzzy, unformed.

You are next to me. You've handed me some pills, or did I get them myself? I can't remember, I don't know how they got here – or how *I* got here, crouching on the floor. *Take them*, you whisper. *Take them and it will calm you.* I want to be calm; I want to stop all of this. But will I end up like you? Frothing on a carpet, back arching like a pinned snake?

The pills are shaking. No, it's my hand, that's why they're making that noise. I don't know what to do.

What would you have me do?

Somewhere in the darkness, I see Miranda. Not as she must be now, older, greyer, wider-hipped, but as she was then, when she visited me in prison.

How upright she was, sitting in that plastic chair, hands pressed together on her lap. How straight and tense, rigid as a board. Her lip quivered at the sight of me. Her eyes fixed on mine, burrowed deep, seeking me out, dragging whatever she could find to the surface. *I want to know why you did it*, she said. *Why you killed my boy. My therapist said I needed closure; you owe me that much.*

My tongue was concrete. My lips stuck fast, unable to speak. What could I have said? Only that I never meant it to happen, that it was as torturous to me as it was her? I must have babbled something, in the end, but she didn't hear me, didn't want to listen. I expected tears, then. A wild outpouring of rage, finger-nails reaching for my neck, my face. But instead she sneered, something that was so much harder to endure. *You can't even give me an apology, can you?* she hissed. *I pity you. You're unbelievably pathetic.*

Pity. That word, worse than *hate.* Worse than anything. She had no right to pity me. It was I who should have pitied her, for her inherent greed, for her willingness to put up with an unfaithful husband for the sake of a few designer handbags and exotic holidays. She was the pathetic one, because she'd lived her life as a trapped creature. I'd dared to be free.

Still, I couldn't answer her, not right then, only convey my feelings through glaring, through the clenching of my fists. Her words kept on flowing; each one a polished rock, thrown at my face. She gave me no time to compose myself.

You're so pathetic that you'd take the life of a child, rather than face me or Henry. You're weak and feeble, and look at you now. It should have been you that died, not him. He was stronger as a child than you'll ever be as a grown woman.

I didn't reply, only raised my hands. It was a defensive gesture as much as anything, a way to ward her off, to repel the foulness spewing from her mouth. The guards grasped me a moment later, tugged me backwards until the chair tilted beneath me and threatened to tumble to the floor. She laughed, though her eyes were wet with some sort of emotion. Pity, maybe. I'm sure her expensive therapist explored it with her afterwards.

You deserve to suffer, you monster, she said, over the noise. *I hope the weight of what you've done never leaves you.*

But I didn't do the thing she was accusing me of. It wasn't like that, it really wasn't. No, that's untrue. It was, in a way. That's the irony of life, isn't it? It seldom exists in blacks and whites, only in ambiguous shades of grey. I am a creature of grey, now. Stuck in neither one place nor another, and unable to progress. Her curse was effective after all, because I *have* suffered, and the weight of it all has never gone away.

Somewhere, in the dark, I hear sobbing. Not Miranda, because she didn't shed a single tear that day, or at least not in front of me. Not Ditz either, nor you, with your terrible, tear-stained face.

It's me, I realise, with astonishment. And with unspeakable, desperate sadness. I'm the one who's crying, because everything is ruined. Because it has been since you died, or perhaps even before that. There's no hope, none at all.

Monster. Butcher Bird. Murderer.

Ava.

I know, as soon as I wake up, that I have had a bad episode. This is what they called it in prison, whenever I got upset about something and they took me to see the nurse.

I haven't had one in a long time. It's been several years, in fact. Stress is the trigger. That and the burden of coping with everything. I'm not mad. They always told me that, and I think they are absolutely correct. I am the sanest person I know; I just have a tendency to get overwrought when people mistreat and abuse me.

The sleeping pills are beside me. I raise the pot and give it a tentative shake. It's still fairly heavy, there's plenty of rattle inside. That's good. I remember in the past that I had dark thoughts during these depressive episodes, and I would hate to think that I'd done anything silly. My head hurts, though, just by the temple. Strange, there's a scab there, in the same place where you hit your head against the coffee table. I must have walked into a wall or something, though I have no recollection of the incident.

Standing is a little difficult. I feel stiff, creaky as a door that hasn't been used in several years. My head spins, and I steady myself against the wall. I need some food and drink; I'm not sure if I had any yesterday. My stomach growls as a timely answer to my question.

Downstairs it is, then. It isn't so hard, once I get my feet moving. The walls feel strange to touch, the space twisted and stretched in places, too tight in others. It will be fine, though. Everything will be fine, as long as I keep moving and focusing.

There's not much food. Bread will do, though the loaf is somewhat hard. I don't have any butter, but I can pour oil on it, or else use a sprinkle of water to soften it. Is that the done thing, or is that odd? I feel as though I've forgotten all these little life skills, and my mind feels unformed and soft as a baby's.

As I pop a slice in the toaster, I hear knocking. It takes me a while to make the connection, but it's the door, of course. I hope and pray it's not the stalker, that I won't have to endure anything more. I can't, I'm stretched taut as an elastic band.

The shape in the glass is female. Not Bill. Margot. I can see that she has her red coat on today, so it must be cold out.

'I wasn't expecting you,' I say, as I open the door.

She looks me up and down, and her eyes widen. 'That's pretty obvious. Robin, what happened to your head?'

'I tripped and fell.'

'You should get that looked at, it's a nasty wound.'

'It's not our meeting today, is it?'

She tuts, then steps inside without being asked. 'I emailed. Dr Holland got in touch. We need to carry out a quick review to see how you're getting on. Also, I thought it would be a good time to talk through your job interview.'

'I can't face it right now,' I tell her, as she marches through to the kitchen. Her gasp is audible, even from the hallway.

'Robin, what the hell happened to the window?'

'Thugs broke it.'

'Jesus. I know this is a rough area, but this is terrible. You'll have to do something about it.'

'With what money?'

'The money the state gives you.'

I sit dully on the chair, eyes fixed on the table. I don't need this; I can't bear to hear her droning, judgemental voice, nagging at me.

She sits, then sniffs the air. 'Were you making some toast? Don't let me stop you.'

'I'm not hungry any more.'

'Well, don't go without on my account. It's good to look after yourself.'

'Go on then,' I say heavily, waving a hand in her direction. 'Get it over with.'

Her frown tells me all I need to know. They're concerned, I can see from her expression. They want to assess how I'm doing, to see if they can send me back to prison and, this time, throw away the key. They think it's for the best, that otherwise I may damage myself or others. That's how they treat people like me, as hazards to be removed as quickly as possible, with minimal fuss. All it needs is the smallest excuse to justify the removal.

'Dr Holland has requested a further psychological profile,' she says slowly, 'as he's worried about how you're handling life at the moment.'

'I'm handling it just fine.'

'Hey, don't shoot the messenger. He's the professional, so I presume he knows what warning signs to look out for.'

'I don't come with a warning, I'm not a dangerous product.'

She doesn't smile. 'Come on,' she says instead, leaning across the table. 'Tell me honestly, are you finding things difficult? You don't seem great today; you're still in your nightdress, it's got a big stain down it that might be blood, and your head is all messed up. Something's not right.'

'So?' I shake my head. 'No one cares. As long as I behave myself, that's the main thing, right?'

'People do care. The rehabilitation process is taken seriously, and there's support in place to help you to—'

'Now you sound like him. I thought you were a bit more real than that.' I'm aware that the words tumbling from my lips will do me no favours, but I don't care. Let them hear what I really think, for a change. Let's see how they cope with me refusing to play their game.

'Dr Holland said you'd been prescribed some—'

'The medication is fine, before you ask.'

206

She rests her chin on her hands and gives me a hard stare. 'Okay. What about the interview? I heard that you didn't exactly fight to get the job.'

'Who told you that?'

'I received feedback, it's standard practice after—'

'She told you I didn't try? She's a liar. It was her who was horrible. She told me I didn't stand a chance, that I might as well give up, because no one would hire someone who'd... someone with my conviction.'

Margot takes a deep breath. She's troubled, that much is obvious, but not about me. No one's concerned about me really. Instead, she sees this as yet another problem in her life, an annoyance to be dealt with, an obstacle to overcome. I am a cockroach, and she badly wants something to spray me with.

'As part of your rehabilitation,' she says slowly, as though talking to a child, 'I need to verify that you're able to function in the normal world. There's a whole checklist of things, and one of those is being able to search for employment or do a job, the other is—'

'I'm searching for jobs. I sent off other applications.'

'I know. I also need to ensure that you're not endangering yourself in any way. I don't like the look of your head wound. I think I'd like to send someone over later in the week, get them to check you over.'

'You mean a psychiatrist or something, don't you? I can tell.'

She doesn't answer. She doesn't need to. This life, such as it is, is falling apart at the seams, it's crumbling under me, and it's so sad, because I was doing well. I was looking after myself, I was talking to people, I was acting how they wanted me to, like a standard human being. But now I realise that I'll never meet their requirements. I'll never tick all the boxes on their checklist. Because I don't fit, I never have. There's no place for me in this world.

'Fine,' I say dully, though my mind is already whirring, making plans. 'You do whatever you think is necessary.'

She flicks through her notes, then frowns. 'It might not be until next week, actually. Everyone's so stretched at the moment, what with all the cuts they're making. In the meantime, I'd like you to take whatever meds Dr Holland has recommended.'

'What if I need help?'

'What sort of help?'

'I just wonder if you'll ever be able to help me. Because I'm alone, really, aren't I?'

She shakes her head. 'Aren't we all, Robin?'

What a response. This planet is unravelling, and all we do is shrug at each other and say, what can we do about it?

I will do something about it. My life is my own, and it's time I took charge of it.

I rest on the sofa. I stare at the walls, at their magnolia blandness, and I drift in and out of sleep. My head lolls. During the moments of consciousness, my temple aches. Yours must have felt like this, after the incident. I have more sympathy for you now; it's a ceaseless pressure and it leaves me disorientated.

The sky turns from watery blue to grey, then slowly to black. The nights are drawing in, and winter will be here before we know it. Coldness. Ice. Snow, perhaps, to cloak everything in whiteness. I remember those snowed-in seasons on the islands: the drifts against the front door, the patterns of the flakes against my solitary bedroom window, my fingers numb when I pressed the pane, cooling to deathly paleness.

A soft thump brings me back from this chill, brittle memory. It's the sound of a letter landing on the doormat, I'd be willing to put money on it. I sit up, exhausted by the inevitability of it. This is how it must be, of course. It isn't as if they're going to leave me alone now, not after they've begun their persecution. It must be from Amber. Who else would deliver something at this time of evening? She's convinced she's got me on the run; I imagine she believes she's already won.

I peer around the doorframe to see the small, white envelope, exactly the same size as before, sitting primly in the middle of my doormat. Sure enough, there's my name emblazoned across it.

My real name. *Ava.* I feel no fear, not any more. She's had her fun with me, she's made me wary, then made me feel as though I'm losing my mind. This will end soon, though; it's time for me to regain control. She will learn to fear me instead, she and Henry both. I'll wait until the time is right, then rip them both to pieces.

The letter is longer than usual. It would seem that Amber has hit her stride and warmed to her task.

AVA,

I HOPE YOU ENJOYED THE PRESENT THROUGH YOUR WINDOW. IT IS NOTHING COMPARED TO WHAT I'VE GOT PLANNED. I WANT YOU TO SUFFER LIKE YOU MADE HER SUFFER. YOU ARE AN EVIL DISCUSTING WOMAN AND I WILL MAKE SURE YOU END UP DEAD IN AN UNMARKED GRAVE. I KNOW YOU HAVE SEEN ME. KEEP WATCHING YOU BITCH, YOU WILL SEE MORE OF ME SOON.

She really needs to learn how to spell. I shall bring it up with her, when I'm force-feeding this bilge down her throat. Choking would be apt for her: all of those poisonous words can finally be silenced as she gobbles them down. She also needs to get the gender right. The last time I checked, you were a boy, not a girl. It's further proof that she's just operating on Henry's orders, and getting it badly wrong.

I open the door. It's dark outside, the road already packed with the parked cars of people back from work. Rain mists the air, making the street lights fuzzy. There is someone on the pavement up ahead, wearing that coat. That hat. The same cocky, knowing posture. It's *her.*

I have courage; I can do this. I step outside, push the gate open, then stand there facing her, hands on hips. Wetness soaks through my socks in an instant, but it doesn't matter. I want her to know that I will face her, and I will win.

It's definitely Amber. I don't know how I could have doubted it before. The figure has the same height and body shape.

The little details confirm it too, like the slightly hunched, defensive shoulders. Now she's facing me, mirroring my pose. Her attempt to intimidate me is laughable.

'It won't work!' I shout. The words are carried along on the quiet evening air. 'I know who you are, you stupid woman. It's been obvious, right from the start.'

Amber's head twitches. I can see it, even from this distance, even though I still can't see her face. *There*, I think, bathed in satisfaction. *Now she knows who she's dealing with.*

'You're a coward, do you know that?' I call, aware that there's a shrill edge to my voice, but powerless to prevent it. This feels too good, and the only thing that would be more enjoyable would be to annihilate her for good. I should have brought one of my knives out with me; there's one by the door that I could have easily grabbed on the way out. She'd soon realise her mistake as the blade slipped through that coat, through skin, through ribcage.

An image comes to mind. Showing Ditz how to make a shiv, like the other inmates did. It was so easy to sharpen everyday items, providing you had the ingenuity to do it. I pressed it to her stomach, and it made me chuckle to see how she recoiled. *It's so easy to finish someone*, I said to her. *Or yourself.* Ditz certainly discovered that truth.

'Aren't you going to say anything?' I scream.

The woman, *Amber*, shakes her head. It's frustrating that she won't reveal her face, that I can still only make out a hint of chin beneath that hat, but I suppose that's a good sign. She's too frightened to do it, to engage with me as equals. She knows I'd destroy her.

'You're revolting,' I shout. 'Look at you, cowering there like a child. Do you think you scare me? Is that what you've been telling Henry?'

A front door opens, somewhere on my left. The light this casts just about reaches me, and I hear muttered voices. It's not much, but it's enough to make me disorientated. My focus shifts, and I'm aware of movement by my side. Suddenly someone moves in front of me, blocking my view. It's a man, big-shouldered and with a ridiculous beard reaching nearly to his chest. I don't know him; I've never seen him before. He's joined by someone else, female, double-chinned, concerned expression, lots of dark hair.

'Are you okay?' she asks. 'We heard shouting.'

'It's that bitch up there,' I say, moving aside, pointing up the street. It's no surprise to see that Amber's gone. I could sense how intimidated she was, and how she realised she was out of her depth. She's probably hiding somewhere now, or else she's run away out of fear.

The couple turn around, then look back at me.

'There's no one there,' the man says.

'I know that. I can see that. I'm not stupid.'

The woman glances at my wet feet. 'You're not wearing shoes. Shall we help you to get back inside?'

'I don't need help. I need that woman to stop making my life a misery.'

Now they're looking at each other, and it's easy to see what conclusions they're drawing. The wrong ones, naturally. Always, it's the wrong ones, because people don't bother to find out the truth. Because it's easier to form opinions based on scanty information and false evidence.

'I'm perfectly fine,' I tell them. 'Not mad, just angry. You don't know what I've been through.'

'Of course not,' the woman says, and reaches for my shoulder. I move backwards, ducking out of her clasp. It's time to go back home, there's no point lingering out here. Amber has gone; no doubt she'll come up with some other horrible plan in a day or so, but for now, she's running scared. The victory is mine tonight, not hers.

'Are you sure you're all right?' the man calls after me, as I walk back down the pavement. There seems little point in replying; he's nothing to me, after all. They can all go straight to hell for all I care.

The world should burn for how it treats people like me.

CHAPTER 22

I wake, and for a moment I think Henry is lying beside me. Not as he must look now, but as he was back then. The smooth ridge of his shoulder. The stubble of hair at the back of his neck. I can almost smell his scent – the vague spice of aftershave, the delicate musk of his body. Then it's gone, spectral-silent, and I realise I'm alone.

I must have dreamt of him. It's unusual, given how many pills I took; dreams are usually numbed to non-existence by the influence of drugs. Indeed, there are still dregs of images in my mind, memories of that one night he stayed at mine when Miranda took the kids to her mother's for the weekend. He reached for me in the morning, and gently pushed my hair out of my eyes. It was tender. It meant something. Or it did to me, anyway.

It's funny, how in these times of quiet and solitude I often have my most piercing moments of clarity. I can see the path forward now, and it relieves me that it's not Ditz's way out. I will not dangle by a rope, nor extinguish myself by any other means. I am too vital for that, and I mean to leave this place, parole terms or no parole terms. They will never find me; not where I'm going.

But first, there are some matters to be attended to, loose ends to be tied. I like to leave things neat and orderly at all times. I mean to deal with Amber, and I may as well do it today. She must learn that every action has a consequence.

To say that I hate her would be too strong. I've never been capable of hating anyone, regardless of how many people have almost driven me to it. She's been manipulated, that's all, just like I was, like countless other women have been in the past. But I won't be as generous as to say it's not her fault. She allowed herself to be used. I did the same, and I suffered for it. Now it's her turn.

It's a simple plan. The most effective ones usually are.

The sun is shining today. It reflects in the puddles in my garden; they sparkle with almost kinetic energy. There are webs too, hanging between the plant pots, glittering with moisture. Leaves laced with jewels. The clouds lolling peacefully by. This planet is such a beautiful place, even though it's so often shrouded in darkness.

I remove my old atlas from the kitchen window and breathe in the air through the gaping hole. This is how we were meant to live – not in our brick boxes, shut away from the elements, but as part of nature. We're at our best when we're deep within it, living as one of the earth's creatures. We were born to soar through the air, to burrow ourselves into soil for warmth. Not to hide behind glaring screens or be concealed in the invisible walls created by mobile phones. For just a moment, I am suffused with love. Not for *them*, those people out there. But for everything else. Everything where people are not. It is a good feeling. I will be all right; I really will.

My sleeping pills are laid out on the countertop. I've done well to save so many of my wonderful *little friends*, lined up neatly in front of me. The Victoria sponge mix is in the bowl next to it. It will be a small cake, to ensure the dosage is concentrated. Too large and the effects will be diminished. My two tins are fifteen centimetres in diameter, which means at least a quarter of a cake is likely to be consumed in one sitting. That should be enough. The tartness of the cherry jam will hide any residual taste.

The pill-grinding takes a long time. I wish I had a mortar and pestle, as Daddy did when we lived on the islands. They make this sort of arduous task much quicker. Instead, I make do with the back of a spoon. It pleases me, to see how resourceful I can be.

213

This is why I survived in prison for all those years. I look for opportunities. I create solutions to even difficult problems. I stand above the others and I *thrive*.

Finally the job is done, and the pill-dust is poured into the mix. The cake goes in the oven, and when it's cooked, I shall shave a sliver off the side, to check that it tastes as it should. There can be no discernible taste, no tang of bitterness. It wouldn't do to arouse any suspicions.

Now the cake is cooking, I need to prepare myself. Bill is no longer attracted to me, that's obvious. However, he may have been genuine when he said he wanted to be friends. He may also be arrogant enough to believe that I accept his terms. This peace offering will do the job. I can be charm itself when I want to be.

It feels like the end of an era, somehow, as though everything has been leading to this point, this moment of completion. Soon I will be born again into another life, an existence without a Margot or a Dr Holland. Without a Bill or an Amber. Without the memories of you to break me anew, every day. I don't know why I didn't dare do this before. I suppose I was still fooling myself that I could be what they wanted me to be: the docile garden bird, happy to hop from fence to fence to accept their scraps.

That's not me, though. It will never be me.

I look pleasing, if I do say so myself. I have dressed in a dove-grey skirt and cream cardigan. Coastal colours, somehow, the crags of the cliffsides painting my body. The stress of the last few days has made me thinner, but that's not a problem; this skirt skims flatteringly over the protrusions of hip bone. My shoulder blades jut outwards as I flex my arms. My wings, I think. I feel buoyed by them, how they pulse and writhe under the skin. My make-up is subtle and elegant. None of the harlot lipstick today. No, this is about friendship and making amends, and I want him to feel warmly towards me. I want a lingering hint of his desire for me still to heat him below the surface. A concern is that Amber has already told him everything. But my suspicion is that she's still toying with me – on Henry's command, naturally. She's biding her time, and as such, she's given me some time of my own. It will be her downfall.

The cake looks delectable when I take it from the oven. I sample a tiny sliver from the side, and apart from a hint of bitterness in the aftertaste, it's fine. The extra sugar has helped to counterbalance the flavour, and after the jam and cream are added, it's virtually undetectable. I'm not sure what will happen to them after they eat it. I'm no expert on these matters. You were different; you were a child, and your body was less able to cope with the drugs. Jean was different too because her heart issues made her susceptible. I want to ensure something happens. They deserve to suffer: Bill for his treachery and selfishness, Amber for her relentless persecution.

What if nothing happens at all? This is a real worry. Maybe the quantity simply won't be enough. They'll feel drowsy, surely, though perhaps not until much later. But I don't want to think about these things right now. They are mere suppositions and aren't based on solid fact. Dr Holland always tells me to examine the facts, not my emotional responses, and on this rare occasion, he's correct. It's not helpful to have unfounded concerns at this stage.

I decide to wait until six o'clock. They will be at home then, I suspect. It has been a long yet satisfying day. I feel good. How I wish that Margot could see me now. She would leave with a very different impression of me. The weak Robin is gone, and I am fully myself again.

Evening closes in, and it is time. Cake tin in hand, plus a bottle of wine under my arm, I lock up the house. I am all action and decisiveness. They won't be able to resist me.

Bill's curtains are pulled, but I can see the warm glow of the light behind them. Indeed, I know him so well that I can sense him in there, watching television perhaps, or thinking about what to cook himself for dinner. Amber is in there too, I'd wager, staring at her phone or reading a trashy magazine. *I'm coming for you*, I think, and knock.

It takes a while for the door to open. Bill peers out, head shining in the hallway light. He smiles uncertainly.

'Hello there, Robin,' he says, taking me in from bottom to top. 'How are you?'

'Very well,' I say, and quickly hold out the cake tin and wine. 'I've come with a peace offering. Don't worry, it's a gesture of friendship and neighbourliness, nothing more. There are no expectations attached.'

He scratches his head, then takes them both from me. 'This is very kind of you. A homemade cake, no less?'

'My mother's old recipe,' I say, with a laugh. 'A good old Victoria sponge with extra jam.'

'That sounds wonderful.' He looks behind him, then frowns. 'I'd ask you in, but Amber's here, and I know that you—'

'That's part of the reason I've come over,' I say. 'I've had a few days now to think about things, and I know I've allowed my paranoia to overcome me. I'd like to apologise to your daughter; my conduct hasn't been good.'

'Really? I'm sure you don't need to say sorry, Robin, but she'd be delighted that you knew she wasn't out to get you.'

Actually, I expect she'll be rather confused about all of this, I think, keeping the same stupid smile fixed in position. 'Well, there's no pressure at all,' I say, 'but it would be lovely to come in for a quick drink, just to talk to her in person.'

He waves me in. It's fascinating how swiftly his posture has changed, from brittle wariness to warmth. What a gullible fool he must be, to imagine that all is forgiven, after everything he's done.

'I'm glad you popped over,' he says, as he gestures to the nearest sofa in the living room. 'I was worried about you. Did you call the police in the end?'

It takes me a while to realise what he's talking about. 'The window? No, there's no point. My ex would just have denied it. He's the reason I was so stressed out, but I've resolved not to let him ruin my life any longer. He's stolen too many years from me already.'

His eyes soften. It's an excellent sign. 'I'll pour us all a glass of wine,' he says, holding up the bottle. 'Amber's upstairs, I'll see if she can join us.'

'Don't forget the cake!' I say. 'I think it turned out rather nicely.'

He grins, then disappears down the hallway. I wait, listening to his mantlepiece clock ticking gently above the gas heater. It really is a disgusting room: dusty, grimy, unwelcoming. After living here for so long, he could have done *something* with it. Given the walls a lick of paint, perhaps, or added a few scatter cushions to this faded monstrosity of a sofa at least. Some people have no standards at all. They're content to live like pigs.

Footsteps clatter down the stairs, and I rearrange my expression into something amenable and apologetic. A moment later, Amber sticks her head around the doorframe. If she's shocked to see me, she does an excellent job in hiding it. But I must remember, she's adept at deception – a fact she's proved many times in the past.

'Hello, Robin,' she says, expression impassive. 'Dad said you were here to see me, as well as him.'

I smile, then stand. This is the moment to deliver the performance of a lifetime, as I know Bill is probably listening in.

'Yes, I very much wanted to see you, Amber,' I begin, voice dripping with authenticity. 'To apologise, you see. I don't know if your father has explained, but I've been having a terrible time with my ex-partner recently, and—'

She waves the rest of my comment aside, in a manner that's vaguely dismissive. 'I know all about difficult ex-partners,' she says, without meeting my gaze.

I bet you do. She's very familiar with Henry, I know that for a fact.

'I hope you'll accept my apology,' I say.

There's a moment of silence. I believe I've thrown her entirely off course. She's remembering our showdown on the street yesterday evening. She can't tally that with what's happening now, and her infantile brain doesn't know what to do for the best. I have the upper hand, at last.

'Who'd like some cake, then?' Bill's voice drifts down the hallway.

'Cake?' Amber says, eyebrow arching.

'I made one specially.'

'What sort?'

'Victoria sponge.'

She nibbles at a nail. 'That would be nice. I'll have a slice, Dad.'

Got them. It's simply too easy. But I mustn't get complacent; they haven't eaten it yet, and things may still go wrong. I won't be satisfied until I see every mouthful shovelled down that gullet of hers, and his too.

Bill brings the cake out on three plates, a fork on each. One for Daddy bear, one for Mummy bear, and one for Baby bear, I think, eying them in their neat row on the coffee table. Only this time, it's not that one is too hot, or too cold. Rather that they're all just perfect for what I have in mind.

'Where did you learn to bake?' he asks, sitting beside me, then handing a plate to each of us.

We had baking lessons in prison, ironically, though most of the inmates were more concerned with flicking cake mix at each other or trying to steal spatulas and mixing spoons for later use. Those lessons hadn't lasted. The government cuts meant that education of all kinds was kept to a minimum after a while.

'My mother taught me when I was younger,' I say, picking up my fork. Bill is the first to try it, a sizeable piece that's taking him a while to chew. Crumbs gather at the corner of his mouth. I can't imagine how I ever found him attractive. He's wrinkled as a tortoise, and those deep crevices around his nose and eyes make him look musty and unclean.

I delicately slice my fork into the cake, then put it to one side. 'What do you think?' I ask.

He nods. 'It's delicious.'

Amber's eating too now, I notice. I raise a tiny piece to my lips, making sure that it's mostly jam and cream. Those haven't been impacted by the pills at all, they were added for taste only.

Suddenly, Bill puts the plate down. 'I forgot the wine, didn't I? Dear me, how could I?'

I hold my hand up in protest. 'Honestly, I'm all right. That's for you and Amber later.'

'You sure? Cup of tea instead, then?'

'No, I'm quite all right.'

Amber wrinkles her face. 'The cake's got an interesting after-taste, hasn't it?'

Damn it. She suspects, I can tell. Not much, but there are warning bells, ringing in that duplicitous head of hers. I should have known; after all, we declared war on one another last night, out on the street. It's a miracle she's eating the cake at all, but perhaps she's more stupid than she looks.

'It could be the bicarbonate of soda,' I lie smoothly. 'I never know quite how much to add.'

She eats another mouthful, and I nod, satisfied. It's difficult to calculate how much they've had so far, but it's got to be the equivalent of around ten pills each, at least. That soporific feeling won't kick in yet, but it won't be far off. I should know; I've consumed enough of them in my time.

I eat another mouthful of jam.

'So, when are you going to get someone in to fix the window?' Bill asks, waving his fork at me.

'Soon, I hope. It makes the kitchen ever so cold.' I turn to Amber. 'Did your father tell you what happened? It makes you wonder who'd do such a thing, doesn't it?'

'Your ex-partner,' she says, glancing at her father. 'That's who it was, wasn't it?'

'Yes, of course. But what sort of a person thinks that behaviour is acceptable? I've never understood it.'

Her eyes narrow. She knows what I'm referring to. We're playing cat and mouse now, and the amazing thing is that she's still eating my cake. I can't quite believe it.

'Your ex-partner doesn't sound like a nice man,' she says. 'Mine wasn't either. But then, I suppose I can be tricky to live with.'

I'll say, I think, stomach turning at the way Bill's looking at her, like a dopey puppy gazing at its owner. 'Poor you,' I say, giving her my most insincere smile. 'It's hard, isn't it?'

'Your bloke was called Henry, is that right?'

Here we go. I knew this would be our battleground, our final fight. She's over halfway through the cake: that must be close to eighteen, maybe even twenty pills now. It'll kick in soon, I'm sure. I remember Jean, how her face became pallid, how she staggered to the sofa and told Daddy that she really needed to lie down, that the room was spinning. That process had been quick: ten, maybe fifteen minutes at the most? I wish I could recollect the details more clearly; a scientist should gather data for future reference, and I failed to do so. But of course, they were different pills. These sleeping pills – it shouldn't take much. I hope, anyway.

She raises an eyebrow at me. I remember now, she's asked me a question.

'He was called Henry,' I confirm.

'I thought you said it was Harry?' Bill says, fork suspended near his mouth.

I flinch. I *had* said that, he's right. 'His real name is Henry, but everyone called him Harry,' I say quickly. Then I turn to Amber. If we gloss over the name, Bill will be distracted. He's that sort of feckless, flitting type, which will serve me well right now.

'I know I shouted his name at you that day, didn't I?' I say, softening my eyes in remorse. 'I'm so sorry about that, it was a real lapse in—'

'Where does Henry live?' she asks.

'I… I don't know these days.'

'When did you last see him?'

'In person? A long, long time ago.'

She frowns. 'It's odd. Why would he bother to do it, if he hadn't seen you in so long? Especially if he left you, and not the other way around?'

'Sorry, Robin,' Bill says, patting Amber's knee. 'I told her a few details, but only to help her to understand what you were going through.'

You betrayed me again, you mean, I think. But it doesn't matter. None of it matters now.

'Why would he go to the effort of throwing a brick through your window?' Amber asks.

She's enjoying this. I shrug, unable to think of an answer. Bill's finished his slice, and the plate is back on the table. He's even scooped up all the crumbs. That's at least thirty, if not more, pills coursing through his system right now. It must be enough for something.

I notice a speck of glitter at the side of his mouth. Drool, just a tiny, shining pinhead, that grows into a stretching line. His eyes are unfocused. It's happening, it's *really happening*. And far, far faster than I'd ever dared imagine. Maybe the pills were more concentrated in his slice. Perhaps he's had something like fifty instead; there's no way of knowing.

The rope of spit elongates to breaking point, then lands on his knee. His eyes follow it there, creased in confusion. Another bubble of saliva follows, this one thicker, frothier. In fact, there's spittle all over his lips, a puffy, dirty cloud of the stuff.

He gargles something, then wipes at his mouth. Amber looks up, then gasps.

'Dad? Dad, are you all right?'

She shoves her plate on the sofa next to her. Two-thirds done; it's probably enough, I should think. But she's showing no signs of the pills kicking in, and that's dangerous. It needs to happen, and it needs to happen fast.

'Dad?' She looks over at me. 'He's having a fit, I think. Robin, find my phone; I'm sure I left it upstairs in my room. Quick!'

'My name's not Robin,' I say quietly.

'Please, just get the phone? He's shaking all over. Dad, can you hear me? Don't close your eyes, I need you to tell me what's wrong. Robin, please?'

'It's *not* Robin.'

Finally, she turns. 'What?'

'My name,' I say slowly, standing, 'is Ava. As you well know, you repulsive piece of shit.'

The confusion on her face is glorious. She doesn't know how I've bested her, she hasn't figured it out. But she's aware that her plans have gone badly, badly wrong, and this is the price she must pay for her actions. She's dragged her poor old father into it all, and what could be worse? Especially if she's killed him. She'll have to live with the pain forever.

'This is all your fault,' I tell her. 'You should have left me alone. You never should have worked with Henry.'

'I don't know who Henry even is!' she screams, then pats her father on the cheek. 'Dad? Dad? Jesus, Robin, was this you? Did you do something to him?'

I spread my arms. I raise them high. They are my wings, and I am in flight. Finally, I am fully me again, back in control. They cannot restrain me; none of them can.

'I did something to you both,' I tell her, with a smile. 'Because you deserved it.'

CHAPTER 23

I have not planned for what will happen next. The meticulous preparation of the cake, yes. The delivery, the eating, all of that was mapped out with a high level of precision. But I haven't given much thought to the *after*, mainly because I wasn't sure what would occur. This, I realise now, is unfortunate. I should have known that Amber, if anything, is unpredictable. She's serpent-sly and has proved it many times, a formidable opponent who shouldn't be underestimated. Fool that I am, I've failed to allow for this.

She picks up her cake from the sofa, and for one moment, I believe she will start eating it again, cramming those last morsels into her mouth, before keeling over next to her father. But that would be ridiculous, of course. Who would do that?

This moment of confusion costs me dearly. I watch as she raises the plate high above her head, but fail to guess her intentions until she swings it downwards, straight into the side of my head. The damaged side. At first I feel no pain, only the stunned shock of the impact, the horror that she dared to do such a thing, that she's still conscious enough to act this way, despite all the drugs that must be racing through her bloodstream.

Then it hits me, a burning, searing pain in my temple. There is wetness too; she must have broken the scab open, made the blood start pouring again. I reel backwards and nearly lose my footing in the process.

'You little bitch,' I hiss, and lunge at her. But she sidesteps easily, and whips the plate at my head again. How could I have failed to notice that she's still holding it? This time, it breaks on impact. Half tumbles to the floor, the other half she holds aloft, like a trophy.

'What did you give my father?' she shouts, pushing at me. I stumble, then trip. I don't know how it happens; I feel my feet are rooted and that no amount of pressure will bring me down. But somehow I am here, on the carpet, my skirt hitched around my thighs, only able to watch helplessly as she looms over me.

'You deserve to die, for what you've put me through!' I shout, holding a hand up to ward off another attack. My words are slurred, but I can't worry about that now. She's trying to kill me, after everything she's done to me already. Why are the drugs not working? They worked with Jean. They worked with you. This skinny little thing should be on her knees right now, foaming and frothing like her father.

'What the hell are you talking about?' she screams.

'You've been stalking me, threatening me, like you're some sort of avenging angel,' I stutter. 'But you're *nothing*. None of your scare tactics worked, you stupid girl. Don't you realise I used to eat feeble little chicks like you for breakfast when I was in prison?'

She raises her arm again. I can't stop her; she's too fast. Why is she so fast? It makes no logical sense at all. Now the jagged half-plate is flying towards me, gannet-dive quick, and I—

I hear groaning. It's me, *me*. I'm making the noise. My vision is blurred, and my head is pounding like an underground geyser, ready to erupt. There are rough fibres under my fingers. Carpet. Why am I lying on the floor, what happened to make me—

She attacked me with that plate. My thoughts are like treacle, oozing and sludging at far too slow a pace. I may be concussed – she certainly hit me hard enough.

Someone's speaking from the other side of the room. A high, panicked voice. Her.

'I'd say it's been ten minutes now,' she says. 'I think she must have put something in the cake. I've eaten it too. Yes, I can feel his pulse, but he's not responsive, not at all.'

If I had to guess, I'd say she was on the phone. Talking to the ambulance service, perhaps. Maybe the police. I need to act quickly. *Think, Ava, think.*

If I sit up, she will see me, and she'll most probably hit me again. But I can't lie here. If she's called for help, someone will be driving to this property right now. The policemen will be at the door, just as they were all those years ago. They'll drag me out to their car, then they'll press their hateful hands on my head to get me into the back seat. It'll be like that day with you, all over again. If that happens, I'll never get away, never make it to that island. That's all I ever wanted, why can't people see that? Just to be away from everyone, to sit on the cliff and listen to the waves on the rocks below, to graze my fingers against wild grass, to make a fire in the evening and rest beside it, entirely on my own. It isn't much to ask for, not really.

I move my head, just a little. Now I can see her, perched beside her father, hand pressed against his forehead. He doesn't look great, I have to confess. His skin has a sheen to it, and it looks grey. Not enough oxygen getting around his body. I think of him pressing down on me, his rough grunt of ejaculation before he rolled off. I wanted him to stop breathing then, if I'm being honest. This is payment for what he did to me.

But do I want to kill him? It's worrying that I'm not sure. I don't see myself in that light, as a cold-blooded murderer. No, I'm sure that isn't my intention. I only want to shake him up a bit, and to make him realise that he can't treat me like that. Men need to learn that women aren't commodities to be purchased, used, then tossed away. He saw me at my most vulnerable, and he walked away without a second thought. Perhaps I *do* want him to die. It wouldn't be anything less than he deserves. But I can't think of this now; I need to think instead about what to do. I shift my head again. There's the plate she used, lying beside her on the sofa. Her weapon, albeit broken. If I can get to that, I may stand a chance.

She's saying something else now. I must remain still, focus hard and listen for clues.

'I do feel woozy,' she says. 'My heart's beating faster too.' A pause, then, 'That's good, that's reassuring.'

Elation soars through me. If she's woozy, her reactions will be slower. But then, I'm not completely alert myself. The room is still out of focus at the edges, and everything sounds somehow muted, as though it's happening far, far away. The 'reassuring' comment isn't great either; they probably told her that someone would be here soon. I've got minutes to act, perhaps only seconds. Speed is of the essence. The skua, when waiting for the penguin egg to hatch, hovers nearby. The parent penguin is aware of their presence, but simply doesn't have the reflexes to protect their young. And so the skua acts, darting forward, seizing the chick in its beak, then flying away.

Actually, that's not always the case. Sometimes they rip the bird up in front of its parents, dismantling its dimpled, naked flesh, piece by piece. Not that this is an important detail, of course. But there's something about the image that fills me with power. Act quickly, I tell myself. The time has to be now.

I pitch myself over to one side, roll to my hands and knees, then stand, ignoring the howl of pain in my temple. She looks up, mouth a small circle of horror, and the phone slips out of her hand.

Now is my moment to attack.

Foolish girl – she misjudges my movements. She lunges at me just as I spin to one side and make a grab for the plate. I hear her groan of pain as she topples forward against the coffee table, and that's good, as it means she's weak. The plate is in my hand now and it feels so strangely light. How did it manage to inflict such damage? It's Amber's turn to find out now. I swing, the perfect arc, like an Olympic discus thrower. The plate catches her on the top of the head. She cries out, but manages to hurl her body in my direction. We fly as one, back against the gas heater. There's a thud of flesh against metal grille – my shoulder blade, slamming against it. My wings – she's trying to clip them.

'No you don't,' she hisses, face centimetres from my own. Her breath is pungent with a hint of jam, combined with something darker. Those pills are starting to play havoc with her digestive system. I shove against her chest and she pulls me with her. We tumble and scramble in a clumsy tangle of grasping hands, flailing arms and kicking legs. I am unbalanced, I can't get my bearings. A fist slams against my head, and the coffee table leg comes into sharp focus. She is on top of me, pressing down, one hand on my throat, the other pinning my wrist.

But she's underestimated me, again. She doesn't understand that I've faced inmates far stronger than her. It's all about the element of surprise, the sharpened shiv between the ribs. The smile one moment, the strike the next. I close my eyes. I flop. Her grip weakens, just a fraction. It's enough, though.

I bring my knee up, right between her legs. A trick to disable a man, usually, but it works just as well for a woman. She releases a guttural, strangulated noise, the garble of someone in a state of astonishment.

'Nice try,' I heave, then swing the plate towards her.

It hits her in the eye. I hadn't been aiming there, but it's as good a place as any. The broken edge sticks fast in the centre of her eyeball, like a shard of glass piercing dough. Wet jelly seeps out of the sides. It reminds me of egg yolk, slick, milky, a mess. If she'd ever been pretty before, she certainly won't be any more.

Someone knocks at the door.

The air warps, each sound muffled and dislocated. I can hear Amber's shrill mewling, but it seems to be coming from another room, or from outside the house. Her once-bright eye is obscured and misshapen. The plate has fallen to the floor, slick with my blood and her fluid.

Another knock follows, more urgent this time, then a muffled voice. It could be the paramedics or the police, but the question is, which? Could it be both? There are blue lights blinking through the curtains, but that could indicate either. I stand. Amber makes an attempt to grip my ankle, but she's easy to shake off. I need to get out of this house now, and the only way out is through the back door. That's my only chance.

There are shadowy figures outside, fuzzed by the frosted glass. For one moment, it seems they are the exact same people who arrested me all those years ago: one tall, one short. One female, one male. They've come for me again, just like before. But of course, I know they can't be those officers; they would have left the police now, or else moved into other roles.

They can probably see me, but there's nothing that can be done about that. I slide into the kitchen. My head's a mess; I can feel the blood congealing against my cheek, but that's nothing compared to the throbbing. That bitch paid for it though. An eye for an eye, I think, and stifle a laugh. She's got her Old Testament punishment. She's learnt the hard way that every action has a consequence.

The back door is locked. Of course it is. I should have known this wouldn't be easy. Daddy always told me that life never was, and that I must man up and get on with it. There's no point whining about things; instead, we must focus on how to improve them. I start searching, looking behind knick-knacks, diving into drawers. There will be a key here somewhere, I know it.

Two loud thumps make me freeze. They're trying to break down the front door. I don't have long.

Help me, I think, more to my inner strength than to anyone else. I can sense you at my back, standing in the corner of the room, wanting me to fail. Ditz, swinging on her rope like wind chimes in a breeze. Jean, pale and gasping as she was during those last few minutes of her life. I'm stronger than any of them, because I'm still here. I continue to thrive. I want them to see me, all of them, and know this to be true. Like the cockroach, like the skua, I fight on and I rise. I won't be crushed so easily.

There, I've found it. A key, tucked into the corner of the cabinet, just behind the salt and pepper shakers. It has to be the right one, it must be. I push it into the lock. It turns. The handle gives under my hand. I slip out into the cold and shut the door silently behind me, just as the front door crashes open.

Bill is so kind, so thoughtful, even as he lies struggling for breath on the sofa. He's left a garden chair right beside the fence. It's not an ideal height, but it will suffice. I can jump, then fling myself over the other side into my own garden. It should be easy, especially in comparison to what I've just been through. But the task is easier said than done. My foot slides off the plastic, and I nearly fall. There's no time for screw-ups, not if I want to get out of this. I need to get to my house, grab some belongings, then go. All in the space of a few minutes at the most.

The second leap is more effective. I lunge upwards, then throw my weight across the fence, arms dangling down, legs still on the wrong side. The wood groans under me. If it comes down, it's no bad thing, but the noise will surely alert them to my presence. As a young woman, I could have done this in a heartbeat. Henry would have laughed to see me, flapping around like a helpless child. He would have run a hand up my leg, enjoying my vulnerability, and would have—

Why am I thinking of him now? This job requires total focus. My feet scrabble for purchase, and I'm aware that every fumbling kick is a clarion call for the police inside. A door creaks open. I hear voices, then a heavy footstep on the patio behind me. *No!* I think, or did I cry it aloud? I don't know, I can't do anything, as I'm stuck on this fence, and I—

A hand grasps my leg. *Henry?* I wonder, for a crazed second or two. Has he come back for me at last, to take me away somewhere safe? Like he once promised?

'We're going to pull you down,' a male voice tells me. 'Don't resist us, we don't want to use more force than necessary.'

It's over. I can't stop the slide of my stomach, back over the sharp edge of the fence. Nor the hands, grappling with my waist, my hips, touching me all over, dragging me back to the ground.

I cry out, a fluting wail of rage, and the sound is immediately lost to the evening air.

My head hurts so badly. I am Robin once again, small, wounded, shaking with cold.

'You need to come with us,' one of the policemen says, taking me by the wrist.

I don't fight against it. This is finished.

CHAPTER 24

Once, I was a little girl. I had a mother and a father, and we lived in a house with ivy over the door and a driveway curling around the double-fronted bay windows. Mother was quiet most of the time, but she loved me, I know that. She used to tell me I could do great things with my life, that I possessed a sharp and enquiring mind. She used to say I could fly high and make something of myself, in a way that she'd never managed. But Daddy often got angry with her. The hallway used to ring with his shouting, and the bedrooms shrank tight around his rage. I'd hide in the cupboard, burrowing into the corner like a chick in a nest. That way I was certain that I couldn't be found.

Daddy and I moved away from that house, to island after island. There were rough cliffs, sand, and endless tumbling grassland. Birds, wailing and crying in the darkness. And I felt the depth of being alone, and understood what the word truly meant. *Alone* meant survival. It meant closing down to everything and everyone else. And *alone*, when under threat, can turn in a heartbeat. Jean Marshall was a threat.

I grew up, but that sense of being alone never went away. It remained inside me like a chasm. It kept me safe. I became grateful for it, because it meant that no one was able to hurt me. Or at least, no one could hurt me and get away with it.

I was so, so foolish to trust Henry. But such is the way with young people. The heart is an ocean of desire; it sweeps up every rational thought in its path. So in return, I hurt his son. I hurt you.

I didn't mean to do it, because you were so young. You could have flown high. Made something of yourself, But that aloneness inside me swelled into agony, it pressed me constantly from within. And then it rushed out of me, all because of Henry and what he'd done.

I nearly lost it all, when they put me in prison. My sense of self, I mean. I became the *alone*, and the abyss gobbled me up. It would have been better to die. I'd done Ditz a favour. Prison is no place for a person in pain.

These are all grey, dead thoughts. They lie inside me like ancient cobwebs, stuck fast to my memories, draped over every waking moment. They coat my dreams. They colour everything I see and do. I am in a cell again. Isn't it funny? After everything, to be back here. It's only a police station cell, but still. The other, more permanent cell, will come later. There will be another trial. They will condemn me again, and again I will suffer.

The fluorescent strip-light is flickering. It should bother me more than it does, but I'm past caring about anything now. There's a bench against the wall; I shall lie down on it.

I just want to shut my eyes and for it all to be gone. I imagine my mother's hand, stroking my brow. But then it turns into Ditz's, pressing with greater and greater pressure against my temple. She wants to pop me open like a plum, to mash me up.

Soon, it will all be over.

'Ava? Can you wake up, please? We need you to come through for questioning now.'

Ava. It's only here that they use my real name. The irony doesn't escape me.

'Ava? Sit up.'

I sit up. Resistance, as they say, is futile.

'Can you accompany us, please?'

What time is it? I can't tell if it's morning, noon or night. The light is sickly; it reminds me of a piss-riddled alleyway, a mouldering sea-cave. Something stinking and unhealthy.

I can't focus in on their faces, but I note that one of them is a man, the other a woman. He has a moustache. She might have blonde hair, or maybe light brown. Not that it matters. I follow them out of the cell and down the corridor. This all feels very familiar.

He reads me my rights, then asks if I'd like legal representation. I don't have a lawyer, a fact they know full well. I didn't have one last time either, and had to make do with the state-supplied goon. Back then, I was so much more frightened. I remember the green plastic seat, the coldness of the table against my elbows. This chair is padded, which I suppose is an improvement.

'Go on,' I say. 'You've got questions. I'll give you answers.'

The male policeman glances at his female counterpart. I wonder if they're romantically involved. They're certainly sitting close enough together. Perhaps he's married; maybe he started seducing her a few months ago, and now she believes that he'll give everything up to be with her. She wouldn't be the first and she certainly won't be the last, because that's where trust gets us all.

'Ava Webber,' he begins, 'do you admit to adding dangerous substances to the cake that you fed Bill Swinson and his daughter Amber?'

'Define dangerous.'

'I'll rephrase the question. Did you add a substance to the cake with the intention of causing harm to them both?'

'Define harm.' I'm warming up to this now, and it's a pleasure to see the irritation in his eyes, wrestling to explode outwards.

The female officer leans forward. 'Ava, did you add anything to that cake that wasn't in the recipe? Like a drug?'

I smile. 'I did.' She'll get my answers. I've already decided that I like her, as she has an honest face.

'What did you add?'

'I added several sleeping pills. Amber acted in a criminal manner towards me, and this was my way of stopping her.'

They glance at one another.

'What do you mean by "criminal"?' the female asks.

'She's working with Henry Hulham. He set her up to torment me. It started with a threatening letter through my door, then progressed to stalking me, then throwing a brick through my window, which is criminal damage.'

'Why didn't you go to the police about the matter?'

'I knew you wouldn't help. Plus, Amber knew my real identity. That would have meant that you'd relocate me again, and I didn't want that.'

She sighs. 'Okay, let's go back to the cake. What was your intention?'

'To stop her. I already said.'

'But it's Bill who's now in intensive care, Ava. Why did you target him?'

I press my lips together. It's a shock to hear that Bill is that unwell. Part of me feels regret for it, because I don't think I intended to make him so ill, but another part of me is glad. There's a lesson in it for him – to treat people with more respect, not just use them, then discard them a few days later.

'Will he die?' I ask.

The male police officer raises his eyebrows. 'That's the key question, isn't it, Ava? Because if he does, that's murder. You know what that means, I take it?'

'I had due cause.'

'You've told us nothing to suggest that Bill deserved what you did to him.'

'He wooed me, then got rid of me when he'd had his fill. Wouldn't you say that's deserving of some retribution?'

He refuses to answer, only nods at his colleague.

'Ava,' she says, in a softer voice. 'You've already confessed that you poisoned Bill and Amber with dangerous substances. You can make things easier for yourself by telling us all the details.'

I laugh. It's a bitter sound, tinny and harsh in this featureless room. 'What does it matter?' I tell her. 'You'll send me back to prison anyway.'

'You've committed a serious crime.'

'I had good reason to. I did it to survive, but you wouldn't understand that. You think it's okay to release someone from prison, then leave them to fend entirely for themselves.'

The male scoffs. 'From the notes, it would seem that you haven't done too badly, Ava. Nice house, free of charge. Benefits. Psychiatric support each week. What more did you want?'

To be truly free, and to have someone understand me, I think. To not feel as though I'm forever to be hated. To escape the torment that I live with, each and every day. But there's no point telling him this. He'll never understand, because he wants people like me to disappear. We're nothing more than problems to be dealt with, dangerous creatures to be restrained.

'I don't want to talk to you any more,' I say, leaning back.

'That's your right,' the female officer says. 'But your co-operation may help your case.'

I shake my head. Even she's lost my trust now. They'll get nothing further from me.

They take my fingerprints, a swab from my mouth, then a few photographs. It takes me back to those days when I was last held in a police cell. How much more afraid I was back then. I remember asking questions, so many questions, and being ignored at every turn, or else told to be quiet. Now I don't bother saying a word. Let them do what they want to. They will anyway, regardless of whether I play an active role or not.

Afterwards, they take me back to the cell. It feels colder than before; I can't help but notice how inefficient the radiator is in here, when compared to the heating in the rest of the building. I suppose that's the idea: to make it as uncomfortable as possible. To punch home the message that crime never pays. Except when it does, of course. When you get away with it.

There's something about the blank walls of a cell that forces you to think. Not just about everything that's led to this point, but about life in general, and what a pointless endeavour it really is. We are born, we suffer every day, we struggle for our little

235

patch of existence, then we die. Or we dare to break the mould. We challenge the status quo, and we say no. It doesn't have to be this way. I don't have to accept it. Daddy always said that, in order to succeed, one must be prepared to take risks and to be ruthless. He told me that he'd risen in his career because he hadn't been afraid to *take out the competition. Like birds*, he said, pointing out the savagery of gulls, pecking at one another for scraps of fish. *Nature is cruel, and so are we.* I always believed this to be true. We are natural creatures, after all, and our actions are driven by our desires and needs. But now, in this dreary, empty room, I wonder. Because this philosophy has never brought me happiness, and that is what I desired most of all. The chance to be someone's lover, someone's mother, perhaps. To mean something to somebody, and to have them care about me. To smile and to feel that happiness, deep down inside. Instead, I am friendless. I crave the solace of the islands, and maybe that is because I *am* the islands. Alone, far from others. Cold and unsupportive. Comfortable only when the ice-wind batters me, when the rain lashes at my surface.

I think about Bill and wonder if he is still breathing. To my surprise, I hope that he is. I didn't want to kill him. A part of me believes that in spite of everything, he deserves some sort of life. Perhaps I acknowledge that it wasn't my place to make this decision. I'm nature's creature, but that doesn't make me a god.

All these wild thoughts will tear me to shreds if I permit it. I need my pills to sleep, all those pills that I ground up so easily into the cake. Pills can make this pain go away, they will calm the voices that clamour and rage inside me. I can't think of Bill any more, I don't want to imagine him lying in a hospital bed, tubes sticking out of him, unable to breathe for himself.

I press my hands against the wall, then rest my forehead against its cool surface. It is soothing, but soothing isn't what I want right now. I want oblivion, an end to this. I bring my head back, then thrust it forwards, as hard as I'm able. The first attempt is too tentative, but it's human nature to protect oneself, even in unbearable anguish. The next, however, is more effective. My vision blurs. Pain rings through my ears and pounds at my eyebrows. I try again, then again, but consciousness still clings on. Thump. Thump. My hands are trembling, my breath a staccato rhythm of desperation. Thump. Thump.

The cell door screams open. Feet pound across the floor, hands grasp at my shoulders and haul me back. I don't resist them; this faceless officer is far stronger than me. At least this way, there's a fair chance they'll sedate me, and that's all I want.

I don't know how long I'm out for. Someone has put a swathe of plaster across my forehead, attached it roughly with sticky tape. I must have made myself bleed, though if there was any mess on the cell wall, they've since cleaned it up. They might have at least taken me to a hospital, just to check I was okay. But I suppose I am subhuman to them, unworthy of even basic care. In a way, I can't blame them. There is something terribly wrong with me, I think, because I know that others don't see the world as I do. Maybe I am the problem after all.

An officer comes in a while later, with some food on a tray. The bread roll is actually quite palatable, but my appetite has entirely deserted me. I sip at the orange juice, but that's it. Then I retreat to the bench and close my eyes. Whatever sedative they used earlier is still fogging up my senses, and I want to make the most of it while I can.

Ava. Ava. Ava.

My name, over again. Funny, how much it sounds like a tern's call when repeated like that. I could almost imagine I was lying on a cliffside, listening, not moving.

'Ava. Time to get up.'

I open my eyes. It's another officer, male again. Thicker-set, older, speaking with a strong Scottish brogue. The others must have finished their shift.

'Why do I need to get up?'

'Because I told you to. Up you get, please.'

This one doesn't mess around. I stand slowly. My muscles feel unpractised; my head pulses and it's hard to breathe. I'm like a fish gasping on the beach.

'Where are we going?' I ask, as he moves to the door.

He refuses to reply, only nods out to the corridor. It's time to interrogate me again, I presume. I remember the ritual from last time. The continual probing, the same old questions, asked in a variety of different ways. I don't know why they're bothering; I've already confessed to what I did.

He takes me to the same room as before. I'd love a cup of tea, but there's no offer forthcoming. I sit in the same seat as before, without being asked. A moment later, another officer joins us, another man, even older than this one. They press record on their device, introduce themselves. I assiduously ignore their names. What does it matter anyway? They're all after the same thing: to ensure I'm locked up again for another twenty-five years or so.

'Ava,' the Scottish officer begins, jabbing at some notes in front of him, 'yesterday you made a statement that Amber Swinson was harassing you, is that right?'

'Yes, that's correct.'

'And you said that she'd been stalking you, throwing a brick through your window—'

'Yes, that's all true.'

He shakes his head. 'Our fellas have had a word with Miss Swinson, and she denied it all. Seemed very confused, actually.'

She would be like that, I think. Then the meaning of his words sinks in fully. 'She's fine, then?' I blurt, forgetting myself. 'She's made a full recovery?'

He frowns. 'Does that anger you, Ava?'

I fall silent. I said far too much yesterday; I wasn't thinking straight. It was the stress that did it, and the emotional trauma.

He waits, then shrugs. 'We found the note attached to the brick, when our lads searched your house. The handwriting doesn't match Amber's. It wasn't her.'

'It *was*,' I hiss. 'I saw her, stalking me along the river, and on my own road. I know that woman wanted to make me suffer.'

He shakes his head. 'You want to know what I think? I think you've imagined all of this, Ava. I think you're unwell, and you've come up with this elaborate fantasy.'

'But you found the note. You saw the damage to my window. Are you trying to tell me that's in my head? Don't be ridiculous.'

The other police officer leans forward. 'We haven't finished telling you what we've discovered. So please, pipe down and let my colleague continue.'

I say nothing, only fold my arms. If I could murder the pair of them with a glare, I wouldn't hesitate to do so.

The Scottish officer waits, then nods, satisfied. 'We had ourselves a visit to the station this morning. From a lady who was rather unsettled, wouldn't you say so, Davis?'

The other officer nods. 'Very unsettled.'

'She wanted to find out if it was true, if you'd been arrested. We of course said that we couldn't disclose that information, but she started to laugh anyway. Said she'd already asked a neighbour.'

'Naturally,' the other officer adds, 'we were curious who she was. Turns out she's known who you were for a long time. And she's got a very big grudge against you. Big enough to lob a brick through your window, it turns out.'

Miranda, I think, growing cold. I'd dismissed her involvement from the start, presumed it wasn't her style. But I made a mistake in imagining her as she was before: implacable, aloof, not the outwardly aggressive type. Her hatred could well have flourished over the years, given how bitter and petty she always was.

'She couldn't let it go, could she,' I breathe. 'It was her husband's fault that her son ended up dead, not mine. Why doesn't she take a good look at him for a change and—'

The Scottish officer shakes his head. 'You're barking up the wrong tree there, Ava. This is nothing to do with Ben Hulham's mother, if that's who you're talking about. This is someone completely different.'

He's enjoying my confusion. Look at him, smirking from ear to ear, his ruddy cheeks glowing in the harsh light. He thinks he's won. I won't give him the satisfaction, or at least not outwardly. Internally, though, I'm scrolling through the faces in my memories. It's a woman, he's given me that much information. A woman with a grudge. Someone from prison? I upset enough women while I was there, it could have been any of them. Another jealous lover of Henry's?

Jean Marshall? Maybe she didn't die. I never saw her body, after all, only the coffin at the funeral. My father had been with her, but perhaps he lied to me, perhaps he secretly moved her to another—

'Ava? Are you still with us?'

'Who was it?' I ask reluctantly. 'Was it a very old person? I don't see how it can be Jean, but perhaps—'

'I reckon you'd remember this lady's maiden name. Ditsfield, it was.'

Ditsfield. *Ditz*. But it can't possibly be her. Her neck snapped, her feet dangled and jerked until she lost consciousness, they'd found her cold and limp, tongue black and swollen, eyes empty. It's not possible: the other inmates saw her being carried out under sheets – there's absolutely no way that it could be her. It's someone playing a trick, a terrible, horrible trick, and—

'I can tell by your face that the name means something,' the officer says with satisfaction. 'This lady told us that you tormented her sister when you were banged up last time. Seems you've got a thing for cruelty, Ava.'

'Her sister?' I whisper weakly. Then the remembrance hits me, powerfully as a sack of cement. They're talking about the famous Babs. The sibling who always cared for Ditz, when no one else would. The saviour, the heroine, now the avenger. It was her, all along.

It all makes sense now. The last note I received said she would make me suffer, as I'd made her suffer. Her, not him. I'd mocked her ignorance at getting the pronoun wrong, but she hadn't. Instead, she'd been referring to Ditz all along. Babs was my anonymous tormenter. I feel small and unformed, suddenly. Foolish, even. I was so sure it was Amber, but I was wrong. How could I have made such an error? What else have I misinterpreted? What other mistakes have I made?

None, I hear Daddy's voice say. *If you lose faith in yourself, you lose all.*

The other officer nods at me. 'I can see you're shocked by that news, Ava. Perhaps poisoning innocent people's cakes isn't such a great idea, eh?'

'Poisoning *anyone's* cake isn't right,' the Scottish officer growls. 'Which is what you'll be finding out soon enough. Because we all know, don't we, that you'll be back to prison after this. You had your second chance, and you used it to harm people.' He turns to his colleague, dramatic grimace in place. 'This is what's wrong with the rehabilitation system, you see? Evil doesn't change. It gets better at disguising itself, that's all.'

'I'm not evil,' I tell him. 'You don't know me.'

'I've been doing this job for long enough to have seen your type before, Ava Webber. Some are just born to be behind bars.'

No, I think, clutching the edge of the table so hard my knuckles turn white. I was born to fly free. It's the rest of you who condemned me to rot in a cell, and that's your fault, not mine.

I think I'm right, anyway. But am I?

I don't know any more, and that frightens me more than anything.

CHAPTER 25

They sentenced me, of course. After the trial, I was sent to a psychiatric prison in Ealing. It turns out that I am mentally unwell, or at least that's the verdict the jury came to. Ealing. It's a new part of the country, at least. I've never been to London before, not that I can see much of it from this cell.

I'm not sure how long it's been now. Two or three months, maybe more. Every day rolls into the next, and the one benefit of this place is that the drugs flow freely. They like to ensure that we ladies are calm, that we don't get overexcited. I've slept better in these last few months than I have done in years. It's medium security too, which is a pleasant change from what I had before. I am allowed to spend time out of my cell. I can watch the television in the day room, or play board games with the other inmates. One lady, with hair so fine I can see her scalp through it, tells me that she likes to make bombs. I can see why she ended up here; she really *is* a danger to society.

They tell me that I suffered an episode of delusion after my release. I like that phrase. Episode. It reminds me of a soap opera, something that's over in a flash, with no hard feelings from anyone. Already, that life is becoming more distant, hazy around the edges, more muddled in my memories. I remember many sleepless nights there, that's for sure. Reading my magazine by the kitchen window. Hearing the garden birds in the summer months. Drinking good quality tea, whenever I wanted to. But it wasn't for me, not really.

I've never asked about what happened to Bill. It's best if I don't; not that I imagine they'll tell me anyway. I sometimes see him here, sitting in the corner of the day room. He still has drool hanging from his lip, and his skin is that same dreary shade of grey. I tell him that he shouldn't feel sad, that we had good times together. We made a decent enough couple; we spent some lovely evenings chatting over a bottle of wine. I won't forget that night he took me out. He made me feel as though I mattered, and that's worth something.

The doctor likes to ask me if I feel remorse, and if I'd like to talk about what happened in the past. The answer is no, to both those questions. There is no point regretting what happened before, or that's what Daddy always used to tell me. We must always focus forward, on our progression, on our survival.

While I don't talk about the past, I often experience it, played out in front of me, crisp and clear as the day it happened. The drugs they give me make me sleepy. They make me care less about everything. But they also give me vivid visions. I see Jean and Daddy, striding across the room, deep in conversation. Sometimes, there are birds above me, flying from one fluorescent light to the other, their shrieks filling the room. Grass billows around my ankles, only to shrink back under the tiled floor when I focus my gaze on it.

I see you, of course. You are always with me, the son I never had. It pleases me to see that you're always holding the chick now, tenderly to your chest, with a smile on your face. You are at peace, I feel. You've moved on, somewhere far, far away from here, and only the echo of your memory remains. Ditz is sometimes with you too, neck straight and unblemished again, her uncertain smile in place. I feel that you two might have been friends, had you been given the chance to meet one another while you were both alive.

But most of all, it's the birds I see. Their singing fills me up; it makes me weep sometimes, though I don't understand why. When I hear them, I am transported to a place far from here. My limbs shrink, my body compacts down on itself, and I am young again. I smell the sea in the air. I taste that salt, and the tang of the bitter wind.

I am Ava, once more.

www.sandstonepress.com

Subscribe to our weekly newsletter for events
information, author news, paperback and e-book
deals, and the occasional photo of authors' pets!
bit.ly/SandstonePress

facebook.com/SandstonePress/

@SandstonePress